Grave Indulgence

Grave Indulgence
by
William Doonan

2012

BookYear Mysteries, First Edition 2012
www.bookyearmysteries.com

GRAVE INDULGENCE
Copyright © 2012 by William Doonan
www.williamdoonan.com

Other Titles by William Doonan:
GRAVE PASSAGE
MEDITERRANEAN GRAVE
AMERICAN CALIPHATE

This novel is a work of fiction. The characters and events depicted herein are derived from the author's imagination.

All rights reserved. No part of this book may be used or reproduced in any manner without written permission from BookYear Mysteries. Contact: Ben Holder at www.bookyearmysteries.com.

Library of Congress Control Number: 2012909209

ISBN Number: 978-0-9831354-1-8

Printed in the USA.

for Carmen

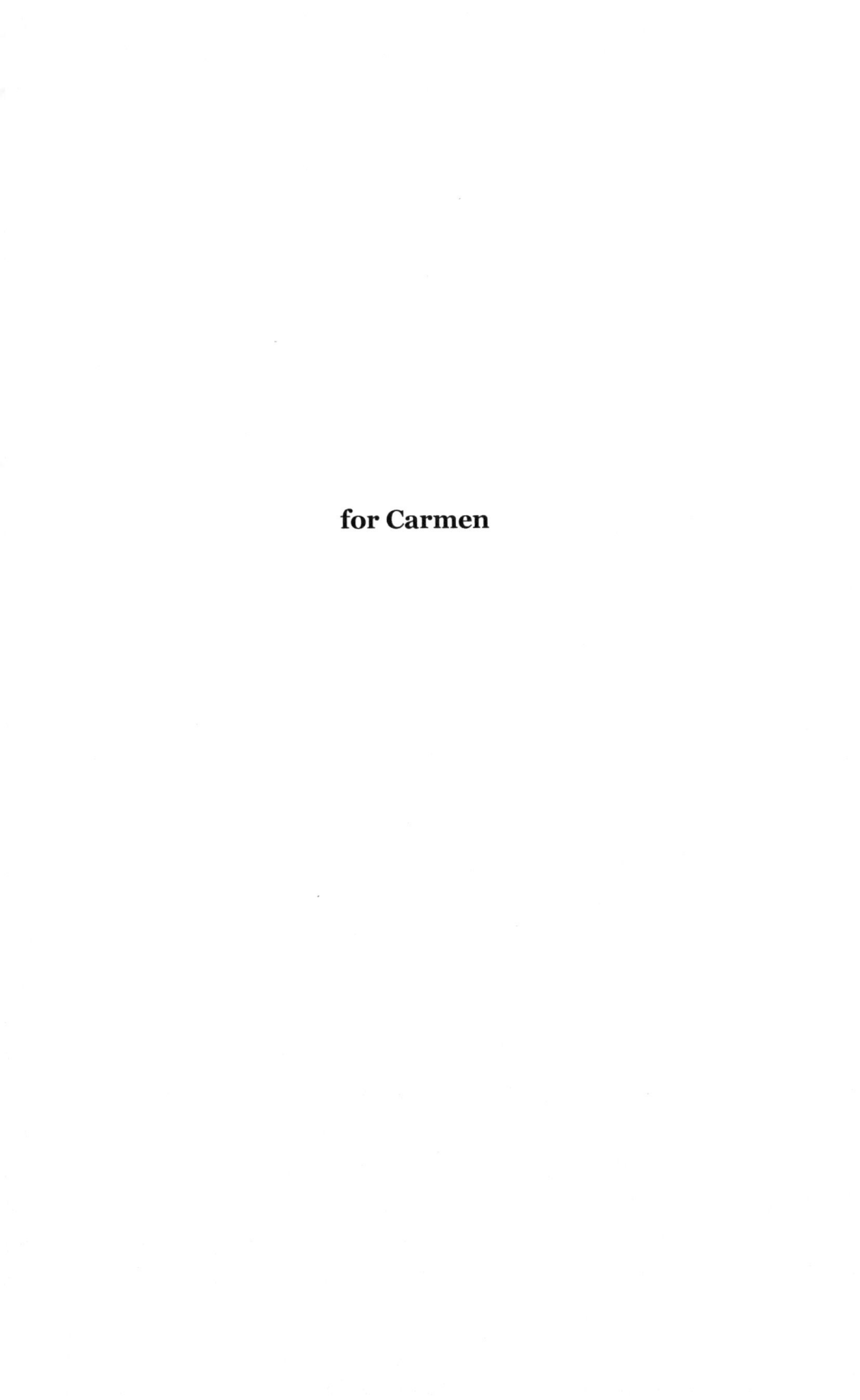

Acknowledgments

I am indebted to a number of people who worked tirelessly to help bring this project to life. Dan Stuelpnagel provided essential insights, edits, and encouragement, helping me hammer the story into shape. Bill Rozell has graciously read and reviewed everything I've written over the last three years, and I'm grateful for his continued support. Bob Bernstein worked with me on the final draft, and has become an invaluable writing buddy. And my family gave me the support and encouragement to keep both myself and Henry afloat.

Indulgence – 1. a state of yielding freely to desire
2. remission of punishment for sins after absolution

Chapter One

Bashir Salib borrowed a billion dollars from his father and threw in half a billion of his own to build Indulgence, the largest cruise ship in the world. At 1,200 feet long, she was larger than a Nimitz-class aircraft carrier. Indulgence had enough cabin space for 5,400 passengers and 2,100 crewmembers. Fully loaded, she was nearly as populous as the Pacific island nation of Nauru. At 226,000 tons, she weighed as much as four and a half Titanics, and her main pool was large enough to hold the iceberg that sunk the Titanic. Indulgence was one day old, and no one had yet been murdered on board. We weren't going to be able to say that about day two.

Indulgence was unlike any ship I'd ever seen. Bashir Salib spared no expense: hard wood floors, granite countertops, ample room for entertaining. I watch a lot of home improvement TV, so I know what I'm talking about. I was sitting by myself in a spacious Italian marble hot tub on Deck 15, two hundred feet above sea level, drinking a gimlet and staring down at the rooftops of Helsinki. It was a fine morning in Finland and I was in a very good mood.

I was looking forward to this cruise. We would be visiting the Scandinavian capital cities of Stockholm, Copenhagen, and Oslo. Then, after an overnight in Dover, England, we would have six glorious days at sea en route to Miami, which was to be Indulgence's home port.

Normally I don't get called in until a crime has been committed onboard a cruise ship, but in this case, I was called in as a preventative measure. Six highly specific threats had already been made against Indulgence. Five were from known terrorist organizations threatening to send her to the bottom of the sea. The Brazilian Intelligence Agency reported the sixth threat. They tapped a mobile phone line, and heard the Syrian Head-of-Mission in Sao Paulo authorize the kidnapping of a retired United States Air Force General, who would be onboard.

Lieutenant General Meg Savoy commanded a squadron of Predator drones in Afghanistan. Pakistan too, though you won't find that in any official paperwork. She was retired now, and looking forward to taking her first cruise. But even retired, she'd make a fine prize for anyone interested in learning more about the drone system. And as I would soon learn, there are plenty of people out there interested in learning about that sort of thing. General Savoy and her family had pre-boarded about an hour ago, and I was planning on having a little discussion with them soon about safety at sea.

My bubble jets fizzled out, so I had to scramble for the button to turn them back on, and as I did so, I found myself staring at row upon row of lounge chairs, just waiting for sun-loving passengers. There must have been thousands of those chairs, all empty. I felt so alone at that moment, just me on a ship that looked like it could hold half the world. If a Biblical flood was imminent, I'd want to be onboard this ship. It was magnificent, and it was stocked with food.

Here's something else special about Indulgence, something you don't find on most ships; almost all the guest cabins were assigned butlers. Butlers! On most cruise ships, only the high-end suites have butlers, but not here. A butler is a nice touch. If you need more mints during the night, or if you need someone to refill the minibar, you can just give a shout

out to Housekeeping. But a butler will unpack your bags for you. A butler will shine your shoes, iron your trousers, arrange your cocktail parties, and manage your spa appointments. I was looking forward to working closely with my butler.

I spotted someone coming towards me, walking around one of Indulgence's three massive swimming pools, so I held up my nearly empty glass. "How about a refill?" I called out. "I'm getting a little parched here."

As he got closer, I could see that he was an Oriental fellow. Mid-forties, he was short and wore a Fu Manchu mustache and the little beard that goes with that. He looked like a tiny Charlie Chan. He was talking into a radio but I didn't have my hearing aid on, so I couldn't hear what he was saying. He kept shaking his head.

"Not getting any younger here," I volunteered.

He came over and stared down at me. "Are you Mr. Henry Grave?"

"I am. Look, I haven't registered my credit card yet, but I'm good for the drinks, I promise. Listen, Sport, a gimlet doesn't need to be mostly lime juice. You have to give the gin a chance to breathe."

He stared at my suitcases which I had assembled next to the hot tub. "Are these your bags?"

"They are, yes. I was looking for my bathing suit, but I think I left it back in Pennsylvania. So I got to thinking, there's really nobody else around just now."

"You're not wearing a bathing suit?"

I shook my head. "I'm as naked as the day the Good Lord made me."

He didn't say much of anything for what seemed like half an hour. "And what day might that have been?"

"October 13, 1925."

He stared at me some more.

"I know what you're thinking, and yes, I have the same birthday as Margaret Thatcher. I sent her a card once, and you know what? She sent me one back. Or someone in her office did. But I think Mrs. Thatcher would agree that dying of thirst is no way to go." I held up my glass.

"Sir, I am not a bartender." He held up a crew ID card but I didn't have my glasses on so I couldn't read it. "Lester Fung," he said. "I am Deputy Chief of Onboard Security. Do you have some identification on you?"

"Not on me, no. I thought I made it clear that I was bathing al-fresco, but my pants are over there on the chaise. I have some identification in my wallet."

He brought me my pants. I showed him my ID.

"You are Admiral Osvaldo Hinojosa of the Nicaraguan navy," he said. "You command a destroyer group?"

Nuts. I looked through my wallet some more and found my investigator's license.

"I didn't know Nicaragua had a navy," he said.

"One of the finest in the world," I told him. "I look good with that hat on, don't I?"

"So this is fake, right?"

"I work a couple of jobs to make ends meet."

"Sir, let me get this straight, you boarded this ship over an hour ago. An officer was leading you to the briefing room to meet with the security team, which is now underway. And after pausing to use the restroom, you slipped away and came up here to drink in the hot tub?"

I frowned. "Well, when you put it like that it doesn't sound so good. I was doing some preliminary research. I like to look around a little before I get down to the nuts and bolts."

"Maybe so, but the captain has asked that you be brought to the briefing room. We have quite a bit of work ahead of us. Can you come with me now, please?"

I stood. "Ready and willing."

He went to fetch me a towel, giving the good people of Helsinki a thirty-second peek at yours truly in the buff.

"I can meet you down there," I told him as I dressed.

"I have to stay with you, but I'd ask that you hurry."

"OK, I'll make you a deal," I said. "We can do this the easy way, wherein you find me a refill on that gimlet. Or we can do this the hard way and you can help me with my skin cream. I'm getting a little rash on my side." I turned to show him. He turned to get my drink, leaving me alone with Helsinki for a couple more minutes.

I followed my new friend Lester Fung to the elevator and we descended eleven decks. In front of us was a huge theater filled with people scrambling to find their seats.

"I think this is the wrong meeting," he said. He took out his phone. "Wait here one second."

"I thought the passengers weren't coming on board for another two hours."

"They're not," he said. "This is just the staff. I need to make a quick call. Please just wait here by the door for one second."

I went inside and took a seat. The theater was massive. I looked up and saw that the mezzanine and the balcony were full. People were clapping.

A couple of the ladies made some catcalls as a handsome man walked out onto the stage. "Thank you, thank you," the man said, taking a little bow, "but I need to get everyone's attention. We have a lot to cover here. First, I want to say that it's been a pleasure working with all of you these past two weeks here in Helsinki. I know we've only been on board the ship for six days now, but hopefully everyone is getting accustomed to their stations."

"What about the air conditioning?" someone called out from the balcony.

"It's back on," he said. "They just needed to figure out where the breaker panel was. Now please let me continue. As you should all know by now, I'm Antonio Grassi, your cruise director. I've met many of you, but since there are more than a thousand of us here on the Entertainment and Hotel Services staff, it's going to take me some time to learn all the names."

"How come there are no eggs on board?" someone in front of me called out.

Grassi shook his head. "I have no idea why there are no eggs. The entire senior staff of Hotel Services is currently scrambling to buy every egg in Finland, which is why all of the rest of you are here in the Entertainment meeting rather than in the Hotel Services meeting. I also don't know where the butter knives are, or why Indulgence is spelled wrong on the bathrobes, so don't ask me any more questions."

I looked around the room to see if I recognized anyone.

"Just a couple of bulletins, and then some reminders," Grassi continued. "First of all, I am delighted to announce that Indulgence has just passed her final certification inspection, and has been licensed and declared sea-worthy by the Finnish maritime authority. So officially, this is Indulgence's birthday."

Shouts and murmurs ensued.

"Yes, so at least we all still have jobs." He leafed through a large folder that was stuffed to the breaking point. "My only other bulletin is that we need to remember that we will not be making port in the Netherlands as planned. Due to logistical issues, the dock facilities in Rotterdam are, as it turns out, of insufficient size to accommodate us. And due to heavy shipping traffic, we will not be able to use the tenders. As such, we will be diverting to Dover, England. The passengers have all been notified of the change of plans, but it is important to remember if anyone asks."

"I wanted to see Amsterdam," someone called out from the balcony. "My sister works in the Red Light District."

A second voice cut through the howls of laughter. "I've seen your sister. If she works in the Red Light District, she can't afford to take the time off."

"Five reminders, then," Grassi continued when the chatter died down, "and this goes for all personnel in both Entertainment and Hotel Services. First, never talk politics with the guests. If you do, eventually you are going to piss someone off, and they are not here to become pissed off.

"Second, never discuss religion with the guests, for the same reason.

"Third, staff members are not permitted to congregate, not in the lounges, not in the bars, not by the pool. If you see too many of your fellow employees in one place, leave. The last thing we want is to give the impression that we have free time.

"Fourth, never be seen walking around holding a beverage unless you're bringing that beverage to someone else. If you want to drink, drink in the Staff Club. If you want to get drunk, do so at your own risk. If you show up to your shift drunk, you go home. And last but not least, if you get in a fight with someone, nobody cares who started it, you both go home."

He got a couple of boos for that last remark.

"I'm serious," he said. "OK, my three guardians have to be in place by noon for the VIP embarkation, and you'll need to stay there through general boarding, so that's a five hour shift. Where are my guardians? I want everyone to know who you are. Remember, every one of you needs to be able to field questions from passengers. This is our maiden voyage but we don't want to look like beginners. OK, Ancient Egypt guardian, can you please introduce yourself?"

A young fellow in the front row stood and turned around, giving everyone a good look at the leather vest and cowboy hat. "Hello, friends. I've met some of you, but for the rest, I'm Max Carder. I'm an Egyptologist working at the American Museum in Cairo. I'll be managing the Ancient Egypt theme area. That is on Deck 8, for those of us who are still trying to figure out where everything is. And tonight we have a show. It's called 'Isis in Love.' Hope to see you there."

"This is important, people," Grassi said. "Ancient

Egypt is a comprehensive theme neighborhood. Moreover, those passengers with suites on Deck 8 will expect us to stay in character for the duration of the cruise. OK, next, where is my Caribbean Quarter guardian?"

A thin colored fellow stood up. "Montrose Royal at your service," he said. He had one of those Jamaican accents that make you smile. "I'm from the islands, a guardian of the loas, the gods who protected the slaves. I'll be sure that our guests enjoy the time they spend with us. Remember, we're located right here on Deck 4, just past the casino. We have a beautiful show tonight called 'Rum Rum.' I hope to see you there."

"Thank you, Montrose," Grassi continued. "Where's my Rainworld Guardian?"

A fellow wearing a safari vest hopped up onto the stage. "I'm Harlan Thorne," he said. "I am a retired professor of anthropology and conservation ecology. I'll be managing the rainforest exhibit. We're doing 'Songs of the Amazon' tonight."

"It's not an exhibit," Grassi reminded him. "It's a theme neighborhood. And you're not the manager. You're the guardian of Rainworld. Be proud. People care about the environment, so be prepared to explain to our guests how committed Indulgence is to the environment. We have solar panels up on top."

I laughed out loud.

"Is something funny?" Grassi looked straight at me.

"No, no," I said. "I was just thinking about an old joke. The one about the guy who fell into the vat of optical glass."

"You think it's funny that we're committed to the environment?"

"No, I think the guy who fell into the vat of optical glass is funny. He made a spectacle of himself." I must have cut some tension because I got more laughter than I expected. I stood up and took a bow. "I'll be in the Lido Lounge every night at six."

Grassi frowned. "I'm pretty sure, but not positive, that

we don't have a Lido Lounge. And this isn't a laughing matter. We make it clear to people that Indulgence is an ecologically friendly vessel."

"Ecologically friendly?" I repeated. "You have to be kidding me. This ship burns a gallon of fuel to sail half an inch. It has probably the largest carbon footprint on the planet, and if you flushed all 3,500 toilets at the same time, you'd flood half of Scandinavia."

I should have been a comedian.

"What section are you in?" Grassi asked.

I looked around. "Come again?"

"Your assignment? Do you actually work here?"

"Me, no. I'm the King of Finland. I just came aboard to have a look."

He spent an uncomfortable moment dumbstruck.

"No, I'm just fucking with you." I told him who I was.

"Yes, we were told there would be additional security personnel on board. To be honest, you're not what I was expecting."

"It's OK," I told him, "I might be better looking than you but I'm not nearly as charming."

"Settle down," Grassi said when the chuckling and hollering was just about over. "Hold on." He leafed through his notes.

"Right, I'm told to remind everyone that in addition to our shipboard security team we have an outside investigator with us. He's from the Association of Cruising Vessel Operators in Washington, D.C. which certifies onboard security protocols. Mr. Henry Grave, who will have Access-all-Areas clearance, was a prisoner of war during World War II. Is that right?"

"I remember it like it was yesterday," I said. "It was cold that winter, my friends. The wind was howling and the Germans were howling even louder."

That got me nothing but stares.

"And please remember," Grassi continued, "that Mr. Grave is undercover so when you see him about, be sure to treat him as you would any other guest."

I felt a tap on my shoulder and turned to find Lester Fung.

"I asked you to just wait outside for a second. I couldn't find you."

"I was here."

"Can we go, please? This is the Entertainment meeting. We're going to a very different sort of meeting."

We left, and I followed him to a bank of elevators. "I'm still trying to make sense of all the decks," Lester Fung told me. "We need to go up a level."

So we did. The elevator opened onto what looked like an extremely high-end shopping mall. I saw coffee shops, a pizza parlor, Indian food, then a camera shop and another camera shop. "They have Indian food here?"

"They have all kinds of food here," he said.

"I'm asking because I haven't really eaten in quite some time. I have that Type II diabetes so I need to keep my sugar up." I pointed to a coffee bar which already had a spread of rolls, meats, cheeses, and cakes ready for the VIP embarkation. "I'm thinking I'll stop here for just a quick nosh."

He said something to me but I had already grabbed a plate from the rack. The place was empty save for one fellow sitting by a window drinking coffee.

"We really need to get to the meeting," Lester Fung insisted, stroking nervously at his mustache.

I piled my plate high with cubed meat and little pastries. "Do you know what's inside the crumpets?" I asked him, but he didn't. When I made my way to a table, I felt his hand on my arm.

"We need to go now," he said. "You can bring the food with you."

I called out to the fellow sitting by the window and asked if he could find me a coffee. Then I turned to Lester Fung. "Listen, Chief," I said. "I'm armed. You are not, so if we get to shooting, you can guess how it's going to turn out. And if you touch me again, I'm going to start shooting."

"I'm sorry," he said, "I'm only trying to do my ..."

"And I'm only trying to do mine," I told him. "And I do it my way. My way involves not being so hungry that I can barely think. Sixty-six years ago I nearly died of starvation in a Nazi prison camp. One day I ate three caterpillars, and that was a very good day, so I make it a point never to pass food, nor allow it to pass me. And by that I mean that if there is a trolley or a dessert cart coming toward me, I can't let it go by until I sample the goods. Do you understand me?"

"I do."

"Good. Now back off or I'll have you transferred to Housekeeping."

He rubbed his hands together, unsure what to say.

The other fellow came over with my coffee. "Sugar?"

"Please."

"My pleasure, sir. Is there anything else I can get you?"

"No, I think I have just about everything I need here. Mr. Fung will be leaving me now, I'm afraid. We'll catch up in about half an hour."

"And what should I tell the captain?" Lester asked.

The man who brought the coffee answered for me. "Tell the captain what Mr. Grave just told you," he said. "And tell him that Mr. Grave and I are becoming acquainted."

Lester nodded. "Yes, sir."

I stared at my new friend. He looked Mediterranean, maybe early thirties. A thin white scar split his left eyebrow in two. "How do you know my name?"

He sat across from me. "I make it my business to know the names of all the important passengers, although of course you're not exactly a passenger. You're here to protect my ship."

"Your ship?"

"Yes. I'm Bashir Salib. And after we've had our snack, I'll show you around."

Chapter Two

I ate more than I should have. I didn't say much while I was eating, and Bashir didn't either. I think he was showing me some measure of respect, and I appreciated that. "Thanks for the coffee," I told him. "I thought you were a waiter."

"Because of my dusky ethnic good looks?"

"Yes, and because there aren't any passengers on board yet."

"Of course. Walk with me," he said. I followed him out into the promenade.

"This is the Rosetta Deck," he told me. "It's the first deck the passengers will see when they board." He pointed to a massive round counter where at least three dozen staff members manned their stations, getting ready for embarkation to begin. "That's Guest Services. Anything you need, you can come here and someone will answer all your questions."

Just past the counter was a cylindrical tank about six feet wide. I looked up but couldn't see how high it went. It was filled with murky water. "I think your aquarium filter is busted," I told him. "You have to stay on top of that; otherwise your guppies will all be floaters."

"Vampryoteuthis infernalis," he said.

"What, now?"

"Mr. Grave, let me introduce you to one of nature's

most incredible animals, the vampire squid from hell."

"That's its name?"

"That is its name."

I got up close and stared into the murky water. I could see something moving around in there, but I couldn't tell exactly what. "Maybe you could have gone with some sea horses or something a little more cheery," I suggested.

He grinned. "Let's see if I can change your mind." He stepped up to a panel attached to the tank. There were two buttons on it; he pressed the first one and the lights flickered on in the tank, revealing one of the strangest looking animals I had ever seen.

"It's like a little octopus," I said, but that didn't really describe the thing swimming in front of me. It looked like a football with tentacles and giant eyes. Bashir tapped at the glass. "There's my girl," he said as the thing swam closer. "When you're ready, Mr. Grave, please press the larger of the two buttons, the one that's blinking."

I did just that, and the squid seemed to explode with light. It looked like an underwater fireworks display. It lasted about ten seconds. Then the squid swam away and the water became cloudy again. "What in the hell was that?"

"That," Bashir said, "was Henrietta. Woodrow tends to linger up at the higher altitudes. The vampire squid is a living fossil, a species more than 300 million years old. They live half a mile below the surface of the ocean, a crushing sunless environment that is nearly devoid of life. And we have the only two in captivity."

"So you press the button and you get the fireworks show every five minutes?"

"The tank resets every hour to give the animals time to rest and recharge, but their entire bodies are covered in light-producing organs, which they use to disorient their prey. Feeding time is at 10:00 in the morning; you don't want to miss seeing that. They get quite excited when we bring out the prawns."

"Who wouldn't?" I followed him past the tank toward what appeared to be a shopping district. "Let me ask you something, aren't you a prince or a sheik or something like that? How did you wind up in this line of work?"

"I am a prince, yes, but I have three older brothers to compete with. My father values proven commodities in his businesses, and in his sons. And I have some catching up to do. My father is the king of Al-Kurbai. Have you been to the Emirates, Mr. Grave?"

I shook my head.

"Even if you had, you would probably not have been to ours. We have very few tourists, and a civil war that has been raging for two decades. My grandfather built a resort hotel on the coast to attract foreigners but it offended many of the local clans. Infidels, alcohol, and scantily clad women."

"A mental picture is forming."

"And when the civil war erupted, the tourists began lining up to stay away, as the old saying goes. And the kidnappings didn't help either. Nor the beheadings."

"Charming."

"No," he said. "It is charming. I love my country. The mountains are beautiful, and the coastline is breathtaking. But the people are scared. Scared of change. The oil changed so much for so many. And so we are trapped in the last century. Unfortunately, unlike some of our neighbors, our petroleum deposits will soon run dry. And when that happens, we will remain trapped in the last century unless we modernize."

"And this is how you modernize? A cruise ship?"

"Oh yes, Mr. Grave. If the world won't come to us, we'll come to the world. You read the papers. You know what they've been saying about Indulgence; a Muslim-owned ship, nobody will sail. Only terrorists will buy tickets, and only to look around for the perfect place to plant the bombs."

I nodded. "I've read the papers."

"But that didn't happen, did it? Indulgence's maiden voyage is completely booked. Not one stateroom will be unoccupied tonight. And this is not a Muslim-owned ship, Mr. Grave. It's not an Emirate ship and it's not an Arabian ship. It is my ship. This is my floating embassy to the world. And it is unlike anything the world has ever seen. Come, let me show you something."

We passed a portrait studio and a women's clothing store, and another store I had never seen before on a cruise ship. "Let me ask you another question," I said. "If someone bought one of those mopeds from that shop over there, could they drive it right out or would they have to wait until the end of the cruise?"

"They're scooters, not mopeds. If you buy one it will be made available to you at every port of call should you wish to use it to explore. But we would keep them in the hold until the end of the cruise."

"Well I'll be goddamned."

We kept walking and came to another bank of elevators. Just ahead was the biggest dining room I have ever seen.

"Magnificent, isn't it?" Bashir said. "It is currently the largest restaurant in Scandinavia."

"Maybe we could stop for a little ..."

"It's not open yet. First seating at dinner tonight will be its grand opening."

We took the elevator up one deck. When the door opened, we walked into a different world. It was two stories high and covered in foliage. I saw trees everywhere and a waterfall in the distance.

"Well I'll be goddamned. You built a rainforest on a ship."

"Welcome to Rainworld," he said. "It's two full acres. The trees and the plants are part of our air purification system, and the fish in the pond and the stream will one day be served in our dining room."

I followed him down a stone-lined path deep into the forest. "It's kind of misty here, like a terrarium."

"Yes, it is all climate controlled. It is eleven degrees warmer here than any other deck. Still cool enough for the passengers, but warm enough for the animals."

"Animals?"

He grinned at my surprise. "We have seven species of birds, three reptiles, and some enclosed areas for our mammals."

We walked across a bridge and came to an enclosure. "Oh, you have got to be kidding me," I said. I could not believe what I was seeing. "Tell me those are artificial, like some kind of robots."

He shook his head. "No, they're real. They were a gift from the Chinese government, technically on loan from the Emirate zoo, but I think they'll be happy here."

"Good Christ," I said. "You brought pandas on a ship." I watched as the two animals reached up to strip leaves from a low-hanging tree. I heard footsteps, and when I turned, I recognized one of the men from the meeting.

"Ah, Dr. Thorne," Bashir said. "I was just giving Mr. Grave a tour, but you know Rainworld better than I do."

"I remember you from upstairs," I told him.

"I remember you, too." He shook my hand. "I feel safer already."

"That makes one of us. I'm not going to be able to sleep tonight knowing there are giant pandas running around. What if they get out?"

He laughed. "They won't get out. I know it doesn't look like a cage, but there's a cage there. The bars and the electrical wiring are mostly hidden behind the branches, but they're there. The pandas aren't going anywhere."

"Well, technically they're going to Sweden with the rest of us," I reminded him.

Bashir gestured toward the forest. "Dr. Thorne is the

guardian of Rainworld," he said. "Perhaps he could lead us deeper into the forest. There are still more surprises ahead."

We followed Thorne deep into the foliage, where birds called out and crickets chirped. At one point he even took out a little booklet to figure out which path to take. "Sorry," he said. "I've been studying the plans for some time but we only just came on board a week ago."

We walked in silence, and a couple of minutes later, the silence changed. There were no more crickets. I had an eerie feeling and I thought I saw something move. I caught up with Thorne and gave him a little tap. "I think we're not alone here."

"I think you're right."

I smelled smoke. We came around a bend and into a clearing where a small campfire had been lit in front of what looked like a straw house. "You have a campfire on your ship," I told Bashir. "I'm not sure that's wise."

"We had it specially designed," he said. "It's actually just a propane gas fire. The wood isn't real, but it looks like a real campfire."

Harlan called out something that sounded Spanish or Portuguese, and a moment later, three Indians wearing T-shirts and loincloths stepped out of the straw house: an older man, a woman, and a young man. They were tiny, none of them over five feet tall, and they sported identical bowl-cut hair-dos.

"Oh, you have got to be kidding me," I said. "You have hunter-gatherers in your onboard rainforest?"

Bashir smiled.

"They're Jipitos," Harlan said. "In fact they're the last of the Jipitos. I've been working with the indigenous peoples of Brazil for decades, and I didn't know about the Jipitos until three years ago. Their tribe has been systematically destroyed over the last decade as loggers and miners began moving further into the Brazilian jungle, bringing disease with them."

"So you brought them here to be part of your zoo?"

The younger Indian munched on a cookie.

"It's not a zoo," Bashir said. "Rainworld is a semi-sovereign territory deeded to the Jipito tribe, what's left of it. By agreement between the government of Al-Kurbai and that of Brazil, we have created an inviolate cultural sanctuary. The accord has even been recognized by the United Nations. This is the Jipito homeland in perpetuity, which they have agreed to share with our passengers."

I shook my head. "It feels wrong."

"I know what you're thinking," Harlan said. "Believe me, I was a little conflicted at first. It does feel wrong, but as I said, I have been working with Amazonian Indians for a long time now; I have seen what's become of a lot of them. Better they should be here than back home sniffing glue by the river, or living in a cardboard slum in Sao Paolo."

The woman said something, then pointed over her shoulder with a TV remote control. The Indian man argued with her. It looked to me like he was trying to shut her up. Finally he gave up and beckoned us to follow him.

Behind the straw house was a man lying on the ground. He was wearing a grey suit and he had a spear sticking out of his neck. He was dead.

Bashir turned white.

"That's the problem with hunter-gatherers," I said. "When not gathering, they hunt."

Chapter Three

Bashir made a few calls while Harlan spoke with the Jipitos. I had a look at the dead man. He was middle-aged, probably Middle Eastern. He was big, muscular without an ounce of fat. I checked his hands and found no defensive wounds. I turned him over and found a holstered nine-millimeter pistol, which suggested to me that the attack was unexpected. His pockets were empty and he had no identification.

"They say they didn't kill him," Harlan told Bashir. "They found him on Frog Island and brought him back."

"Then where is the blood?" I looked around. "There should be a trail of blood."

He shook his head. "Jipitos have many taboos against the sight of blood. They would have cleaned it up." He spoke with the older Indian who confirmed the cleanup.

"Or maybe they just killed him," Bashir said.

"Easily resolved," I suggested. "We need a security team ..."

"On its way," he interrupted.

"And they can bring some Luminol. If they pick up traces of blood on the path to whatever Frog Island is, I would be inclined to believe these guys. Do they keep many spears around?"

Harlan shook his head. "They don't do any actual hunting. A little fishing maybe, but the spears are kept under glass in the exhibit. I don't know if they actually made it to the exhibit yet. We're still unpacking everything."

"Is that right? So there might be a few spears poking around."

"There might be," he admitted.

"Fantastic. Do you know who the dead man was?"

"No," he said. "I've never seen him before, but like I said, this is all new. We've only been onboard a week, and before that, we were in orientation in Helsinki for another week. But there are a lot of people working on this ship, and I don't know too many of them yet."

Bashir got off the phone. He looked ashen. "I have my chief of security coming down. We have to clear this up right away. We begin general boarding in little more than an hour."

"That might be a problem," I told him. "We're still in port, so the Finnish authorities have jurisdiction. They will want to conduct an investigation, so you won't be sailing today, and probably not tomorrow either."

"No, no." He shook his head. "We cannot let that be the case. If they detain the ship, it would be a disaster, financial ruin. Our own team is more than competent to conduct the investigation. Also, we have you."

"I appreciate your confidence," I said, "but the law is not ambiguous as to who has jurisdiction when crimes are committed in port."

"I am aware of that." Bashir took a deep breath. "I have phoned my legal advisor who is currently researching a workaround. If none can be found, I will do as you suggest and contact the harbor police. But for now, let me bring my own resources to bear on this if you will."

I didn't know exactly what he was getting at, but I was willing to play along for an hour or so. Bashir's phone rang and I could hear him giving directions. A few moments later, a uniformed man stepped into a clearing. He was one of those guys who look to be made entirely of muscle with maybe just a little sinew. "Aver Golan," he introduced himself. "I'm the ship's chief of security. Sorry to meet under these circumstances."

"I like your accent," I told him. "You're Israeli."

"I am, yes. As is most of my staff."

I turned to Bashir. "That's quite a thing, a Muslim enterprise counting on Israeli operatives to keep it safe."

"They're the best in the word at what they do," he said. "And I'm a businessman before anything else."

Golan examined the body while Harlan brought him up to speed.

"He's not carrying any ID," I told Bashir. "You have no idea who he is?"

He seemed to consider his next move for an undue amount of time.

"I am part of whatever loop this is," I told him. "So if you know something, now is the time to tell me."

"His name was Nasr Wakim. He worked for my father."

"He did, did he? In what capacity?"

"In the capacity of ... factotum."

"What, now?"

"Wakim performed a variety of services for my father, a variety of ..."

"You mean like a butler?"

Bashir stared at me. "No, very much not like a butler, he was more like a chief of staff, a right-hand man."

"Then what was he doing on board?"

"He was protecting this considerable investment," he said, opening his arms wide as if to take in the entire rainforest. "He was protecting me."

Golan took out his phone but Bashir waved to him. "Please don't make any calls just yet. I need to think."

"So what was this Wakim doing down here?" I asked.

"I have no notion," Bashir said.

"Why didn't he have an ID?"

"That's a great question." Golan turned to Bashir. "Perhaps the killer stole his ID. Is that what you think must have happened?"

Bashir lowered his head.

"I told you," Golan began, "that you cannot have anyone onboard without identification. There are still at least three or four people running around without paperwork. I have asked you to identify them to me, but you have not. I will insist on it now, or I will ask the Finns to intervene."

"Alright," Bashir said forcefully. "I will give you the names and stations of my handlers. This was my father's idea, not mine." His phone chirped, and he turned away to answer.

I turned to Golan. "Do you want this, or do you want to give it to the Finnish maritime police?"

He stared at the body. "We can probably bring in as many resources as they can. In addition, it is almost certain that the murderer is on board, so it is our problem. And it's our ship. I'd say yes, I want this, but I suspect technically it's not our call."

I agreed with him.

Bashir snapped his phone shut. "That was legal. Here's the position they're taking: because we are still in Finnish territorial waters, we cannot assume jurisdiction. However, because the murder transpired within the confines of the semi-autonomous Jipito nation, the Finns cannot assume jurisdiction either. If we were at sea, the case would be ours. But in port, only the Jipitos have the authority to investigate. Or they can delegate authority to whomever they wish."

"That sounds a little dicey," I said as Harlan translated for the Jipitos. The older man shrugged and peeled back the wrapper on a candy bar.

"He says OK," Harlan told us.

Bashir clapped his hands. "Good. Then it's your case,

Golan. Please work closely with Mr. Grave. And please process this quickly before the guests arrive. I'll be in my suite if you need me."

I waited for him to leave. "This is a very inefficient way to kill someone," I told Golan.

"Yes. These tribal people like to make a show of it."

"Tribal people? You think it was the Jipitos?"

"No," he said, "the other tribal people, the Emiratis. This is some inter-clan feud. The Emir has four wives from four different parts of the country, and every time he picks a new favorite son, another wife feels publicly shamed. So she cries to her uncles who are all too ready to pick up their guns and rocket launchers."

"And is Bashir his current favorite son?"

"Oh, yes." Golan nodded. "Bashir has a mind for investments. He's made his father a lot of money."

I heard birds chirping overhead, and I had to remind myself that I was on a ship. "How did you get involved with this?"

"I've worked for the old man, the Emir, for a dozen years. Before that, I was a consular officer for the Israeli government and I got to know him. He's quite a guy. Moderate and shrewd, he's the kind of man this part of the world needs. He asked me to keep an eye on his son's new venture."

"It was an offer you couldn't refuse."

"Something like that. I told him I'd see it off to a good start. I'd take the job for three months, but no longer. I have young children; I don't want to miss them growing up." He made a few phone calls and I sat with the Jipitos in front of their hut eating puff pastries and thinking things through. We had just about finished eating when two security officers showed up with kits to process the crime scene.

"Can you ask them if they saw anyone?" I asked Harlan, and he did. The Jipitos shook their heads in unison. Harlan asked them a few more questions and then translated for me.

"They said they heard some grunting and a scream, and then they went to check it out. That's when they found the body."

"Can they show us where that was?"

Harlan said a few words in Portuguese and we were off. I borrowed a can of Luminol and followed the Jipitos down the path, spraying the Luminol every few minutes, which added an eerie blue glow to the already surreal rainforest. The blue glow indicated the presence of trace amounts of blood, which confirmed that the Jipitos were telling the truth. The man hadn't been murdered behind their hut.

We walked in silence over a low bridge and around the edge of a small pond. It was all very pretty. If you looked up you'd think you were looking at a night sky instead of the underside of Deck 8. Still, for a two story rainforest, it seemed quite a bit larger than it was. You would have to look up past the foliage to notice, but all around the rainforest's perimeter were stateroom balconies.

We crossed another bridge onto an island in the middle of the pond. The Jipitos led us off the trail to a grove of trees near the center of the island. There were frogs everywhere, bright yellow frogs about the size of a quarter.

"Don't touch them," Harlan told me. "They're pretty but they're toxic."

I made quite sure I didn't touch anything as we moved further from the trail. We came to a pile of artificial rocks where you didn't need the Luminol to see the blood. It was everywhere.

The Jipitos marveled at the Luminol and asked if they could have the can. It wasn't mine to give, but what the hell. I've always felt it was bad luck to say no to a hunter-gatherer.

"Nobody is supposed to be off the trail, right?"

Harlan nodded.

"Then why do you need artificial rocks back here?"

"I don't know. It could be a junction box." He poked around the rock pile and found a door. Inside was a panel with several buttons and a circuit breaker.

"What's it for?"

"I have no idea," he said. "I've never been over here before except to look around."

I pushed a button and we heard a buzzing noise from up in the trees. "What the hell?"

"It's probably not a good idea to keep ..." Harlan began, but I wasn't listening. A moment later, a rope ladder dropped from the tree canopy.

"How about that," I said. "This looks like fun. I'd climb that if I was fifty years younger."

Harlan grabbed hold of the ladder. "Oh, you know what this is?" he said. "This is one of the howler monkey nests. The ladders are in case the zookeeper had to go up into the nest for some reason."

"You have howler monkeys?"

"No, no." He shook his head. "They didn't work out. We got them all the way to Helsinki, permits and all, but they were too nasty. Most of their waking hours were spent masturbating, so they got returned. That was the end of Monkey Island. Unfortunately, the only other species available on short notice was poisonous tree frogs, so Frog Island it became. Only we have to be sure the passengers stay on the trails."

"Is that right? Well, up you go."

He chuckled. "You're kidding, right? You want me to go up there?"

"Yeah. I already did my cross-training for the day. Off with you now. Don't touch any frogs."

He didn't look too happy about it but he climbed. I stood there staring up at him as the Jipitos played with the Luminol.

"See anything?"

"It's kind of dark," he called out.

"I'll try to find a light." I pressed another button and heard a buzzing noise. Harlan screamed.

The Jipitos ran away, and I pulled out my gun. "What happened?"

"Don't press anything," I think he might have said. I didn't have my hearing aid on, and I was still hoping to find a light switch. I pressed another button and he screamed again. I did not know what was going on.

He came down the ladder fast. "What the hell?" He was out of breath.

"What happened? What's up there?"

"Nothing is up there. But the button you pressed, it's part of the electrical perimeter to keep the monkeys where the passengers could see them. If they stayed in their nest too long, one good press of the button would motivate them to get out."

"Is that right?"

"It is, and it really hurts."

"I'm sorry," I told him as Golan came running up.

"I heard screams."

Harlan told him about the monkey nest.

"And it was empty?"

I put my gun away, and as I did so, I noticed a sticky liquid on the ground under the rope. It was all over Harlan's shoes. I pointed it out.

Golan knelt down and smelled it. Then he looked up at the ladder.

"What is it?" I asked.

"It's khat. It's a narcotic popular in parts of Arabia. You chew the leaves, and spit."

"That's a lot of spit," I said. "Someone was waiting up in that monkey house for a long while, someone with a monkey on his back." I laughed for about four minutes, but nobody else seemed to find it funny.

Chapter Four

Over the next several hours, as embarkation proceeded, Indulgence took on an estimated 285 tons of passenger weight, 9,000 bottles of wine, and all the eggs that were available in southern Finland, which was an alarmingly low 7,200. We were going to need to find more in Stockholm.

I made my way to my cabin on Deck 11. I won't lie to you, I was disappointed to learn that it was an inside cabin. But once I opened the door, all my disappointment evaporated. It was lovely. I've been in some great cabins and some not so great cabins. Once I had my own suite with a hot tub and two bars. Then again, one time I shared a crew cabin with a flatulent Filipino who played video games all night long. This cabin was somewhere in between, though much closer to the former than to the latter.

My bed was queen-sized, my desk was large enough to do some actual work on, and my TV was nonexistent. That was a bit of a shock. I stared out the window for a full forty seconds, watching the palm trees sway in the wind as little sailboats flitted back and forth. Then I remembered that Helsinki doesn't have a lot of palm trees, and I had an inside cabin. I grabbed the remote control to confirm, but sure enough, my window was actually a TV, fully loaded with premium channels.

Continuing my tour, I found a full tub in the bathroom, and a terrycloth robe that had the word "Undulgence" embroidered on the back. Either someone had made a very costly spelling error, or my knowledge of the English language was incomplete.

I found the couch appropriately firm, the bed as well. Across from the bed was a full-length mirror, and I looked good in it. It was time for the acid test; I opened the door to the minibar. And I smiled. No tiny cube fridge here, this was one of those half-size fridges, the kind you might find in an English kitchen or a fraternity den. It was well stocked with soda and beer and white wine and my new favorite, Captain Manuel's Spiced Rum. I was glad my requests had been taken seriously.

My bags had arrived safely, but sadly, my butler had not yet unpacked them. I understand from long experience that things get very busy on cruise ships on embarkation day. So I was willing to give my butler a little slack.

Several folders had been placed on the desk. The first contained my full access ID card, which I was going to need in order to move freely about the ship. And I intended to move freely about the ship. I also found the passenger manifest and a booklet containing a detailed list of staff and crew members and their stations. The second folder contained the analyses of the threats that had been made against the ship.

I also found my dining room table assignment. As I had requested, I would be dining with retired Lieutenant General Meg Savoy, her husband Tuck, and their grandson Casper.

I mixed myself a rum and Coke, turned my window/TV back to the beach with the sailboats, and opened up the staff booklet. Twenty-one hundred staff and crew members is more than most ships have passengers. Managing that kind of workforce was an industry unto itself, and I knew for certain that if I rode an elevator down further than the passengers were allowed, I would find a wiry middle-aged man known as the chief steward. He would be Serbian or Romanian or maybe Russian. His name would be Yuri or Vlad or Brutus, and if it wasn't, he'd still answer to Yuri or Vlad or Brutus. Every ship had such a man. And on every ship, that man is feared.

Look at him the wrong way and you will be baking apple dumplings all night long for a month, never mind that you are an assistant art director. Show up for work one Sunday morning with your shirt untucked and you'll be showing up for work Sunday night too, ironing shirts and learning to curse in Polish with your new friends in the laundry. Talk back to him, complain about your roommate snoring, ask for a better-fitting uniform, or mention that you've really been bussing tables for a long time, and a ticket will manifest itself in front of you. It will be an airline ticket, one way, coach, and he will have willed it into existence that very moment. It has your name on it, and it's a ticket home.

There's no bullshit below decks. Don't get me wrong, it's a giant twenty-four hour party down there, but nobody is playing around with the rules. The stakes are too high. Have fun but behave, and you can keep coming back.

And come back they do. Cruising is an exciting career. If you can take the pressure, and if you can kiss up to the occasional crabby passenger, then you can make some good money. But then, good money is always a relative thing.

If your mother is back home in Riga feeding your children well because you have a little something to send home each month, you're going to want to keep your job. If you trust your wife around the swarm of unemployed fellows standing on the corner of that new apartment complex a comfortable distance from the Manila slums, you might be thinking hard right now about the private school your daughter attends, the one with the books. And this job might be something you'll want to hold on to.

But if you're an American, this isn't the job for you,

unless you're an officer. The rules are too strict, the hours are too long, the pay is not that good, and you'll just get plain fed up with all the Oriental food.

I was looking through the list trying to find someone I knew, someone I might have bumped into on another cruise, maybe someone I could get some straight answers from. I had just refilled my beverage when I found her. Isla Rossdale was the managing director of the Karnak Art Gallery. Art galleries are huge profit centers on cruise ships, and a good director can make nearly as much as the captain. Isla was good. Some years back, she nearly sold me a Picasso.

I checked my handy ship's plan and located the gallery on Deck 8, which was also the Ancient Egypt theme deck. It was time for me to get to work, so I finished my drink, pocketed my new ID card, and after a brief nap, headed out to find an elevator.

When you work the cruise ships, as I do, you tend to run into the same people over and over again. Once you take to this life, it's hard to give it up. I first met Isla Rossdale about a dozen years ago aboard a ship called the Marla C when a young woman went overboard twenty miles outside Martinique's territorial waters. The young lady was a newlywed traveling with her husband. By the time I got onboard, he had already confessed to pushing her over the railing of their stateroom verandah. I knew he was lying.

But that's neither here nor there. Back then, I had a huge crush on Isla Rossdale but there were a number of impediments to our love, such as her marriage, my advanced age, and her inability to recall that my name wasn't Murray. I was certain that once I solved the case, she would be impressed and want me. As it turned out, she didn't. But I'm pretty sure she'd remember me. I'm charming.

I was unprepared for the sheer number of people I found moving through the corridors. And yes, they were mostly older passengers. Let's get that out of the way right now. Cruising is a mature man's pleasure, but far more often than that, it is a mature woman's pleasure, as the ladies tend to outnumber us older men by at least ten to one. That's something I was unprepared for as I began maturing and then kept at it, but it's been a wonderful bonus to the aging process.

Embarkation was by this point nearly complete, and passengers were scurrying every which way. There's a science to boarding a ship. You won't find it written down anywhere but all the cruise lines do it exactly the same way. First, you stand in line waiting to board. You give your ticket to the young man at the counter and say goodbye to your luggage. It will make its way to your cabin later. Walk through a metal detector. Have your picture taken in front of the gangway, then walk up the gangway and through another metal detector. Have your picture taken with the cruise director, and then a staff member will walk you to your cabin. Spend three minutes checking out the contents of the minibar. Confirm that premium channels are available on the TV. Pee, wash hands, and then exit cabin in search of free food. Trust me on this, I'm a veteran.

Embarkation might be a crazy time, but it's also your best opportunity to scope out the passengers and have a look at the lovely ladies you'll be spending the next couple of weeks with. And let me tell you, there were many hundreds of them, each better looking than the last. I was smiling, thinking about this, when I heard a whirring sound. It was nearby and getting louder.

I turned, and that's when I saw her. She was an older woman, a good deal older than me, and she was riding a Rascal. Judging by the whine of the motor, I knew she had the joystick to the metal. She came at me fast, swerving at the last minute, but she still ran over my foot. I could hear her cackling as she rode away.

Just then, the elevator door opened, so I didn't give the incident any more thought. When I finally made my way down to Deck 8, I stepped out of the elevator into a different world.

Ancient Egypt had come to life. Already, about half of Indulgence's fifty-four hundred passengers had arrived for the pre-departure party. They were listening to the band, staring at the sculptures, and ogling the serving girls who were dolled up in semi-tasteful-yet-skimpy goddess uniforms. All the lighting was faux-torchlight. All the lettering was faux-hieroglyphics, and all the structures looked to be stone blocks, but were probably faux-stone blocks. I saw enough gold plating in the decor to sink a lesser ship. I joined my fellow passengers gawking and marveling, and I nearly bumped into a fellow wearing a King Tut mask carrying a tray of stuffed mushrooms. I couldn't let him pass.

Towering over the entire kingdom were four two-story high statues of Ramses II, two on each side of the ship. They faced a giant sphinx made of ice that presided over a central bar offering free champagne. Past the Ramses statues were pyramids that rose high above us on each side. And near the tops of the pyramids you could see the guests peering down from the balconies of what were very likely some expensive suites.

Each of the pyramids was itself a shop. I saw Egyptian-style jewelry for sale in one, and non-Egyptian-style jewelry for sale in another. Other pyramids proffered Nefertari's Swimwear, Seti's Sushi, Memphis Margaritas, Khufu Tattoo, Cleopatra's Cappuccinos, Anubis Fish Tacos, and Amenhotep's Tuxedoes. I had no idea the ancient Egyptians were so cosmopolitan.

You know what the folks in the cruising industry got right? The fact that people on vacation will spend more than people who are not on vacation. You might think twice about buying a $6,000 watch back at home, but hell, you're on vacation, so why not splurge? Every shop had customers in it. I came to the end of the hall where another Tut waiter wielded a platter of bite-sized quiches.

"You're my man, Tut," I told him as I took two. The last

pyramid shop didn't have any customers at all, just a pretty little thing standing inside the doorway looking forlorn. She brightened as I approached. Most women do.

"Have you thought about making Indulgence a special part of your life?" she asked. She was gorgeous.

"What, now?"

"Many of our guests find that fractional ownership is the ideal way to enjoy all the marvels that Indulgence has to offer. If you'd like to step inside, I can show you just how affordable it can be."

I quickly turned off my hearing aid, closing my eyes as I did. I spun around as fast as I could but I could already feel the pull of this siren. I knew that if I looked at her for another moment or listened to so much as ten seconds of her song, I'd be hooked forever. Time shares have a bad reputation. That's why the industry changed the name to fractional ownership. They are relatively new to the cruising industry but are making headway.

The companies hire the prettiest girls imaginable and equip them with highly organized sales pitches that are nothing less than spells. Shake your head as much as you like, but half an hour later you'll be the proud owner of something you never thought you needed and will probably use only once, kind of like a treadmill for your condo, only many times as expensive. I ran.

Near the stern, two obelisks made of ice towered over the entrance to the Nile Enchantment Theater. The Egyptologist I had seen earlier in the meeting was holding court. As I passed, he handed me a brochure for a show called 'Isis in Love.' I couldn't help appreciating the scanty clothing on the slave girls.

I relieved another Tut of three crab cakes, passed a pyramid selling New York-style malteds, and found myself in front of the Karnak Art Gallery. I spotted Isla right away. She looked great. She was up front talking with some customers about a blocky art print that hung on the wall. They were interested. I would wait.

I wandered into the next pyramid, Narmer's Wines & Spirits, which was nearly empty. "Let me get a piña colada," I told the girl behind the bar. That's when the lights went out, all of them.

Chapter Five

It's worth remembering that a pyramid inside a ship has no natural light, so when it gets dark, it gets really dark. I was standing right by the doorway and I couldn't even see the doorway. I heard several shouts of alarm but no actual screams. It took only about fifteen seconds for the emergency lighting panels to pop on, and then all the lights came back.

"We have no piña coladas," the girl behind the bar said, not missing a beat.

"What, now?"

"No piña coladas, only wine."

"It says wine and spirits on the sign," I told her. "Hey, what's with the lights?"

"It does say that," she said. "But so far we only have wine. And I don't know what happened with the lights. I was right here with you the whole time."

Her nametag read 'Lyudmila.'

"Have the lights ever gone out before, Lyudmila?"

"What before? You are the first customer ever here. Wine bars are not popular when there are girls walking around outside giving free wine."

I had no idea what she was saying. I remembered I had my hearing aid turned off so I turned it back on. "You said something about free wine. I'll have some of that."

"Not free wine," she told me. "Free wine and champagne is outside. Here you have to pay. There is better wine here but you already have a glass of champagne in your hand."

"But it's empty," I told her.

"It is not."

"What's that?" I pointed behind her. She turned to look and by the time she turned back my glass was empty. "How about a refill for old time's sake?"

I didn't quite get a smile but something close. And I got a free glass of wine. Lyudmila even got me a plate of nuts which I was enjoying when the captain's voice came over the ship's public address system.

"Good evening, ladies and gentlemen," he began. "This is Captain Norgaard speaking to you from the navigation bridge. First, on behalf of the officers and the staff and crew, I'd like to welcome you to Indulgence. As you know, this will be our maiden voyage and we look forward to a wonderful cruise.

"I would also like to apologize for the brief power failure we just experienced. One of our transmission lines was still connected to the Helsinki power grid as we were switching over to our generators in preparation for sail-away. And the transition was not as smooth as we had hoped. We will be leaving Finland behind in approximately thirty minutes, and setting sail to our first port of call, Stockholm, Sweden. If you have any questions or concerns, please feel free to speak with any member of the crew, or consult one of the information kiosks you'll find at each of the elevator banks.

"Once again, welcome to Indulgence. We look forward to a wonderful cruise."

"What's the captain like?" I asked Lyudmila.

"I met him only one time. He is a very nice old man."

"Old like me?"

"Maybe not so old," she said, almost cracking a smile. "I am not meaning to be rude."

"Hey, are you OK? You don't look so happy. I'll bet I know why, you miss your boyfriend, and/or your husband."

She shook her head. "No boyfriend and no husband, and I am twenty-eight years old. Why should I not look unhappy?"

"No boyfriend? No husband? How can that be? You're gorgeous, but you could lighten up on the gloom. If you do that, you won't last a week without someone proposing to you."

"Do you want to have a bet with me?"

"I do," I said. "I'll bet you a glass of wine."

She shook my hand.

"So how about it?" I said. "Want to tie the knot with me? I could make you happy. I dance and tell jokes and I have cable TV. I'd keep you warm at night."

"Very funny man." She blushed. "Do I have to answer now?"

"Take your time," I said. "My heart is yours. At least until we get to Copenhagen, then I'm on the block again. I love you, Lyudmila, but I can't wait forever."

She moved off to attend to some customers who had wandered in. I stared out the doorway at the throng of humanity pressing by. I wondered what the ancient Egyptians would think of all this. This is what their culture would have evolved into had the Assyrians and the Greeks and the Romans and the Muslims not invaded, and had they been somehow transported to the Jersey shore. They're probably all rolling over in their museums right now.

"One for the road, Lyud?" I asked when she returned. I held up my empty. "A bet is a bet and you lost. You got a marriage proposal so I get a glass of wine."

"Cable TV," she said as she poured. "You have premium channels?"

"I do."

"HBO?"

"And HBO II."

"Showtime?"

"Of course," I said, leaning in to whisper. "I also get Playboy Channel. And Spicy Mumbai."

"What is Spicy Mumbai?"

I wasn't sure how to answer politely. "It's kind of like Playboy Channel only with Indian ladies. I'm not sure why I get it. I keep thinking that I'm going to call up and have them take it off. I mean, why pay? But then every now and again, they show you something so special. Listen, I have to leave you for now. Think about what we talked about, OK?"

She assured me she would.

I wandered through the corridors of Ancient Egypt for a bit longer. I was getting good at spotting the Tut waiters, and I managed to score two more puff pastries, six mini-quiches, and one stuffed mushroom before I headed back to the Karnak Art Gallery.

Isla spotted me as soon as I walked into her pyramid. "Murray," she called out, holding out her arms. "It's been a long time."

I hugged her back. "You know my name isn't Murray, right?"

"I do. And I'm glad to see that you're drinking wine and not that noxious beverage you had me try. What was that drink you invented, a Puerto Rico Avalanche? That was vile."

"It's not vile. A Puerto Rican Iceberg. Rum and cool whip; it's refreshing. I'll probably have one later."

"Disgusting. But you can't be here on business, right? I thought for sure you'd be out of that line of work by now. Please tell me you retired, and you are here to enjoy the good life. I could find a nice etching for you."

"No, no. Apparently you have to save money in order to retire. It seems I forgot to do that. But I've started socking a little bit away each month. I figure a couple of dozen more years and I'll be on my way. So how's about it, I don't know anyone else here. Can we talk for a bit?"

She looked back at her customers. "It's kind of busy tonight, maiden voyage, first customers. Could we meet up tomorrow? I'd love to catch up."

I raised my arms for another hug. "How much time does it look like I have left?"

"OK, OK." She whispered something to an assistant and came back. "You have to make it look like you want to buy something."

"Oh, I do. I do want to buy something." I followed her to a case housing a little wooden sculpture of a man holding onto a cow. "I've been looking for something to put on the mantel. I was thinking maybe a man holding a cow."

"You have an eye for quality," Isla told me. "It's Middle Kingdom, original, of course. The Egyptians had by that point stopped most of the pyramid building. They were focusing less on funerary architecture and more on grave furnishings."

"Well I'll be goddamned."

"It's quite a dramatic shift in focus," she continued. "Think about it. Instead of working to be sure your god king lives forever, you can focus instead on what you want for your own afterlife. Artisans made representational images of the things people wanted with them when they died."

"And someone wanted a man holding a cow?"

She stared at me. "Henry, in all possibility we'll be dead for a very long time. Do you want to have to hold onto your own cow, or would you prefer to have a groomsman to do it for you?"

She had a point. "I'll take it," I said. "Get the paper before I change my mind."

"It lists for $16,000. It's worth $2,700 but I'll let you have it for an even $10,000."

"You drive a hard bargain," I said. "I left my checkbook back at the intersection of Penury Lane and Pauper Boulevard. Can you lend me a few bucks?"

"Very funny. So why exactly are you here, Henry? There hasn't been any trouble on this ship, has there?"

I assured her that there hadn't been. "I'm just keeping an eye on some Arabian King's investment. You know, make sure nobody walks off with the keys while we're in port."

She was quiet for a moment. "I still think about that girl back at Martinique, you know. Do you ever think about her?"

"No," I told her. But in truth, I've thought a great deal about Debbie Weimar over the years.

"Did anybody ever figure out why she jumped?"

I stared at the Egyptian cow herder and hoped that Debbie Weimar had someone with her to help navigate the afterlife, on the off chance such a thing existed. "No." I shook my head. "I don't think so."

"Poor thing."

I nodded in agreement. "She was taking anti-psychotic drugs, but her husband swore she had it under control."

"He also swore he pushed her over the railing, didn't he? How did you know he was lying?"

"Remember on those older ships sometimes the lifeboats were hanging overhead? You don't see too much of that anymore but it used to be common."

"I remember."

"Well there was one of those lifeboats hanging out there with a nice view of Debbie's verandah, and I got to thinking there might have been someone in that lifeboat when she went overboard."

"Why did you think that?"

I told her to hold on for a moment when a Tut waiter passed. I flagged down an Isis and came back with two flutes of champagne.

"I can't drink on the job," Isla said.

"And I wasn't offering," I told her. "OK, lifeboat maintenance is a regular part of any duty roster, so someone had to climb in that lifeboat every couple of days. And if you were up there, you might start thinking it was kind of peaceful, maybe the only place on board where you could be by yourself."

"Yeah?"

"Do you remember what Debbie Weimar looked like?"

Isla nodded. "Beautiful girl, about nineteen years old, right?"

"She was twenty-seven. Now imagine you're up there lounging in your lifeboat and this beautiful girl plops herself into a lounge chair just beneath you. Well, your life just improved tremendously. You might be tempted to do a little more maintenance tomorrow. You might even tell a friend."

"You think like that, don't you? You're a pervert."

"Maybe," I said. "A guy can get lonely at sea seven thousand miles from Manila. So I started questioning the maintenance crew. It didn't take long. She even knew they were up there, and she didn't care. I heard that from at least half a dozen guys. She just wanted to lie in her lounge chair."

"And then she jumped."

I nodded. "And then one afternoon she lay out there tanning, drank two iced teas, then climbed up on the railing and swan-dived into the Caribbean."

"And the guys saw it."

I nodded. "They didn't want to say anything because they were afraid of losing their jobs."

"Then why did the husband confess?"

"I don't know why he confessed," I told her. "He said he promised her mother he'd take care of her, and he had failed at taking care of her. And he didn't want people to think badly of her."

"That's true love." Isla said. But I didn't know what it was.

"You're sure the husband wasn't involved?"

I nodded. "I spent twelve hours sifting through every picture the photographers had taken until I found one with him in the background. He was at a pineapple carving class when it happened. He just couldn't face the fact that he was learning to make whimsical fruit sculptures while his wife killed herself."

I finished my champagne while Isla went to talk with a customer.

"Wow, you totally bummed out my evening," she said when she came back.

"You brought it up," I reminded her. "So let's change the subject. How do you like Indulgence so far?"

Isla shrugged. "We're going to have to see, I guess. We've only been on board a week. We've had some glitches but I think we're over the worst of them."

"Glitches?"

"Mostly minor. Somebody didn't pull the right visa paperwork for the Russians. They got Ukrainian visas instead which weren't going to work. Then, let's see, for some reason there were no gas lines to the pool deck, so the hot tub wasn't hot and the grills didn't work. And, of course, we're on our third captain."

"Third captain? How do you have three captains without even sailing out of port?"

"It seems the little prince isn't as hands-off as he promised to be. Have you met Bashir?"

I nodded.

"He more or less fancied himself as captain. He wanted to be the final authority for all decision making, and that's not how things work on a ship. He's been slow to pick up on that."

"So the first two captains quit?"

"That's right. Have you met Captain Norgaard?"

"No," I said. "I haven't gotten around to it yet."

"You'll like him. Lovely man. He's about your age. They coaxed him out of a comfortable retirement community at some Norwegian spa. He has a one year contract and a license to nap."

"So Bashir is effectively the captain?"

"Right," Isla said. "That's where it gets interesting. Bashir makes the decisions but he doesn't tend to make them without consulting this other guy Golan who is the head of security."

"Him I met."

"If you ask me, he's the guy with the most juice on board. I think he answers to Bashir's father."

"Interesting chain of command."

"It is," she said. "Henry, I have to wrap up some sales. In fifteen minutes the dinner swarm begins, and it will be desolate here. Let's make plans to meet later or tomorrow."

I was momentarily terrified. I have found myself at the tail end of a dinner swarm more often than I care to admit, and I had no idea what it would be like on a ship this size. Many cruise ships, Indulgence included, had set dinner seatings about two hours apart. You don't show up late because it messes everyone up. In fact, showing up late for dinner is probably the biggest faux pas a cruise passenger can make. Other passengers will already be sitting at the table, and you can only munch on a breadstick for so long. The pressure to arrive on time is so great that most passengers will do anything to avoid being late, even if that means arriving ten minutes early, when the dining room has not yet opened.

The result is a crushing press of aged humanity known onboard as the dinner swarm. The elevators clog, the stairways fill, the atria become florid with the mingling aromas of aftershave, cologne, eau, and perfumes pungent enough to choke a dove. Everyone wears their finest finery; gowns, dinner jackets, tuxedoes, you might even see a corset if you look closely. If you didn't know better you'd think you were lined up for a casting call, looking for a role in a show about rich old people. There are more baubles and gems and jewels per square inch here than in any other part of the world. If you melted down all the gold, you could ransom an Inca. Don't even get me started on the diamonds.

I did not want to find myself at the tail end of the swarm. No, sir. It can take twenty minutes to load people into their seats, and that's after the doors open. No, the place to be is at the head of the swarm, so close you can smell the bowl of after-dinner mints just inside the doors. That way, when the doors open, you get to the table first and you get your choice of rolls. Also, you get your drinks faster.

I needed to change so I hurried to my cabin. Once I got inside, I flipped the lights on and was surprised to find a Tut waiter standing there. He was holding a tray of pot stickers with a little bowl of dipping sauce.

"Are you my butler?" I asked. Then he punched me in the face. I passed out.

Chapter Six

I heard voices and the barking of dogs. Both the voices and the barking were in German; the logic of dreaming allows this. I was wearing two shirts, but I was still freezing. My friend Paul Gentile had been shot by the guards a week earlier and I wore his shirt over mine. Thank you for that, Paul, though I sure miss you. And I was doing exactly what Paul was doing when he got shot, searching for potatoes on the wrong side of the stalag fence. By the winter of 1945 the fence was falling down anyway, and none of the guards cared too much about fixing it. Most of the time they didn't care if you went out looking for potatoes either, though at some random times they did, as Paul learned. I was holding four little tubers that I had just dug up. I'm not sure if they were actually potatoes but I didn't care. A guard started shouting at me to come back so I did. He reached out for my potatoes and I pulled away. That's when he smacked me in the head with the butt of his rifle. When I woke up I had a throbbing headache and no potatoes, and I was far more saddened by the latter.

"Mr. Grave," someone called out. I felt some gentle prodding and woke to find myself in some sort of hospital.

"My potatoes," I said, but nobody seemed to have any useful information about them.

Someone took my pulse. "I'm Dr. Faber," he said. "I'm

the ship's doctor."

"What, now?"

"Can you tell me your name?"

I told him. Aver Golan was sitting next to my bed. I waved.

"Do you know where you are right now?" the doctor asked.

It was coming back to me. "Not Germany."

"You're in the ship's infirmary, Mr. Grave." He had me count some fingers. He tracked my eye movements and took my blood pressure. "You took a nasty hit. Do you know what happened?"

I told him about the Tut waiter.

"Did you get a good look at him?" Golan asked.

"I did, yes," I said. "He looked Egyptian. Regal, even kinglike. He was wearing a mask, remember?"

"Did you see anything else?"

"No. He was carrying a tray of pot stickers. They could have been samosas. Sometimes you can't tell the difference until you taste them, but I think they were pot stickers. He punched me before I got to try one."

I tried to sit up but the pain kicked in. The doctor helped me back down onto the bed. "I'm afraid we're going to have to send you home," he said. "You've taken a very bad blow. And at your age, it can take awhile to recover from something like that."

"I've been through worse," I told him. "I'm not going anywhere."

"I'm afraid it's not a request," he said. "You know as well as anyone that nobody can countermand the decision of the ship's doctor, not even the captain."

"Under normal circumstances, that would be the case," I told him. "But I think the chain of command here is a little loopy. I also need to call my son. He's a doctor. Hey, I need to get to dinner. I'm supposed to be having dinner with the general and her husband."

"I think you might have missed dinner," Golan told me.

My spirits sank. "How long was I out?"

"We have you on the surveillance cameras leaving the art gallery just before 6:00," Golan said, "and the housekeeper found you in your cabin when she came to turn down your bed. That was at about 6:30."

"That's quick work."

"We'll need you to look through your things to be sure nothing was taken, but I think this was just about sending you a message."

"Well the message could have been clearer. It's rude when people don't tell you how they really feel about you."

"The message was pretty clear," Golan said. He held up a sheet of ship's stationary with a single line scrawled on it in pen. "I'm going to kill everyone on board," it said.

"We found this sticking out of your jacket pocket. Presumably you didn't write it."

I assured him I did not. This message complicated matters for me in two ways. First, it confirmed that my assailant knew who I was, and that's a problem for anyone working undercover. Second, it was a direct and possibly credible threat against the lives of the passengers. And my job required me to pass that information on to my employers who would require that Indulgence pass that information on to all the passengers.

Golan shook his head sadly. He knew what I was thinking. Most of the passengers would disembark in Stockholm, and the cruise would be largely over. Indulgence would be over too, because nobody would be willing to risk sailing on her again, not for a while. There are plenty of other ships out there. Who needs this kind of hassle?

"Maybe I did write it," I told Golan. I grabbed the sheet of paper and stuck it in my pocket. "Or maybe we didn't find it yet." Life is all about taking chances with the fate of others.

Don't ever let anyone tell you otherwise.

The doctor gave me a shot of something for the pain and it worked almost instantly. I felt a little dizzy when I sat up but the sensation passed quickly enough. "I'm going to give you some pills," he said. "Take no more than two at a time."

"We'll talk with the servers who were working the Ancient Egypt party," Golan told me. "But I'll tell you right now, we won't find out who this is. We've got lots of those masks. Is there anything else you can tell me about your assailant? Any characteristics you remember?"

"Yeah, he was an albino and he had a club foot. Come on, he was just a normal guy, normal height."

"Then we won't be able to find him."

"Oh, I'll find him," I told him. "I'm going Tut hunting." I jotted a series of queries on a piece of note paper and handed them to him.

"What's this?"

"It's some information I'm going to need before morning." My ears were ringing. "Can you get one of your guys to work on it? He'll need a computer. It's morning in Washington, D.C., so he should be able to get this done in a couple of hours. Tell him to call my employer. The number is right there. Ask for Beth Obradors. She works with me. She can find out anything."

Golan shook his head. "This is somewhat irregular."

"So am I. Some days I'm like clockwork, but most days, well, you don't want to know about most days."

"I don't have anyone who can work on this tonight," he said, "but I'll put someone on it first thing in the morning."

"No, no. We need to move this along. That fellow who works with you, he can work on it. Fester Lung is his name."

"You mean Lester Fung."

"That's what I said. He told me he'd be happy to help me."

Golan took a deep breath. "You've been through a lot

tonight. I promise we will share information with you, but I'm going to be leading the onboard investigations, so I won't be able to assign my people to work for you."

"You might want to check on that," I suggested.

He shook his head. "I run ship's security. I make the decisions. We share information with you and your organization. That is the nature of our contract."

"Technically you might be right," I said, "but here's how I see things. In about two weeks, Indulgence is scheduled to arrive in Florida, which half of the world's cruise ships call home. When you dock in Miami, you will be asked to provide a form certifying your ability to respond to crimes at sea. I am here to underwrite that certification. If I choose not to sign my name to that form, Indulgence will not be allowed to return to Miami, or for that matter, any American port."

Golan stared at me.

"It's not the end of the world," I told him. "There are a couple of European ports that will still let you in without our paperwork. Albania is lovely this time of year; the fig harvest is sure to delight. And of course, you can pretty much still have your way with West Africa. Senegal is doing a jazz festival this year."

"This sounds like a threat, Mr. Grave."

"It's not," I assured him. "It's not. I'm a nice man. By the end of this cruise we're going to be good friends, you and I. We'll probably meet up every summer to go bow hunting. But for now, I need you to work with me. So have Fester work on my queries."

"Lester."

"That's what I said." I patted my holster. "Can I have my gun back?"

Golan looked up.

"You didn't take my gun?"

He shook his head.

"Good Christ."

I went back to my cabin about half an hour later, when I felt stable enough to walk. My butler still hadn't unpacked my bags. I called my son Teddy in Boston and I told him what happened. He told me to come home, but in the end, he gave me a list of symptoms to watch out for. If I got dizzy, I should sit down immediately. If I got confused, I should find a quiet place and just try to piece things together slowly. But half my days are like that anyway.

I promised Teddy I'd be more careful. My head was pounding, and then something odd happened; colors started behaving differently from how they usually behaved. Believe me, I know how strange that sounds, but I have lived my life thinking about colors as visual sorts of things, and now it was as if they had some sound to them. I would learn later that this condition is called synesthesia. But at that moment, I did not know what was happening to me. There was a palm tree on my TV that sounded like rush hour traffic, so I changed channels and found a documentary on vampire squid, which was fascinating. But when that thing lit up like Coney Island on the fourth of July, it sounded like a thousand typewriters clicking away at once. And I didn't even have the volume turned on.

I watched that show for about an hour and a half, enough to become an expert on vampire squid behavior. I was feeling very tranquil, very relaxed, and it occurred to me that my pain medication might have something to do with that. If so, I was a big fan.

I made a mental note to ask Teddy about the medicine the next time I spoke with him. But first, I needed to get organized. I had a killer to catch, and I didn't have a lot of time. In twelve days, Indulgence would spill out her passengers onto a dock in Miami. And the killer would be among them, presumably not dressed like King Tut.

Here is the thing about crimes at sea: when they go

cold, they go cold forever. Once a ship reaches its destination, the passengers settle their tabs, stuff any remaining bottles of shampoo and scented lotion into their bags, hand off envelopes filled with two twenty-dollar bills to their favorite waiters, eat all the Belgian waffles remaining at the breakfast buffet, have one last picture taken with the celebrity guest, and then they vanish into the wind. Or into a taxi, or a bus if they signed up for airport transfer, but they'd be gone, and gone with them would be any actionable evidence of a crime.

No, I needed to get a move on, put some miles under my gumshoes, and get a little detecting going on. I got my backup gun out of the cabin safe. Then I ordered room service but I fell asleep before it got there.

Chapter Seven

If you have never been to Stockholm, it is about time you visited. Built on fourteen separate islands connected by bridges, Stockholm is often called the Venice of the North. It's quite a spectacular place to visit, if my shipboard newsletter was any authority. I wouldn't know. I didn't get to see much of it.

I was a mess when I woke up. A peek at my bathroom mirror confirmed my suspicions. I had a black eye. It was puffy and ugly, and I'm puffy and ugly enough as it is. I was also starving, so I got myself together quickly, picked up the folder that had been slipped under my door, and headed up to the top of the ship, to Deck 15; the Riviera Deck.

A nice smorgasbord was being laid out in the little bistro just past the main swimming pool, and I was so hungry I didn't even linger to stare at the lovelies sunning themselves in the Scandinavian summer sun. I couldn't believe I had missed dinner. Breakfast too. In all my many years at sea, I have never missed dinner. I was hungry, and the sensation was not pleasing.

"Can I help you select your brunch?" a young man called to me. His nametag read 'Hiram' and indicated he was from Lima, Peru. He was frowning. "Have you hurt yourself, sir?"

"I have, Hiram. I have. I have slipped in my bathtub, but it's not as bad as it looks. I can get my own brunch. How come there's nobody here yet but me?"

"We haven't opened yet, sir. Not for another half an hour, and most of the passengers are ashore, but I'll be happy to get you started."

I picked up a tray but he took it from me and started walking with me around the table. "What do you like to eat here?" I asked him.

"Personally I like the potato pancakes and the meatballs."

"Let's start with that." I watched as he ladled meatballs onto my plate. "Keep it coming, Hiram."

I also got some rolled up slices of ham, a fair assortment of cheese, some cubed salami, hummus, a hardboiled egg, and a couple of slices of bread. I would have gotten more but an alarming percentage of the offerings were cold fish dishes, and no offense to the Scandinavians, but cold fish is among my least favorite food.

"What do you have for beverages, Hiram?"

"I can get you whatever you like, sir. Would you like a table inside or outside by the pool?"

"Oh, by the pool." I followed him out to a table next to one of Indulgence's smaller pools. Several children were splashing in the water. I ordered some orange juice and a Bloody Mary as a woman in a bikini flew by overhead.

"Make that two Bloody Marys," I told Hiram. "Can I ask about the flying girl? Or is my neurological damage worse than I feared?"

"No, sir," he said. "She's on the zipline. It's like a ride. You fly all the way to the stern over the big pool. Would you like to try it?"

"I would not. Now be off with you. I need my drinks."

"Yes, sir."

"One more thing," I called after him. "What's the name

of the fellow who runs the Vile Enhancement place?"

"The what, sir?"

I couldn't remember. "Vile Enhancement?" I tried again. "It's the Egypt Theater."

"Do you mean Nile Enchantment? That's the theater in the ancient Egypt neighborhood?"

"That's the one, yes. The guy who runs it, what's his name?"

He shrugged bashfully. "I can find out, sir." He turned and spoke into his radio as I dug into my brunch, which I found quite acceptable.

"Dr. Max Carder," Hiram told me. "He's our onboard Egyptologist."

"That's the one. Can you have him come up here? I need to have a little chat with him."

Hiram looked momentarily uncomfortable. "Sir, I'm sure if you ask at Guest Services, they can let you know when he might be available, but I can't really ..."

I shook my head as I chewed a meatball. "Hold on, hold on." I got out my ID card and handed it to him.

"You're Boris Yeltsin?"

"What, now?"

He stared at the card, then at me. "This is your picture but this is a Kentucky driver's license for Boris Yeltsin."

Nuts. "I think that's the wrong card." I fished through my wallet.

"What could you possibly use this for?" he asked. "Why would Boris Yeltsin be in Kentucky?"

I sighed. "I don't know. I thought it would be more useful than it is."

"Boris Yeltsin is dead."

"Is he?" I found my investigator's license and my Indulgence ID card and showed them to Hiram. "I should probably get rid of that one then. Listen, have Dr. Carder meet me up here right away. If he gives you any grief, tell him I'm the guy that had the run in with one of his Tuts."

"One of his what?"

"Tuts. He'll know what you mean. Now get him and then get my drinks. I'm an old man, I haven't got all day."

I stared out at the skyline of Stockholm, which looked to be quite lovely, almost as lovely as the young lady who dangled over my head, apparently not yet getting the hang of the zipline. "Are you going to make it?" I asked her. "If you're going to be there for awhile, I could order you something."

"Don't rush me," she said. "I think it's stuck."

"What's your name?"

"Emily."

"That was my first wife's name," I told her. "She died."

"I'm sorry to hear."

"It's not really your fault. I'm Henry. Come visit when you get down. I'll buy you a drink."

"OK. What happened to your eye?"

"I fell in the tub," I told her.

"That sucks." She started moving again at that point, and I soon lost sight of her.

Hiram returned promptly with my drinks but I had to wait almost half an hour for the good Egyptologist to make his appearance. I spent that time wisely, reading the folder of information that Lester Fung had researched for me.

Max Carder's eyes were red, and he looked tired. He had his leather jacket on, but instead of the cowboy hat, he wore an Atlanta Braves cap. "I heard what happened," he said, shaking his head.

"Did you, now?"

"I met with Mr. Golan about an hour ago. I'm really sorry. I wish there was some way I could help."

"We'll get to that," I told him. "Have a seat. I'll buy you lunch."

"I haven't even had breakfast yet," he said. "We had our

second show at midnight and we didn't wrap it up until nearly 3:00. Then they had me up for a 7:00 meeting. I had no idea the hours were going to be this long."

"Sit." I flagged down Hiram who came right over. "Can you bring us some more meatballs and some rolls? Egg rolls too, if you have them, and eggs. And a couple of egg creams. We have some catching up to do."

"Have we met?" Max Carder asked, as he watched Hiram scurry off.

"Not officially," I told him, "but I feel like I know you. I was at the meeting yesterday when you introduced yourself."

"I remember now," he said. "You're the King of Finland."

"In the flesh. Where's the cowboy hat, Max? The Atlanta Braves are Indians, so which side are you on?"

He took off the cap to show me his nearly bald head. Only a tuft of hair remained at the center. It was awful. "I started going bald at fifteen," he said. "I started wearing the cowboy hat at sixteen, but it looks silly in the morning."

"I see what you're getting at," I told him. "Hey, how many of those Tut masks do you have onboard?"

"Like I told Mr. Golan," he said, "I really don't have anything to do with catering. The restaurant manager would have more information about catering attire."

"No, no. The masks are not normal catering attire. They're stage props. You are the manager of the King Tut Theater, so the buck stops with you when it comes to stage props."

"Nile Enchantments," he said.

"Excuse me?"

"The name of the theater, it's not called the King Tut Theater."

"How many masks?"

"We brought thirty. Catering asked for twenty-four, which we gave them. As of this morning, all thirty are accounted for. So my best guess is that one of the waiters assaulted you."

"It wasn't one of the waiters," I told him.

"How can you be sure?"

"He had samosas. Or pot stickers." I read from the information that Lester Fung had prepared for me just to be sure. "Waiters weren't serving either of those things, so this guy wasn't a waiter. If he was, he would have just brought a tray of whatever he was serving. But the guy in my cabin had pot stickers, which are available from room service. So he was not a waiter. OK, so you had thirty masks and they asked for twenty-four. Where were the other six masks?"

"In the prop room."

"Was the prop room locked?"

"It wouldn't have been, no. The actors were rehearsing all day for the show."

I leaned back in my chair. "So it might have been possible for someone to slip out with a mask?"

He looked frustrated. "I suppose so. The staff has only been on board for a week, so we haven't, you know, fallen into a groove yet. Like I said, I'd love to help you but I really don't know anything else."

I ate quietly, religiously, in glorious silence for a few moments, until Hiram returned with the rest of our food. "Dig in," I said as I dug in. "So how did you wind up with this gig? I mean, the transition from professor to onboard entertainer can't really be understood as a good career move."

He paused, fork halfway to his mouth. "I would hardly call myself an entertainer," he said. "I'm an Egyptologist. We have exhibits on board. I will be interpreting them for the passengers, as well as lecturing on hieroglyphics, religion, and all facets of Egyptian culture. It's actually quite a step up the career ladder if you ask me."

"I'm sure your faculty colleagues are green with envy."

"I'm not sure I like your tone," he said. "My career decisions are not your business."

I pulled out the second sheet of information that had been prepared for me. "Dr. Max Carder," I read. "Where did you get your Ph.D.?"

"I pursued my graduate studies at Yale," he said. "I'm a legacy. My father was a professor there."

"I see that." I reread the information. "But you didn't exactly answer my question. You were clever, but I asked where you got your Ph.D. And that's not the question you answered."

He stiffened and put his egg roll back on the plate. It was already more than half way to his mouth by the time he did that, so it seemed to me to be an unfortunate decision. "I'm not thrilled with your tone," he said, standing up, "and I really don't have to sit here and have this conversation with you."

"Yes, you do," I told him. "You really do. I'll make it fast and we can be done. Otherwise I have to make it all official, with a video recording and witnesses, and it might lead to some public admissions that you'd rather not have on record, and which I have no interest in. I just want to move my investigation along, and you're a big part of it right now, so sit. Eat your food and answer my questions."

He grumbled but he sat.

"Millard Fillmore University," I began. "What's the campus like there, lots of green space? Bearded guys playing guitar on the quad? Coed girls with tambourines playing along? Lots of pillow fights?"

He stared at me.

"I got carried away."

"It's an online university," he said curtly, "and it's nothing to be ashamed of. Yale wasn't a good fit for me, and Fillmore allowed me to transfer my credits."

"All six of them." I read. "You got kicked out of Yale after your first semester of graduate school. So you got a Ph.D. from a mail order university and you were unable to find employment for some time."

"I pursued several nonacademic opportunities."

"Yes, at Best Buy. Then you worked as an adjunct professor at several community colleges until last year when you were hired as a visiting assistant curator at the American Museum in Cairo, which contrary to what you wrote on your employment application, is not affiliated with the American University in Cairo."

"It is affiliated," he said, "but the relationship had not been made official yet."

"I see." I ate another egg roll. "So you're pretty lucky to have this gig. Otherwise you might be back on Long Island selling VCRs. Let me ask you a question; is it ever worthwhile to get the extended warranty?"

"Is there something you need from me?" he asked, "or do you just plan to belittle me all morning?"

"The belittling is just to put you off guard," I assured him as I pushed a bank statement across the table. "I need you to explain something for me. I had a look at some bank records. Your parents left you some money but that's long gone. You've never had more than $3,000 in the bank until three months ago."

He stared at the page in front of him. "Bank records are private," he said.

"Yes, yes they are, but they're not secret. There's a difference. You opened a new account three months ago. It's one of those internet-only banks. I've not yet tried one of them myself. I'm more of a traditionalist. When I open an account, I want a toaster. But that's neither here not there. Max, where did you get $200,000?"

He shook his head. "It's not your business."

"I like to pry."

"I don't have to answer. I don't have to answer any of your questions."

"You do. Yes you do. I'm a man of great power as well

as stamina, resolve too. I guess what I'm trying to say is that I have a lot of juice. I am conducting a murder investigation, and you're going to answer my questions, or I'll have you fired and put ashore before I finish my Bloody Mary. Now, where did you get $200,000?"

He took a little time, but that was fine. "I gamble," he said.

"What kind of gambling?"

"Table games, mostly craps. Some Blackjack."

"If I have fifteen, should I draw another card?"

"Almost always, depends on how many face cards you've seen."

"Hold on," I got out my pen and my little notebook. "I want to write that down. I always forget. So you won two hundred grand gambling?"

"That's right."

"Where?"

"Luxor. In Vegas, last Christmas."

I laughed. "I like that. You went to Luxor because you're an Egyptologist."

"No," he said, "because I found a hotel deal online, and they let me use my frequent flyer miles. OK? Is there anything else you want to ask me?"

This was going nowhere. I drank my beverage. "Are you going to be doing any gambling onboard?"

He shook his head. "Not allowed."

"A sensible rule," I told him. "OK, be off with you. Are you going to eat those hardboiled eggs?"

"Knock yourself out," he said as he left.

Sometimes even the most promising of leads hits a dead end, but I'm a patient man. I held up my glass and waved to catch Hiram's attention. "How about a top-off?" I called out, "while I'm still young."

Chapter Eight

I am always anxious to test the limits of an Access-all-Areas ID card, and there's no better way to do that than to knock on the door to the bridge. Indulgence's bridge was on Deck 12. It was at the bow of the ship, as bridges traditionally are. But it still took me nearly twenty minutes to find. There's no big door with a sign on it, of course. Passengers are not allowed on the bridge, not anymore. Not with today's security protocols. But I'm not really a passenger, I explained to the duty officer who appeared at the unmarked door, and it took him only about thirty seconds of walkie-talkie chatter to agree and let me in.

I've been on a lot of bridges, but this was spectacular. It looked like something on a spaceship. Everything was blue and grey and polished to a shine. I saw Bashir Salib standing by the window. He was talking on his cell phone and staring over the bow at the ferries that darted around Stockholm's harbor. Behind him, three uniformed officers sat at an immense console in front of a bank of monitors. Above them, flat-screen panels displayed maps, images, and numbers, lots of numbers. And just behind the three officers was a larger chair. It was elevated above the others and it looked comfortable, lots of chrome and lumbar support, so I climbed aboard. It was heavenly. I wondered if the seat went back.

A young man with several stripes on his sleeves approached. "Raynor Arneson," he announced, holding out his hand. "I'm staff captain."

"That's a fine thing," I told him. "If I've learned anything during my years at sea, it's that the staff captain is the third most important person on the ship. You can't leave port without a doctor. And there would be nobody to man the captain's table without a captain. That makes you an important fellow."

"I suppose it does," he said. "Welcome to the navigation bridge."

"You have a lot of buttons here," I observed.

"Yes, we do. We have the most sophisticated navigation system in the world, more complex even than that of a nuclear warship."

"What are all the images on the screens?" I pointed overhead. "I've never seen so many."

"Diagnostics." He pointed to the first screen. "Then traffic, electronic navigation, heading, rate of turn, and finally, closed circuit television."

"Wow." I stared out the immense front window. "From this high up, it doesn't even look like we're moving."

"We're in port."

"You're good," I told him. "If you had to, could you sail the ship yourself?"

"If I had to, yes. I would need an engine crew, of course. And we would have to be in open water. It would not be possible for a single individual to sail into port, or to dock. The ship is simply too big."

"Have you ever chewed any Middle Eastern narcotics?" I asked.

"Excuse me?"

"Never mind. So what's new here today? Can I get a look at this morning's security briefing?"

"I'm told you can get a look at whatever you like," he

said. He pulled up a file on the monitor in front of me.

"Bomb threat." I read in the section with today's date. "8:19 a.m., it was called in from a disposable cell phone in Stockholm."

"That's right."

"And what's this? It's marked with a green flag. What does L.C. stand for?"

"Low credibility. Our threat assessment team in Zurich does a statistical analysis of each unique event. This one was deemed to be of low credibility."

"So you won't be searching the ship for bombs?"

"We search the ship for bombs every morning and every night, but we won't be evacuating the passengers."

Bashir spotted me and made his way over. "Your eye looks terrible," he told me. "I'm sorry this happened to you. I'm going to personally do everything I can to make sure you are safe."

"That makes two of us," I said as the staff captain left us. "I asked Fester to gather some information for me. He was apparently unable to find much on the man who was killed. I'm going to need to know all about him."

"Who is Fester?"

"He's part of your security team. Oriental fellow. He's very helpful. You told me the man who was killed was your bodyguard. I need his name, some detailed information about him, and who his friends were. Cabin number too."

Bashir ground his teeth, it was kind of a nervous thing he did. "As I explained, his name was Wakim and he worked for my father. I'm certain he didn't have any friends on board."

"Then I want a list of his enemies."

"How much time do you have?" Bashir asked. "He was killed to send a message to me, to frighten me. There are people who want to see me fail."

"How many people?"

He nodded his head a few times. "I have three brothers.

I'm the youngest by many years, but my father favors me. As such, my brothers are hostile. Two are hostile always, the third, only occasionally."

"Hostile enough to kill you?"

He pointed to the scar in his eyebrow. "When I was six, my brother Hamid wanted to teach me to fence." He held up his left hand, and I saw that he had no pinkie. "When I was sixteen, I lost Hamid's favorite nine iron. He was not pleased."

"What a dick," I said. "What's Hamid up to these days?"

"Minister of Defense. Our brother Sadiq held that position for two decades until he mysteriously fell out of an airplane last summer."

"You can't be too careful. So you think Hamid is behind the threats to Indulgence, including this morning's bomb threat?"

"Possibly," he said. "Or it could be Nezim. But I know how they work. They try to intimidate their rivals. And I'm not easily intimidated."

"That's grand to hear. So the fellow who got stabbed, I need his cabin number."

"That won't be necessary," Bashir said. "My people have already searched his cabin. They will make their report available to you, but I can tell you that they found nothing of interest."

"I'm going to need his cabin number," I repeated. "I decide how to conduct my own investigations. It's just the way I do things, you know, not letting other people decide how I should conduct my own investigations."

An officer approached us. "Excuse me," he said. "Are you Mr. Grave?"

I nodded.

"There's a phone call for you, sir."

"A fine morning to you," I said into the mouthpiece.

"Yeah, you too. Is this Henry Grave?"

"It is. Who am I speaking to?"

"This is Lost and Found. Did you lose something recently?"

I thought about that for a moment. "Can't think of anything," I said, "but I appreciate you staying one step ahead of things. It's service like this that makes all the difference. That's what keeps the passengers coming back again and again, sometimes for decades."

The line went silent for a moment. "How about your gun? Did you lose a gun, asshole?"

"Who is this?"

"I'm the guy that took your gun. How's your eye?"

I grabbed Bashir's arm with one hand and started writing with the other, and I accidently dropped the phone. When I picked it up, it had turned off. I turned it back on.

"That was the guy." I told Bashir about the call. "Can you trace this?"

"Definitely." He pressed the redial number. "It's from one of our courtesy phones." He called out to one of the watch officers to bring up the surveillance camera images.

Two minutes later, I got another call. I pressed the speakerphone button.

"Hang up on me again and you're dead," he said. "You and I have something to talk about."

"Then let's meet," I suggested. "We can have lunch. I'm buying."

"No, I'll be having lunch down here in the crew mess. Now listen to me, you need to get the passengers off this ship. If they're still on board when we leave Stockholm, I'm going to start killing coneys one by one. And I'm going to use your gun to do it."

"Would I have to get off too?"

"What?"

"Would I have to get off too?" I asked. "Stockholm is cold. If we were in Puerto Rico, I might take you up on your offer, but my knees ache in the cold." I cupped my hand over the mouthpiece and whispered to Bashir. "Is there any way to get something to drink up here? A vodka tonic would be swell."

"Listen to me," the man on the phone said angrily, "I know who you are. You have an obligation to protect the passengers. You can't ignore a credible threat."

"You've got that right," I told him. "I just don't find you credible. Maybe if we got to know one another. Hey, do you play Bingo?"

The line went dead.

"Why would you antagonize him?" Bashir stared at me as if I were a lunatic.

"What?"

"You could have kept him on the line until security apprehended him."

"Are you joking? He's probably seen at least one television show in his life. Nobody making that kind of phone call is going to stay on the line for more than half a minute."

The watch officer waved to Bashir and we both went over to his station. "The calls were made from two different courtesy phones," he said. "The first one was at Guest Services, and the second was from the casino. He has his back to the camera on both."

I stared at the monitor. The man on the screen wore a sunhat and the same robe that everyone else on board was wearing. He was careful not to turn, and when he left, he moved quickly.

"Security is on the scene," the officer said. And he wasn't kidding. We watched the screen as two security teams moved past the courtesy phones.

"They're not going to find him," I told Bashir.

The watch officer played the phone conversation out loud for all to hear.

"What's a coney?" Bashir asked. "He said he was going to kill coneys."

"Haven't you ever been to Coney Island? A coney is a hot, hot, hot dog that will make your mouth water."

He stared at me. "Why would someone want to kill a coney?"

"Beats the hell out of me," I told him, remembering my last visit to Coney Island years ago. I think I ate three of those hot dogs that day. "Our mystery man said he was going to be eating in the staff mess. He wants us to think he's part of the crew, but he's not."

"Why do you say that?"

"He's using the jargon wrong. The word is cone, not coney. If he really was part of the crew, he would have threatened to kill a cone, not a coney."

"So what's a cone?" Bashir asked.

"A cone is a passenger; it's a term you hear below decks, but never in front of the passengers."

"Why are they called cones?"

"You have to avoid them, like traffic cones. You know, you're doing your job, let's say carrying a tray of drinks to some guests by the pool, and sure enough, a couple of passengers are coming at you and they're going to have thirty questions about the buffet or what time the after-dinner show starts, so you do your best to swerve to avoid them. You know, like you would a traffic cone."

"Charming."

"Hey, you asked."

"What did he mean when he told you to do your job?"

"He wants me to shut you down," I said. "If I have any reasonable suspicion of a credible threat to passengers, then we have an obligation to inform them that they are in danger."

"So that they could leave," Bashir said quietly.

"That's right."

"So what will you do?"

"Well, I've been working on trying to get a vodka tonic, but that's not happening with any great speed. After that, I'm going to go find this guy."

"You don't think he's a credible threat?"

"No."

"Why not?"

"If someone hangs up on you and you call them back, you lose credibility."

"But he does have your gun."

"Yes," I said. "And I'm going to get it back. This guy is an amateur. Are you a gambling man, Bashir?"

"What do you mean?"

"If you're playing Blackjack, and you have fifteen showing, should you draw another card?"

"I would not have the faintest idea," he said.

"I always draw another card in that situation," I told him. "He placed the second call from the casino. He's on camera."

"He had his back to the camera," Bashir reminded me.

"Cruise ship casinos are independently operated," I told him. "They employ their own people, they bring their own uniforms, and they have their own surveillance cameras in addition to yours. Lots of them. Let's go talk to the good folks at Bally's. I'll meet you down there."

Chapter Nine

I never got my vodka tonic. My head was throbbing so I headed back to my cabin to get some of those pain pills the doctor gave me. The door was open when I arrived so I lingered in the hall for a moment until I saw the girl from Housekeeping peek out.

"Sorry," she said, "almost finished."

"I just need to get into the bathroom," I called out. "Is that OK?"

"It's your stateroom, sir. Is there anything else you need?" She frowned when she saw me up close. "What happened to you?"

"No, no. It's nothing. I was doing a little kickboxing this morning."

She made a pouty face. "Are you sure you're OK?"

"Leila," I said, after consulting her nametag, "I'm going to be just fine after I take my pills. How about you? What's a pretty girl like you doing changing sheets?"

She stared at me for a moment. "I'm changing sheets."

"That's a good answer," I said. I swallowed three pills and moved into the room. I saw that the full-length mirror was actually a door, and it was open. "What's in there?"

"Sorry," she said. "It's just easier with them open. That's the door to the adjoining cabin. Some people travel with children or family. The door lets you turn your stateroom into a suite."

"I didn't even notice it was a door," I told her. "Hey, you're kind of cute, did I mention that?" She was, too. She couldn't have been more than twenty years old. Romanian, if I was getting the accent right. I've always had a thing for Romanian girls. They're so mean.

"Thank you, sir," she said. "I'm just finishing up here. Do you need any fruit?"

"No, I'm good for fruit."

"I refilled your minibar," she said, closing the mirror. "All of it."

"That's wonderful news. Hey, who's on the other side of the mirror?"

"A woman. I can't remember her name. She's traveling alone. I only met her once."

"Maybe I'll knock on the mirror later if I'm feeling lonely."

"Maybe you could knock on her door. Otherwise it might be strange."

"You're probably right," I said. "Hey, you want to stay and hang out for a bit? I have fruit."

"I have twelve more staterooms to clean up," she said.

"Maybe tomorrow?" I asked, but she was already out the door. "Wait one second," I called after her. "Can you tell me the name of the butler? I haven't met my butler yet, and I'm telling you, these bags aren't going to unpack themselves."

She gave me that pouty smile again. "I'm afraid there are no butlers back here for the inside staterooms."

"What, now?"

"Sir, these are economy staterooms. There's no butler service here. But if you need something, I'll be happy to assist."

I couldn't believe what I was hearing. "But who is going to unpack my bags? Who will be arranging my cocktail parties? Are my spa appointments going to manage themselves?"

"Did you want to visit the spa, sir?"

"No, not really. OK, off with you. Leave me to my sorrow."

"Yes, sir."

I sat there for a moment staring at the TV, wallowing in self-pity. I was watching one of the news channels, not CNN but the other one, and there was a cruise ship on the screen. Our cruise ship, I realized, as I grabbed for the remote to turn up the volume. The title "Sheik-up?" appeared on the screen.

"...maiden voyage now comfortably underway. Although many industry insiders doubted a ship of this size could be profitable, Bashir Sahib forged ahead with his plans. Offering, quite truthfully, something for everyone, Indulgence is already booked solid for the rest of the year. She leaves Stockholm this evening, bound for Copenhagen and then Oslo. Then, after two days in port in Dover, she'll cross the pond to Miami to begin a series of two-week Caribbean and South American cruises.

If profit forecasts are met, Indulgence will also become the most profitable cruise ship afloat, and it is perhaps that distinction that led Al-Kurbai king, Sheik Abdullah bin Salib to name Prince Bashir as his new Minister of Finance, and second in line to the crown. Bashir's older brother Hamid replaces Nezim as Crown Prince in this dizzying dynastic deliberation."

The screen switched to an image of a turbaned man sitting in front of a bank of microphones. He was speaking in Arabic but switched to English for the last couple of words. It was hard to hear because a boat whistle was blowing in the background. "It is not only my will," he said, "but the will of God, that my son Hamid will tend the flock, while my son Bashir enriches it so that we all may prosper."

There was much clapping, and then the announcer was back. "Let's wish them luck," he said. "And let's hope Bashir

Salib brought along enough shuffleboard mallets to keep all his passengers happy! We'll be right back with the latest in high fashion from Milan."

Shuffleboard! Curse it. No matter what you put on your ship, I don't care if it's a submarine, a rock wall, a replica of the Valley of Kings, or even a full-fledged rainforest, you're still going to have to fend off the shuffleboard comments. It sickens me, though it is kind of a fun game.

My plan was to head straight to the casino, but in my haste, I left my cabin without my handy deck map, so I didn't know where I was. I knew that I had to head down but when I got in the elevator, I wound up going up. I don't know why that sometimes happens, but it does. I found myself back up on the Riviera Deck, at the stern, by one of the pools. There was a tennis court, but nobody was playing. I passed about sixty people doing those tai chi exercises that take forever. I've never had the patience for something like that.

It was a little cold out so I headed indoors. I passed a bar that was sadly closed, but I found an arcade where all the teenage passengers were congregating. Maybe they have different video games at sea, because that's what was grabbing the attention of the younger generation. Decades from now, these kids will be holding babies in their arms telling them how lovely Sweden was, when all they got out of Sweden was yet more hand-to-eye coordination.

Let me tell you something, I was feeling happy, almost blissfully so. I even found myself giggling. I wasn't entirely sure why, but the whole world seemed to be working just perfectly for me at that moment. And I like to celebrate such moments. I needed a drink.

Beyond the arcade was another bar, called Oxygen. I was just about to step inside when I caught a glimpse of something out of the corner of my eye. I turned to look; it was her, the lady on the Rascal. She was sitting by the railing staring out at Stockholm. Suddenly she turned and looked me straight in the eye. Then she came at me. Let me tell you something, with a skilled hand on the tiller, a Rascal can move fast, nearly five miles per hour. I spend a lot of time around the elderly, so I know what I'm talking about. I moved as fast as I could, darting back into the arcade and out the other side, but she stayed with me. I didn't know who she was or what she wanted, but by the insane look in her eyes, I knew she'd never stop until she caught me, or until she had gone about twenty miles, which is more or less the maximum range for a Rascal.

I slipped into a men's room, and waited about ten minutes before I dared to nudge open the door. The coast appeared to be clear. I was safe, at least for now. I headed back to that bar I had passed, and stepped inside. Strange decor, I thought. Everything was white.

"Welcome to Oxygen," a young lady welcomed. "Is this your first visit?"

"My first visit? This ship has only been in the water for a day and a half."

"That's true, sir. But we've already had some repeat customers." She handed me a menu. "Are you familiar with our flavors?"

"Oh, I get it." I read her nametag. "Polina, this is one of those vodka bars, isn't it? Well that's a fine thing. Give me something dry."

"I have just the thing," she said, handing me a little hose. "It's called Mediterranean Sunset. It has light olive undertones."

"Bring it on. What do I do with the hose?"

She fiddled with a machine under the counter, and handed me what looked like a pair of headphones. "You snap it in right here," she said.

"What, now?"

"You're all set."

"What, now?"

"Your oxygen. You just slip that over your head and start breathing."

"I'm already breathing."

"Sir, this is an oxygen bar. You breathe oxygen through the tube."

I think she was a little dotty. "I'm already breathing oxygen, Polina. It's filling up my lungs as we speak. Why would I want ...?"

"Just try it," she said, so I did.

Wow. It was something else. "This is like regular air, only better."

"It's refreshing, isn't it? You'll feel reinvigorated."

"I feel three years younger already. Hey, just about right now, me with a nozzle sticking out of my nose, I'll bet you look better than me. How about that vodka you were going to bring me?"

"I'm afraid we don't serve alcohol in here, sir."

"You don't have a bottle back there?"

She shook her head. She had long red hair and it was pretty. I told her so.

"Do you have a lot of oxygen back in Russia?" I asked.

"No, just what's in the air. Do you like it?"

"Like it? I'm never going back to the old stuff. Can I get some of this to go?"

"I'm afraid not. But you can come back twice a day."

"I'll be back three times a day." I stared out the window at the pool, where bathers in little rafts rammed into each other. "What the hell is that?"

"Bumper pool," she said. "It's like bumper cars but with little boats. Each team must get as many boats to the other end while blocking the other team."

"That's fascinating. What else is going on today?"

"Lots of wonderful things." She reached for the shipboard newsletter. "After bumper pool there's water polo."

"Do they use real sea horses?"

"Excuse me?"

"Nothing. What else?"

"It's almost lunch time, so there will be a lull for a bit."

"I like lulls. We could take a walk, you and me. You could tell me about Poland."

"I've never been to Poland," she said as she continued reading. "After lunch we have water ballet, jazz-aerobics, bridge for beginners, The Spanish Main, golf swing masters class, Know Your Universe, afternoon comedy jam, Scrapbooking Secrets, Whale Tales at Stuff-a-Whale, a couple of movies, a hieroglyphics workshop, talent show try-outs, Our Fragile Ecosystem, Everyone Loves a Banana Split, Holiday in Holography World, Magic & Madness with Murray, You Too Can Play the Uke, Stone Tool Making in Rainworld, Brew a Better Beer at YouBrew, How to Win at Roulette, Zipline Zecrets, rock climbing, Piña/Piña, ballroom dancing, swing dancing, salsa dancing, Hip Hop dancing, Teen Treasure Hunt, and Bingo."

"What's Piña/Piña?"

"I'm not sure. I think they hollow out pineapples and make big cups from them."

"Is that right? So that's all, there's nothing more to do?"

"I'm afraid not." She handed me the newsletter as a gorgeous little strawberry blonde took a seat at the bar. "There's more this evening. You can read about it."

The woman smiled briefly and looked at the menu. I couldn't keep my eyes off her. She was quite petite. Her sleeveless top did justice to a light bronze tan, and her full lips pursed alluringly as she frowned at me.

"Don't get your hopes up," I told her. "All they have is air."

"All they have is oxygen," she said. "I was in here this morning. I'm already addicted." She turned to Polina. "Honey, I'll have the same thing I had earlier."

"It's a little forward to be calling me honey," I said, introducing myself, "but I like that in a woman. Don't let this tube sticking out of my nostril hang you up. I'm a good looking man."

"I was talking to Polina," she said. "I'm Anne. You're breathing very deeply, Henry. You should take it easy or you'll get woozy."

"Woozy. About ten years ago I had a root canal and they sent me home with some kind of medicine that made everything funny. I kind of feel that way now. I'm happy, happy to meet you, Anne. Don't tell Polina we're a couple. She desires me."

"She's right here in front of you. She can hear you."

"I can hear you," Polina agreed. "And I'm happy for the both of you. I'll try to get by without you."

"Don't you get started too," Anne told her.

I moved over and took a seat next to her. "Don't be mad at Polina," I said. "These last six seconds or so have been rough on her, but she'll find love again. Let me buy you a drink, Anne?"

"They don't serve drinks here," she reminded me.

"We could go somewhere else. I have fruit in my cabin. Plus I'm high as a kite."

"Everyone has fruit in their cabin." She took the nozzle Polina had prepared and snapped it into the holder so that it rested just under her nose.

"So it doesn't actually go in the nose?"

"No. Normally not. Listen, I'd love to chat with you more but I am waiting for someone."

"So sad. He's a lucky man."

"Yes he is."

"Tell me who he is so that I can congratulate him when I see him."

"I don't know his name, but I'll recognize him when I meet him."

"What, now? You're looking for love?"

"Yes I am, Henry."

"It could be me."

"It's not. You're too tall for me."

"Too tall? In all my sixty-one years, I have never had anyone tell me I was too tall."

"Sixty-one years? Give me a break. You're like ninety-nine years old if you're a day. I'm fifty-two but I look forty. And I'm five foot one, so yeah, you're too tall."

My hose went limp. "That's mean," I told her. "Hey, Polina. My air tube has no more air in it."

"First timers only get a small dose. We don't want to over-stimulate you. You can come back this afternoon."

"I might do that," I said. "I'll check first to make sure Miss Mean Lady isn't here."

"I wasn't being mean," Anne said. "I just don't want to waste my time with banter that isn't going to go anywhere. I'm looking for a shorter man. Besides, you already have a girlfriend."

She was right about that. I'm a big flirt, but the love of my life, Helen Ettinger, keeps me warm at night. At least when I am at home. "How do you know I have a girlfriend?"

"You dress well. Single men your age are slobs. Married men your age have long since given up any pretence of fashion. It's nothing but track suits. You at least have some style."

"And the substance to back it up," I told her as the nozzle popped out of my nose.

"Maybe so, but you're incredibly old, so you have to leave me alone now."

"I can do that," I said. "Insults roll right off my back, like rain drops. Except huge biting insults. They're more like hailstones, cutting deep into the bone. Good luck finding short love."

That's when I remembered what I was supposed to be doing. "Polina," I said, "where's the casino?"

Chapter Ten

A substantial portion of Deck 4 had been dedicated to the gaming arts, as casinos now call their proffered vice. I passed row after row of silent unlit slot machines, which was kind of sad, really. Their cousins back in Atlantic City and Vegas and Macau are nearly always lit, nearly constantly ringing, calling out. But it is the lot of cruise ship slot machines to spend a great deal of quiet time because regulations do not permit gambling while a ship is in port.

They do permit gambling lessons, however. I walked in on a virtual university of gambling. Class was in session. I passed craps lessons, roulette lessons, and poker lessons before coming to the casino office. Folks were cheering. They weren't even winning anything, but at least they weren't losing.

I knocked on the door. Golan let me in. "I heard about your phone call," he told me. "You shouldn't have hung up the phone."

"I didn't hang up. I dropped it. Did you find anything?" I followed him back to a bank of monitors where Bashir and a heavyset fellow were scrolling through video footage.

"This is Mr. Potts, the casino messenger," Golan told me.

"You can call me Cordell." Potts didn't even bother to

turn around. He tapped at an image on one of the screens. "I think we have your man. I'm just looking around for a better mug shot."

"It's a little blurry," I said. "Can you clear it up?"

He spun around in his chair. "It's a nearly perfect high-resolution image."

"Is that right? Wait, I need my glasses." I found them in my jacket pocket. "I was upstairs breathing nitrogen. I must have taken them off."

Potts lit a cigarette as he typed with one hand.

"Do you need to smoke right now?" Bashir was irritated.

"It helps me think."

I stared at the image on the screen. The man wore a robe and a hat. Glasses too, but if he was trying to hide his face, he wasn't doing a great job of it. "Do you recognize him?" I asked.

Both Bashir and Golan shook their heads.

"Here we go," Potts said. "Let me direct your attention to screen number three."

"Which one is that?" I asked.

"It's the third one. Start counting at one and you'll get there. This is from the camera near the forward doorway, so it's after he ditched the robe and the glasses. He still has the hat on but there he is."

And there he was. The man on the monitor turned to look behind him but when he turned back again, his face nearly filled the frame.

"I could count his whiskers." Potts danced a little jig in his seat.

"I still don't recognize him," Bashir said.

"I don't either." Golan leaned in. "If you send me the file, I'll take it up and run it against the staff photo ID files. If we don't hit there, I'll run it against the passengers. It's just a matter of time."

"How much time?" Bashir asked. "I'd like to have him

in custody before we sail for Copenhagen."

Golan looked at his watch. "Go have lunch. I'll hope to have something by the time you finish."

"That works for me," I said. "I'm famished. What are we having?"

"There are twenty-four restaurants on board," Bashir said. "Have whatever you like."

I moved for the door. "By the way, congratulations on your promotion to … to the thing you were promoted to."

"Minister of Finance."

"That's the thing. That's a pretty great thing. Are you excited?"

He smiled nervously. "I'm still trying to make sense of it."

"Did you get my message?" Golan asked.

"No," I said. "What message? Where?"

"I left a message on your stateroom phone about twenty minutes ago. You asked Lester to let you know if General Savoy and her family re-boarded. They did, about half an hour ago. They made lunch reservations at Noku."

"What's Noku?"

"It's a restaurant. Deck 5 forward."

"I'm on my way. Call ahead, will you? Put me at their table."

I did not get lost, and I deserve some credit for that. I was feeling lightheaded and more than a little bit intoxicated, which was odd since I hadn't had very much to drink lately. I attributed my addled state to my recent injuries, and I followed my nose, and the trail of re-boarding passengers, to get some lunch. It always astonishes me that folks will pay out a great sum of money to cruise the world but they won't buy their own lunch ashore. How often do you get to Sweden? Ask yourself that question. If you are like most people, the answer is once or twice in a lifetime. Unless you're Swedish, in which case it would be considerably more often. But why the hell wouldn't you just grab something ashore?

Judging by the uncluttered bamboo décor and the little bonsai trees at the entrance, Noku was a Japanese restaurant. I had to wait in line but not for long. The Russian girl at the desk had no trouble finding my name because she had just written it on the list herself.

"Right this way, sir." She led me to a long table with one empty seat. "Can I get you started with some miso soup?"

"You sure can. And bring me a little something to drink. What goes good with miso soup?"

"Mineral water or perhaps lemonade?"

"Don't play with me, little girl."

"You could have a sake."

"If I have to, I will, but it's not my favorite. Just bring me a beer for now. Something Korean or Belgian." I smiled my biggest smile as I took my seat. "Hi folks, I'm Henry. I fell in the tub and hurt my eye. It's fine, really. Just wanted to get that out of the way."

"I'm Tuck." The man across the table shook my hand. "This is my wife Meg, and our grandson Casper."

Tuck was a tall man, well over six feet tall, and that was a good thing because the wife had to be six feet if she was an inch. She had grey hair and grey eyes, and she looked to be in better shape than I've ever been in my life.

"Casper, that's a fine name," I told the boy. He looked to be about ten years old, a little blonde fellow.

"Does it hurt?" he asked. "Your eye?"

"No, no," I said. "It's not as bad as it looks. You should see the other guy."

"You were in the tub with another guy?"

"What, now?"

"You said you fell in the tub."

"I did, yes. So Casper, did your parents take you out to see Stockholm this morning?"

"They're not my parents. My parents are back home in San Francisco. My grandparents brought me because it was my birthday."

"Well, happy birthday. I'd buy you a drink but you're probably only about six years old."

He stared at me. "I'm eleven. How old are you?"

"Casper," the grandfather began, "it isn't polite to ask people how old they are."

"But he asked me," the boy insisted.

"It's fine," I told him. "I'm eighty-five. I know I don't look it. I'm spry. I do circuit training. So did you get out into the city?"

"We went on a double-decker bus," he said. "We went all over, and we got to see a real old wooden ship that used to be under water. It's called the Vasa. It sunk hundreds of years ago. It had lots of cannons."

"Is that right? That sounds like a lot of fun. So you folks are from California?"

"We're from Maryland," Meg Savoy said as a waiter came with my soup and my drink. "Our son lives in San Francsico."

"Have you looked at the menu, sir?" the waiter asked.

I hadn't. It was in front of me. "What are you all having? I'm in the mood for a burger. Maybe some fries and some mashed potatoes."

Casper laughed. "You can't get a burger here."

"Why not?"

"Because it's a sushi restaurant."

"What, now?"

The waiter pointed to that very fact written in bold on the top of the menu. "Noku is the finest sushi chef at sea," he said. "If you like, I can have him bring you a sample plate."

"No, no." I read the menu. The only thing worse than cold fish is raw fish. Actually I've eaten a lot worse under duress. "Hey, can I get some of that vampire squid thing in a sushi? That would be something, wouldn't it?"

"No, sir," he said. "I'm afraid that is not on the menu."

Nuts. "OK, I'll have the peppered tuna and the Kobe beef. You cook it, right? It doesn't come raw like the puma, does it?"

"The beef is cooked to your taste," he said, "and the tuna is seared."

"That's a fine thing. And can you bring me another beer? This one is already empty."

"You haven't touched it yet."

"True, that's very true. I'll be touching it soon."

"You're going to drink two beers at lunch?" Casper asked.

"I might have three. So Maryland, you say. I'm from Pennsylvania. What do you do in Maryland?"

"I'm retired from the military," Meg Savoy said. "Tuck was a developer. Now he's a state assemblyman."

"Is that right? I ran for Congress in 1972. I lost. I was in the military too. I was a corporal in the army. How about you?"

"Air Force."

"She's a general," Tuck said, standing up. "She's good at giving orders. If you will all excuse me for now, I have to check my messages before I go play bridge."

"Wow, so you outrank me," I said when he left.

"I do. Were you in combat?"

"No, no. Well, technically yes, but I was captured before I got the chance to do anything. I spent the tail end of the war as a guest of the German government."

"World War II," Casper said. "Did you meet Hitler?"

"No. So what about you?" I looked past the boy. "Did you see combat?"

"I'm just an analyst. I spent most of my career poring over spreadsheets."

"Air force spreadsheets," I said. "Well, that could be

interesting. I was watching a show about those remote control airplanes that they have now. You can have a pilot halfway around the world sitting at a computer flying the little planes. Did you ever see those?"

She used her chopsticks like an expert. "No. I didn't have anything to do with that."

"But what about the picture of you in front of the Predator?" Casper asked. "The one you have in your office.

"It was a gift," she said. "Casper, can you tell Henry why we aren't going to be seeing more of Stockholm this afternoon?"

"We're going to Rainworld," he said excitedly. "Have you been to Rainworld yet?"

"I have," I told him. "It's pretty great."

"Casper loves rainforests," Meg beamed. "He wants to turn his bedroom into one."

"Do you know that one out of every ten species in the world lives in the Amazon rainforest?" Casper asked.

"I had no idea."

"Including more than two and a half million species of insects."

"I'll bring spray if I go," I assured him.

"And it's getting smaller every year by twenty square kilometers."

"That's a lot."

"No, I mean twenty thousand square kilometers."

"That's more."

"They're going to have a stone tool making demonstration today. The Jipitos are going to make spears."

"Yeah, they need to replace the one they lost."

"What?"

"Nothing." The boy spent the next ten minutes yammering about rainforests. I wanted to either eat or steer the conversation back to Meg Savoy but I couldn't figure out a way to do either. "Want to trade war stories?" I asked.

She stared at me. "Are you nuts? The war is still going on. Anything I could tell you is classified. But you can tell us some stories. If you were captured, you would have been sent to a stalag, right?"

"That's right, Stalag 7A. I spent the winter of 1945 in Moosberg, Germany. It was cold."

"The Allies lost a lot of captured servicemen to disease and hunger in the stalags," she said. "We studied it in the academy. It must have been horrific."

"It was." I got out my wallet. "It was horrific. But one day one of those unmanned Predator drones flew overhead, and I felt better just knowing that the US Air Force was on its way."

"That didn't happen," she said. "You're not who you say you are."

"I am. I'm just more." I handed her my investigator's license as our meals came. "This doesn't look like puma."

"It's tuna, sir," the waitress said. "And the Kobe beef is here."

Meg Savoy didn't even look at my license. "Mr. Grave, I knew who you were the moment you came in. I was briefed about your participation in shipboard security. But I must say, had I not been briefed, I might have mistaken you for a very strange old man."

"No, no," I told her. "I'm not strange, and I have information that confirms my identity. I know about an illegal phone tap at the Syrian consulate in Sao Paulo, for instance. I know that somebody would very much like to get their hands on you."

She turned to her grandson. "Casper, did you wash your hands before lunch?"

"Yup," he said. "I sure did."

It was my turn. "Can you do me a favor, kid? Could you go find that waiter and ask him to bring me some extra kimosabe sauce?"

"You mean wasabi sauce."

"That too, I can never get enough of the stuff."

Meg Savoy nodded and he took off. "You're not exactly what I was expecting," she said.

"Story of my life."

"That being said, I am authorized to share pertinent information with you. This is highly unusual, you understand, but your boss, Mr. Underhill, is highly regarded in the Department of Defense. He and the Secretary of the Navy are close friends."

"They do paintball together or something like that."

"They fish," she said. "So your vetting process went quite smoothly. You have what we could call a limited, temporary, and conscribed, top secret clearance."

"That's grand to hear." I took a bite of my food. I closed my eyes. I might have been all wrong about sushi; it was good. "I read through the protocols that Mr. Golan set up, and I think they are adequate. But let me ask you this, why would someone want to come after you?"

She threw up her hands. "Because I'm a woman, maybe. Because I designed half of the command and control software. Because two months ago we lost a drone north of Karbala. We sent a recon team to the landing site but the drone was gone by the time they got there."

"It crashed?"

"If you read the reports, that's what they would say. But it didn't crash. It lost power but it landed intact. Someone took it, and whoever that is now has a functioning Predator."

"So it still might be able to fly."

She nodded. "We've lost seven drones in the last two years to crashes; five of them went missing before we were able to recover the wreckage."

"A little duct tape, some spackle, and they could potentially be airborne again."

"That is more or less our fear. What's more, if our

enemies can figure out how to formulate, encrypt, and transmit command and control signals, they could, in theory, hijack the entire fleet. They could then turn the weapons on anyone they wanted."

"How many drones are there?"

"I'm pretty sure you don't have the clearance to be asking these kinds of questions."

"Don't worry. The Nazis couldn't break me, and neither could my second wife. I'll take your secrets to my death."

"On the books, almost two hundred, but we have at least twice that. These are potent weapons. They can detect the heat signature of a human body from 10,000 feet. They can fly at 135 miles per hour and stay aloft for up to forty hours. They have a range of 2,000 miles and carry Hellfire air-to-surface missiles. Let me be blunt, Mr. Grave, the only thing standing between the insurgents and the restoration of the Caliphate is me."

"You're not really retired, are you?"

"No."

"Still active duty?"

"Yes, but I'm on vacation. I'm still allowed to take vacation."

Casper returned with my sauce. "Do you want to come with us and watch the Jipitos make spears? Ruspewe said he would show me how to make a blade out of glass."

"Ruspewe?"

"He's one of the Jipitos. He's nineteen but he's the exact same height as me."

"Right, he's the son."

Casper bit into his sushi roll. "The three of them are the only members of their tribe still alive. Isn't that sad?"

"Makes me want to cry." My head was on fire from the wasabi. "Good Christ. Casper, can you get me water, please? Would you go ask the waiter?"

"Why don't you just drink your beer?"

"On fire here," I reminded him. "Time is precious."

"So why take a cruise?" I asked when he stepped away. "Isn't it risky?"

"I'm not going to live in a box," she said. "If they can grab me here, they can grab me anywhere. You have to understand, Mr. Grave. I've been dealing with these kinds of threats for years. You get used to them after awhile."

"You don't give them much credibility?"

"I do," she said. "I've been in combat long enough to have developed great respect for the capabilities of our enemies. I think their threats are very credible, but as I said, I am not going to live in a box."

Casper returned with my water. "I think you're using too much wasabi," he said.

"I think you're right." I drank the water and much of the beer. "One more thing I'd like you to think about," I told her, "if it was me coming for you, I'd K-I-D-N-A-P the B-O-Y."

Casper stared at me, his eyes wide open. "Kidnap who?"

Meg Savoy stared at me too. "How old do you think children are when they learn to spell?"

I hadn't really thought about that. "I'm just joking," I said as jovially as I could. "But maybe I could kidnap you later and we could go see a movie."

"No way," he said, already recovered. "We have our day all planned out but maybe in a couple of days. Tomorrow we're going to Copenhagen. Do you want to come with us?"

"I'd love to," I told him. "But I have to get some work done."

"You shouldn't work when you're on vacation," he said.

"Don't get me started." I wrote my cabin number on a napkin and handed it to Meg Savoy. "If anything looks out of place, anything makes you feel uncomfortable, you give me a call."

She nodded.

"By the way, I'm sitting at your dinner table," I told her.

"So wait for me. And don't eat all the rolls."

We finished our lunch. The Kobe beef was exceptional. I left most of the sushi on the plate. I hate wasting food. I remember a time when there were starving children in France and Greece, and starving soldiers in cold prison barracks with thin blankets that were no match for the rain. Peppered tuna would have been a gift of life. I try not to think about those days, but I'm never successful for long.

Chapter Eleven

According to my paperwork, Indulgence's security office was on Deck 3, just behind the aft elevator bank. Lester Fung opened the door when I knocked.

"Fester, my man!" I shook his hand. "Thanks for the information you pulled. It's been very helpful."

"My name is Lester," he said as I pushed past him. "Is there something I can help you with?"

I walked along a row of desks and through an open door. In front of me were three empty cells. "You have three cells. I've never seen more than one."

"This is a big ship."

"It is." Each of the cells had bunk beds, a toilet, and a sink. "How often do you fill up all three at once?"

"We've only been in the water for a day and a half," he reminded me.

"That's true. Hey, do you like sushi?"

"I love sushi, why?"

"I just had it. It's really not my favorite."

"There are like thirty places to eat on this ship. You could probably find something else to eat."

"That is a fine suggestion. Hey, there's this older lady who has been chasing me. She rides a Rascal and she's really mean. Do you know who she is?"

Lester shook his head. "I don't."

Nuts. "Which desk is Golan's?"

He pointed to a large workstation in the corner. "I think he's up on the bridge. Is there something you need?"

"I'm glad you asked. Can you get food down here?"

He pointed to a phone. "Just call room service."

"Do I have to dial 9 first?"

"No."

"Can you do it for me? I'm shy. I want a cheeseburger, well done, French fries, French onion soup, and a piña colada. Get something for yourself too, at least an appetizer. I'm buying."

He did a little squawking, but before long, he picked up the phone and placed my order. I sat at Golan's desk and read the files he had open on his screen.

Lester came over. "I really don't think ..."

"What's this one here?" I double-clicked on a spreadsheet.

"That's the start dates and duration of individual crew contracts," he said when it opened.

"Why are all the numbers the same?"

"Again, we just put in the water, so all the contracts are more or less in sync. What is it that you're looking for?"

"Don't know. Let's have a look at some of the crew." I picked a name at random and double-clicked the mouse. A split second later, a smiling face filled the screen. That smiling face belonged to Wagus Bardzecki of Lodz, Poland, age thirty-four.

"That's the bastard," I told Lester. "Wagus is behind all this, I'm sure of it. Look." I scrolled through his personnel file.

"Head waiter, six years at sea," Lester read. "Promoted seven times, twice won best-in-shift awards, father of three. Yeah, he sure seems like a criminal mastermind."

"I might have misjudged young Wagus." I moved on to the next file. Osvaldo Barillas of Los Angeles, California, age forty was a dishwasher. An ex-soldier, this was his first tour of civilian duty. "We have an American here," I told Lester. "You don't see too many Americans below decks. What's the deal with Mr. Barillas?"

"I don't think I've met him," he said, "but we're starting to see more ex-military looking for cruise ship work. It's mostly guys having a hard time making the transition. They do well with the structure on board."

"Is that right? Hey, you heard about my phone call today, right?"

"I did, yes. Mr. Golan is still trying to identify the man on the casino video."

"Still? Why is it taking so long?"

"I'm not sure."

"You can get feeds down here for all onboard security cameras, right?"

"Yes, but not the casino's cameras. Those are on a different server."

"Show me the bridge."

He slid the mouse over an icon on the right side of the screen and opened up a list of files. He clicked on one and brought up an image of the bridge. I saw Staff Captain Arneson sitting at the helm, where I myself sat earlier.

"Can you back it up a couple of hours? I want to see who was on the bridge when I was there."

It took him only about ten seconds to move quickly back to the moment I stepped onto the bridge. "What are you looking for?"

"I want to know who was there. Do you know all these people?"

"Yes. That's Bashir Salib standing at the window. The guy standing by the door is the duty officer. I don't know him. The three watch officers I know but I can't remember their names, and there is Captain Arneson coming over to talk to you. Why do you ask?"

"Because nobody knew I was going to the bridge. I didn't have a meeting there. I didn't even have any plans to go there. And I got so lost on the way that I guarantee nobody followed me."

"And?"

"And yet someone called me there moments after I arrived."

Lester nodded. "I see your point."

We looked back at the screen. Arneson was talking with me the whole time. The duty officer didn't move from the door. The watch officers were doing whatever watch officers do, but they were not wearing headsets or talking to anyone. One of them picked up a phone from the console and put it to his ear. A moment later he came over and handed it to me.

"There's your phone call," Lester said. "And the only other person on the bridge talking with someone not on the bridge was this guy."

I nodded as we stared at the image of Bashir Salib standing by the window, talking on his cell phone.

"I want to know who he was talking to," I said. "Can you get audio, maybe isolate his conversation on the file."

"No. We do not have audio on the bridge. This doesn't make any sense. You think Bashir told someone you were there, and then that person called you?"

"It would seem. Maybe Bashir is betting against himself. How well do you know him?"

"About twice as well as I know you. I've met him three or four times. He's nervous, anxious, seems pretty smart. But I never got the impression he was running some kind of a scam."

"Let's go visit him," I suggested. "Do you know where he lives?"

"I do, but he doesn't allow visitors in his suite. That's one of his very specific instructions."

"Listen, I don't care about his instructions. When I

come on board, I go where I want, and this is where I want to go, so take me there."

"Let me call ahead first," he said, picking up the phone.

I grabbed his arm. "No, it's going to be a surprise visit. But can you call catering back and ask them to bring my food to his suite?"

"You're kidding, right?"

"I have the diabetes. I need to eat regularly. Otherwise I don't stay regular. I'll tell you all about it sometime."

"That would be nice," Lester said, but he made the call.

I followed him to the elevator. He slipped his ID card into a slot on the panel and pressed the button for Deck 13. "It's a private deck," he said. "Only guests who have suites there have access."

"Do those guests have butlers? I don't have a butler for my cabin."

"Yes, they have butlers."

"Bastards."

The elevator opened onto a massive foyer. There were only two rows of doors, one on either side of the ship, and between them was a vast space, uncommon at sea. On almost every cruise ship I've ever sailed on, the hallways are narrow, only a few feet wide, but this must have been sixty feet wide. The massive space was sectioned off into seating areas, library nooks, card tables, a paneled section with plexiglass walls that extended halfway up and then a fume hood – it was a high tech cigar room! Beyond that, was a very elegant bar, all teak, with nobody sitting at it. Nobody.

A young woman frowned as we approached. "Good afternoon, gentlemen," she said in a heavy Russian accent. "Can I provide you with the beverage of your choice?"

She looked familiar but my gaze didn't linger for long, drawn as it was to the immense display of exotic and expensive bottles behind her. "Well I'll be goddamned." I stared at the single bottle on the top shelf. "Fester, have a look at this. This is the rare Springbank Single Malt. This is one of the finest Scotches in the world, and one of the most expensive. This stuff spent thirty-two years maturing in an old sherry cask. Think about that, Fester."

"My name remains Lester," he said.

"Do something effectively and I'll call you Lester," I told him.

"That makes no sense. I've done nothing ineffectively."

"I was a boyish fifty-three when this was poured." I turned to the girl. "How much is this?"

"It's free, Mr. Henry. Every thing on Deck 13 is free."

"Is that right? Well pour me a shot, and one for Fester too. And pour one for yourself, for knowing my name. How do you know my name?"

"You asked me to marry you," she said. "Just last night."

I stared at her nametag. "Lyudmila, I never forget a face. Did you accept my proposal?"

"No," she said. "What happened to your eye?"

"Kickboxing."

Lester shook his head. "None for me, I'm on duty."

"I insist," I told him. "Try it for me. It will take thirty-two years off your life. You owe me one."

"Then I'd be eleven years old, too young to drink, and I don't owe you one."

"You're filling me with gloom, Fester. It's bad enough that Lyudmila's face can't even crack a smile, but I'm trying to win her heart. Work with me. If things go well, she'll take me back to Poland with her."

"I'm from Novosibirsk," she said.

"Somebody is from Poland," I ventured. "I just can't remember who."

Lyudmila poured two shots and set them on the bar in front of me.

"You're not going to have one?"

"They would fire me," she said. "And I can't marry you.

I'm too young for you."

"You're not," I assured her. "You're perfect for me. I wouldn't have asked you if I didn't think you were ready."

"That's not what I meant."

"In any case," I turned to Lester, "looks like it's just you and me. Don't let me down."

He gave it a moment of thought, and we drank.

In the end, a gypsy woman once told me, no, I think it was my neighbor Glenda from Rolling Pines, she's the one with the goiter - in the end, all you will remember are the moments, strung together like pearls on a necklace. They are the moments of your life, the only things you can truly call your own, other than debt. Sitting there, drinking that Scotch, I understood what she meant

My life puttered before my eyes. There I am at the age of four, my Pops pulling me in the wagon as we head to the Fourth of July parade. I'm eating popcorn. Then there I am graduating from high school. My wedding to Emily and the next moment are so close together; our honeymoon to Niagara Falls. Later, I'm on a transport ship headed for England. I'm scared but I'm OK because I know what I'm doing is important. Later still, I'm walking along a cool Belgian sidewalk late one evening looking for pretty Belgian girls to flirt with, nothing more, and I walk right into a German scout's pistol.

The subsequent moments define my life, but I will not dwell on them here. I have work to do. One moment stands out, the moment I drank the most angelic concoction that I could imagine, a beverage so light and yet so potent, forever poised between liquid and a dream. I wanted to preserve this moment, to make it last for an eternity if I could, but Lester shook me out of it.

"Did you fall asleep?"

I frowned. "Yeah, I think a bit. It was good, wasn't it?"

He smiled, at least now I knew he could. "It was very good. Thanks. If anyone asks, I'll blame you."

"That's what my second wife told me when she spliced the cable TV line from the neighboring condo."

"Did she get in trouble?"

"Oh, yeah." I nodded. "And she blamed me. Lyudmila, we have to be off. I want to thank you for your hospitality. I will find you later and ask you to marry me one last time."

Chapter Twelve

"Bashir's suite is on the starboard side," Lester told me. "It's the owner's suite."

"That's kind of funny," I said. "Almost every cruise ship has an owner's suite but since most ships are owned by corporations, there really isn't a single owner. So it's rare for the owner to occupy the owner's suite."

"Yes, it's absolutely fascinating."

"Lighten up, Fes. You're bringing me down. Who else lives up here?"

"Elite guests." He led me past a library, then past a massage station where three Oriental fellows beckoned with hot towels. "These are the most expensive suites. Some of them are for comps. Some are for celebrities."

"Do we have any celebrities?"

He nodded. "We do. Countess Anna Wilhelmine of Hungary is on board. She is staying for three months."

"A countess," I said. "I like the sound of that. Is she traveling alone? I could woo her; I've never been with a countess. No wait, I have."

"She is traveling alone, but she's about ninety years old so I don't think ..." He paused. "I mean ... I mean maybe you would enjoy each other. You're about the same ..."

"What are you trying to say?"

"No, she's fascinating. She was some kind of spy for the Allies in World War II, so you have a connection there. Her book is for sale in the bookstore. She claims she was in bed with Winston Churchill when they heard that Hitler committed suicide."

"I'll be sure to pick up a copy. Who else?"

"It's mostly comps; the highest grossing cruise travel agents from different regions, some corporate execs, some media people but nobody I've ever heard of. And the oceanographer that managed to capture those disgusting squids that Bashir wanted for the lobby."

"Is that right? How hard is it to catch a squid?"

"Apparently pretty hard when they live half a mile deep. You have to bring them up in pressurized tanks otherwise they explode when they reach the surface."

"Who knew?"

Lester shrugged. "The only real celebrity is Emily Ashberg, the pop singer. She is eighteen years old, and she has her whole entourage with her, about twelve kids. They have three suites, and they drink the day away."

"So sad."

We stopped in front of a double door. Unlike the other doors we passed, it was unmarked, no number. Lester knocked.

We waited a few moments and Lester knocked again. "Use your master key," I told him.

"I am under direct orders not to. I could get fired."

"Good Christ, give it to me," I said, and he did.

Lester followed me into the most lavish cruise ship suite I had ever seen. What can only be described as a parlor was ringed by floor to ceiling bookcases. A writing desk sat against the far wall next to an elaborate spiral staircase that led up to places unknown.

A doorway to the right led to a sitting room with a giant television set and a large verandah. A doorway to the left led to a dining room with another large verandah across from a bar that ran the length of the room. I noticed two anomalous features simultaneously. A single meal had been set out on the table; a burger with French fries, French onion soup, and a piña colada. It was precisely what I had ordered.

The second thing I noticed was a giant sitting at the bar. He was tapping a hardboiled egg with a spoon to get the shell off. Within easy reach of him were a newspaper and a nine-millimeter handgun.

"Did one of you gentlemen order this feast?" He had thick white hair and he wore a dark red corduroy jacket. And he had an English accent, the regal kind, the kind you hear when you accidentally turn the TV to public broadcasting.

"I think it's mine," I told him. I took a seat. I didn't want to be rude so I made sure I put the napkin on my lap. "Hey, I think you're the tallest fellow I've ever seen, and you're not even standing up. What are you, about eight feet?"

"I'm 2.4 meters tall," he said.

"What's that in feet? I can't do metrics."

"I have no idea."

"I'd like you to meet my friend Fester," I told him. "I think you're going to like him."

"Lester," Lester said. He moved in as if to shake the man's hand but stopped short when he saw the gun. "Can I ask who you are, sir?"

"Abelard," he said, removing the egg from its shell and popping it in his mouth. "My name is Abelard." Then he stood, and I was sure he was the tallest man I had ever seen. An easy seven feet, he was in good shape. He looked to be in his early sixties. He shook Lester's hand. "You work for Mr. Golan, don't you?"

"I do. I'm Deputy Chief of Onboard Security. We're looking for Mr. Salib."

"Because you work for Mr. Golan, you are certainly aware of the very strict instructions that he has shared with his staff. Those instructions prohibit you or any member of the staff from entering this suite for any purpose."

Lester stood there for a moment. He looked like he was thinking through his options. I ate my soup, which was delicious.

"Want to come over here and join me, Abelard?" I asked. "Are you a drinking man? I ordered this piña colada, but I just had some thirty-two year old Scotch and I'm still basking in its afterglow, so I'm disinclined to chase it with something so pedestrian, so mockingly fruity. What I'm getting at, is that this piña colada could be yours for the asking."

"That's very kind of you," he said, "but I have to watch my sugar."

"Me too. I have the Type II diabetes."

"As we age, we have to pay attention to more and more," he said. "Are you armed, Mr. Grave?"

I nodded. "Oh, yes."

"Then I'm going to have to ask you to remove your weapon and place it on the table. There are no weapons allowed in here other than my own."

"I can't do that," I told him. "I lost one already. But don't worry, Bashir trusts me. He's around here somewhere, I'll bet. You could call out and ask him."

"I'm not interested in Mr. Salib's assessment of your trustworthiness," he said "but if you won't give up your weapon, you'll have to leave."

"No. Here's how this works," I began. "I get to go anywhere I want on this ship. If I want to bring my gun, I bring my gun. If I want to bring my Fester, I can do that too. Now that that's out of the way, can you give me a sense of what you do here? Because I read the passenger and crew manifests, and I don't remember anything about a big old giant running around."

He stared at me.

I ate my fries. "Hey, how about something from the

minibar for my friend? You could stand to be a little more hospitable, Abelard."

"Can I get you a beverage, Mr. Fung?" He reached into a bowl and produced another egg which he began cracking.

"I'm fine," Lester said. "Mr. Grave is right. I don't think we have you listed on any of our manifests. Can you tell us what it is that you are doing here?"

Abelard took a drink of water and put down his spoon. "I share some responsibility for the well-being of a certain individual on board this ship."

"You mean Bashir?" I asked.

He didn't respond.

I heard someone at the door, and a moment later Bashir himself walked in. He was surprised to see us. "What are you doing here?" he asked.

"I'm having my lunch," I told him. "The soup was first rate. Abelard and I were just catching up. Hey, would you like this piña colada? I hate to see it go to waste."

"You're not supposed to be here. Mr. Fung, you have very specific instructions ..."

"Save it." I cut him off. "I have some questions, so sit."

"Excuse me? You don't tell me what to do in my own suite. This is my home."

I kicked a chair out from under the table. "Sit. I need you to tell me who you were speaking with when I was on the bridge earlier."

"What? I don't know what you are talking about." He turned to Abelard who had resumed his egg cracking. "I don't recall talking with anyone."

"Give Lester your phone," I told him. "Lester, do you know how to work these phones? Tell me what number he called when I was there."

"I'm not going to give anyone my phone," Bashir said. "You are a guest. I brought you in to help me, not to accuse me."

I finished my fries and moved on to the burger. "Bacon," I said. "It's delicious. I didn't even ask for it and there it is. It's the little things that will have people coming back for more. That is if they have anything to come back for. The phone, now, or I'll pull your security accreditation. Once you cross the Atlantic, you won't be able to dock anywhere north of Patagonia. Oh, and you'll probably never get to be king either because your investment will fail. What do you think they'll do with this ship after that? Mothball her until you can find a buyer, or just sail her right into the ship-breaking yards in Bangladesh for scrap?"

I looked up at Abelard as I said this, but he didn't pay me any attention at all. I remember thinking that this was odd, but at that very moment, I heard a ferryboat whistle somewhere in the harbor, and I started to understand what was going on.

Bashir fumed. He did some teeth-grinding, but he handed his phone to Lester. I stood up and carried my burger over to the full-length mirror at the far end of the room. Abelard eyed me as I moved. "I got punched in the eye last night," I told him. "I think the bruise is starting to go down but I can't tell for sure."

Both he and Bashir grew noticeably tense as I stood there in front of the mirror.

"I have this same mirror in my cabin," I said, standing inches from it. "It opens onto the next room. This one does too. And it even has a peephole in it. If you look really closely, you can see a tiny bit of light coming through."

"Mr. Grave," Bashir said, "you have my phone, and you have my full cooperation. I ask that you now please leave my suite."

I turned to Abelard. "I thought you were here to protect him, but you're not." I got no response to that. "OK, you asked for my gun. I'm going to take it out and hand it to you now, so don't get alarmed."

He stood again, and I swear he was even taller than he was a few minutes ago. He looked down at me as he took my gun. "You must take a great deal of care at this point," he said. "You don't know what you're about to get involved with."

"I have a suspicion." I knocked on the mirror, and when nothing happened, I knocked again. I waited about a minute.

It opened slowly, and standing there was one of the loveliest women I have ever seen. She had slate grey eyes, and wore a jeweled bikini. Her skin was so pale, she was nearly translucent. She stepped back and held the door open.

Chapter Thirteen

"Who is this man, Abelard?" Her accent was American, from somewhere in the South.

"He works for Bashir."

I introduced myself.

"Yes, yes. I know who you are," she told me. "I remember your name from the security protocol documents."

"Well, that's grand. I'm going to come in and visit with you for a bit. What's your name, sweetheart?"

"Amaranth," she said. She took my hand and led me down a hallway lined with mirrors. It was dark, lit only by candles, and everywhere I looked I saw her in the mirrors. We turned a corner and passed under an arch, emerging in a different world entirely.

Candle lanterns hung from the ceilings, and the floors were covered with woven rugs. Incense filled the air. In the middle of this massive room, a man sat on cushions watching the news on a flat-screen TV as he smoked from a water pipe. He looked up when he saw me. He turned and called out something in Arabic.

Amaranth let go of my hand and nestled into him. She whispered in his ear. He smiled as he caressed her hair, then he picked up a remote and switched off the TV. "Please," he said, patting the cushion next to him.

It took me a minute but I sat. Amaranth smiled at me. "We don't get many visitors."

"I would have come sooner," I told her, "but I'm just only finding out now that you exist."

The man took my hand in his. "You are an old man," he said, "older even than myself, and I am seventy-five years old."

"I've got you by a decade," I told him, "but you look good. I'll bet you eat right. I'd watch the smoking if I were you."

He sucked on his pipe. "It's a habit I picked up in the desert. But that was long ago. Do you know who I am?"

"Yes," I said. "You're Bashir's father, the king."

He nodded. "I am Abdullah bin Salib. I was told it would be possible to remain hidden from others."

"I watched your news conference earlier. I heard a boat whistle in the background, and I heard it again just moments ago. It's the ferry that takes tourists to the Vasa museum, to visit the old warship."

"It did not occur to me to think of that," he said. "Did you go ashore today?"

I shook my head.

"I remained onboard as well," he said, "but I would have liked to visit. I'm told the royal palace here is the largest in the world. It has six hundred and eight rooms, just one room more than England's Buckingham Palace. That is quite a bit larger than my palace back in Al-Kurbai which has fewer than forty rooms, I think. I can't recall the exact number."

"Hey, home is where you hang your turban, right? And this ship has something like twenty-six hundred cabins, so I'd say right now Indulgence is the largest palace in the world."

He stared at me, and then burst into a howling laughter. "I like that very much," he said.

"So, what are you and the missus up to here? Why hide on a cruise ship?"

Amaranth frowned. "I'm not his wife."

"Grand-daughter?"

"Not even close," she said. "I'm his concubine."

"Is that right? I didn't think they had those anymore. So does that make Abelard chief eunuch?"

They both stared at me.

"Well I'll be goddamned. You folks really are old school. Backing up a bit here, how would I go about getting a concubine for myself? Because I think that would be great."

She looked me up and down. "I don't think that's likely. You don't look like you travel in the right circles."

The king held up a hand and she fell silent. "I am here looking after my investment," he said. "The girl accompanies me. She brings great joy to my heart."

"Mine too," I assured him, "and I've only just met her. So who is guarding the kingdom while you're on vacation."

"I am not on vacation," he said. "I am very much working. My sons are watching over my people in my absence. We are in touch many times each day."

"What about the son you just disinherited, Shazam?"

He opened his mouth, but nothing came out for a moment. "Nezim."

"Right, aren't you worried that Nezim will be angry that he's not crown prince anymore?"

He shook his head. "Nezim does what I tell him to do, always. He was an effective crown prince, but his business skills are not what I would have hoped. As Minister of Finance, he was a disappointment. My investment portfolio became tattered. It is my hope that Nezim will prosper in his new role."

"What's his new role, if you don't mind me asking?"

"Minister of Endangered Wildlife. It is a most important position."

"I'm sure it is. Do you actually have any endangered wildlife in your country?"

"Oh yes." He nodded. "Our wild jird populations have

declined considerably."

"What's a jird?"

He turned to Amaranth and whispered something in Arabic.

"It's a gerbil," she said. "It's one of the only animal species indigenous to Al-Kurbai."

"Is that right?"

An older woman entered the room carrying a tray. She placed it in front of us and backed out of the room, bowing. Amaranth poured us each a cup of tea from a silver pot.

"So you work for Bashir?" she asked.

"In a manner of speaking," I told her. "A man was killed on board yesterday. I'm trying to find out who did it."

She nodded. "King Abdullah was very fond of Wakim. We were shocked when we heard the news."

I frowned. "Who's Wakim?"

"The man who was killed."

"Right. So what can you tell me about him?"

The king fiddled with his water pipe and prodded Amaranth to relight it for him. "I will answer your question, myself," he said. "Wakim was like a son to me. His father was a commander in my armed forces. When he was killed in a military engagement, Wakim came under my protection. When he matured, he joined the unit his father founded, a special branch."

"What kind of special branch?"

"A covert branch, which is all I will tell you."

"Then what was he doing onboard?"

"He was looking after me."

"He was looking after you. Do you know who killed him?"

"I do not," he said. "If I did, this carpet would be littered with his fingernails."

"Is that right? That's a disturbing image. But make sense of this for me, please. Why would someone want to kill him?"

He looked down at his lap. "Nasr Wakim was a phantom, my phantom. Killing him drives a dagger into my heart. It is a private message, from someone close to me."

"And what exactly is the message?"

He held up his hands. "This venture, this ship ... many people disapprove. They call it decadent, immoral. They call it a ship of whores."

"My goodness."

"There are many who would like to see Indulgence fail," he said, puffing on his pipe.

"Then let's start by giving me a list of names," I suggested.

"No." He exhaled. "My people will take care of this. You'll forgive me, but these are matters best left to my own consideration."

I drank my tea. I thought about reading him the riot act as I did with Golan, but instead I held my peace. I didn't feel ready to threaten him, and I wasn't convinced he was the kind of man who was easily threatened. "I was in a German prison camp," I told him, "in 1945. It was the tail end of the war and our side was winning. Even the guards understood that.

"There was this one guard named Walter Bremmerman who I didn't know very well. However, one day as the war was coming to an end, I was standing outside trying not to fall asleep, and he came over and handed me a carton of raisins. And that meant a lot, because the guards had almost as little food as we did. Inside were ten little boxes of raisins. I ate two whole boxes before I said a word. Then I asked him why. Do you know what he told me?"

The king nodded slowly. "I would think he told you that he understood the shoe would soon be on the other foot, and he wanted to be sure you would treat him kindly."

"More so. He told me he knew he would spend the rest of his life trying to make sense of what he had become. And he wanted to know if I would consider being his friend."

"And did you become his friend?"

"I did," I said. "I told him that for three more cartons of raisins and one of cigarettes, he could count me as a friend for life."

"Your friendship was purchased quite inexpensively."

"No," I told him. "I've thought about this a lot over the years. If he offered me a million dollars and I accepted, then my friendship would have come cheap, because I did not need a million dollars. But I was starving to death, and I needed food and vitamins, and those raisins very likely saved my life. I intended to give away two of the three cartons, but in the end, I ate two myself and only gave away one, I'm ashamed to say. For what it's worth, I gave away the cigarettes."

"And did you keep up your end of the bargain?"

"I did, yes. We wrote to each other for years, sharing stories. And I even visited him in Berlin, much later. By then it was as if we had always been friends."

Amaranth refilled my cup. "So the point is that a few well-placed raisins can make a world of difference?"

The king said something to her in Arabic. He said it softly but it was a rebuke of some sort because she sat back stiffly. "The point," he told her in English, "is that by sharing stories, you can make a friend."

I drank my tea.

The king pulled hard on his pipe. "One summer day," he began, "I was just nineteen years old, the same age perhaps as you in the story you told?"

I nodded.

"We rode on horseback, my father and I, into the hills to the estate of one of the Osman princes. They were the sons and grandsons of the Ottoman rulers who fled Istanbul when the British came in your World War I. My grandfather had agreed to let them live in Al-Kurbai provided they followed our laws.

"So my father and I were paying a social visit to the last of the princes, a man called Beyd, who was dying from all the red wine he would not admit to drinking."

I shook my head. "Too much alcohol can kill a man."

"Yes," he said, pulling again on his pipe. "We ate a nice meal with Beyd Osman. I remember it because I had never before tasted truffles, which I quite liked. And as we prepared to leave, Beyd pulled my father close and begged him to care for his slave when he died."

"His slave," I repeated. "You have slaves?"

"We do not," he said firmly. "But Beyd Osman did, an English boy of nearly ten years old. He was a slave of the kind the Ottomans preferred, one who had been castrated."

I shivered. "Abelard."

He nodded. "My father took him that very day on his horse. And the next day he burned Beyd Osman's house to the ground. It took my father five years to locate the family, and during that time, Abelard lived in our palace as my brother. I missed him when he finally left on an airplane to rejoin his parents. We wrote to each other nearly every day. It was ten years before he came back, before he came back to our family."

We spent some quiet moments drinking our tea.

"I understand why you would put your trust in him," I said, "and I hope we have made some small progress today to become friends ourselves."

He reached out and put his hand on mine. "It is late afternoon. I must observe my prayers. I will ask Amaranth to see you out."

It took me longer than I had hoped to stand up. I generally don't sit on the floor if I can avoid it. My knees ache and then I have to put the Bengay on them. I followed Amaranth back through the hall of mirrors to the door. I won't lie to you; I couldn't help but stare.

"It's been a pleasure," she said.

"Let me ask you something," I said quietly, standing in

front of the door. "You can just nod if you like. Are you being held here against your will?"

She stared at me for a moment and then burst out laughing. "Good day, Mr. Grave." She opened the door and pushed me back out into another universe.

Chapter Fourteen

Abelard said nothing as he returned my gun. He was apparently too busy with his egg cracking.

"How many of those are you going to eat?" I asked but he didn't even look my way. Bashir and Lester Fung were nowhere to be found.

I had many questions, so I marched back toward that private bar; thinking that my questions were the kind best mulled over a glass of thirty-two year old single malt. But I was getting a little anxious, so instead I took the elevator down, hoping to make my way to the security office to find Lester.

I closed my eyes for no more than a minute, and when I opened them, the doors were open, and I rushed out only to find that I was on the wrong floor. I was back in ancient Egypt, and there was a line of people waiting to get back on the elevator. I pushed my way through the aged throngs, keeping an eye out for anyone who bore even a passing resemblance to King Tut. Fortunately, nobody did. It was slow moving in front of the pyramid shops; they were doing a brisk business.

I smiled at a pretty girl just outside one of the pyramids, and she smiled back.

"Have you thought about making Indulgence a special part of your life?" she asked

I think she was coming on to me. "If your name is Indulgence, that's exactly what I've been thinking about," I told her.

She laughed. "Many of our guests find that fractional ownership is the ideal way to enjoy all the marvels that Indulgence has to offer. If you'd like to step inside ..."

I moved away quickly, putting some distance between myself and the time-share harpy. I ducked behind the sphinx, and was startled by a tap on my shoulder. I turned to find a young man holding what looked like a pair of deflated balls.

"Would you care to stuff a whale?" he asked.

"What, now?"

"Stuff-a-Whale." He smiled like some kind of lunatic. "It's great fun. First you pick out a whale that fits your personality. Then you stuff it."

"Son, whales aren't empty," I told him. "Did something happen to your balls?"

He wrinkled up his face. "It's not a real whale, sir. It's a stuffed whale, one you make yourself." Then he stuck his hand inside one of the balls and started wiggling it around like a shapeless hand puppet.

"You pick out a heart," he continued, "then you pick out some sunglasses or maybe a nice sun hat."

"What the hell are you talking about?"

He pointed to the pyramid shop behind us. "Stuff-a-Whale."

"Well I'll be goddamned. Why would I want to stuff my own stuffed whale?"

He wrinkled his face again.

"Good Christ," I said, "this is like the pizza place that sells you the pizza you have to bring back home to cook. Or that, just have a look over there, will you, what do you see?"

"YouBrew," he said. "It's great fun. The brew master works with you to craft a personalized microbrew."

"So it's more things that I have to do myself," I said.

"Do I look like I want to do more things myself? Hey, how about this – 'Pull a Tooth?' Next time you get a toothache, you don't even have to go to the dentist."

He pursed his lips. "Well, that doesn't sound like fun."

"Exactly. I don't know how to make beer, that's why I pay others to do it for me. I don't know how to stitch my own underpants either, so that's why I trust the work to specialists. And you want to bring us all back to the middle ages where we all have to shave our own ducks? I don't think so. Good day to you, sir."

I had to get out of there before I ran into anyone else, but it was slow going. YouBrew was knee-deep in amateur brewers. I spied a bank of elevators just ahead, so I moved quickly. I jumped into one just as it was about to close. The elevator was crammed full. I pressed the button for Deck 3 and I got out with everyone else when the door opened. But we weren't on Deck 3. I didn't know where we were. It looked like some kind of hideout for pirates.

A man wearing a sword strapped to his belt came at me eagerly. "Welcome to the Caribbean Quarter."

"Hey, you look familiar. Have me met?"

"Aye, we have, sir. I be Antonio Grassi. I be your cruise director."

"Is that right? Why be you talking like a jackass?"

"I be a pirate in the Caribbean Quarter. Have ye visited us before?"

"I'm not entirely certain where I am," I told him. "I was just up at Shave-a-Duck and I'm trying to make it to Deck 3."

"Ar, this be Deck 4," he said. "Caribbean Quarter. Deck 3 be the one below. Does ye like piña coladas?"

"What's not to be liking?"

"If you be heading over to Pirate Cove, ye can get a piña colada that you drink out of a real pineapple. It's delicious."

"Hey, why is it dark in here?"

He leaned in to whisper. "We keep the lights dim to

make it look like Port Royal in the evening. Port Royal was a pirate city in Jamaica." He strapped a plastic parrot onto my shoulder.

"It's a plastic parrot," I said.

"Aye, a pirate's best friend."

I left him at that and headed down Privateer's Lane. It was crowded, and it took me a few moments to get my bearings. The ground was painted to look like cobblestones, but the rest of it looked like a Disney Ride.

Overhead, girls wearing little bodices waved from balconies, which was nice. Other balconies featured more mature women, and some men too, reclined on lounge chairs. I'm pretty sure those were actual cabin balconies and not part of the exhibit. Lanterns lit my way as I passed a pirate bar, and I smelled something wonderful. I passed a jewelry store, a leather goods store, a handbag boutique, and a duty free liquor store before I came to the source of the smell. In a clearing made to look like a waterfront, I found a fire pit with a pig roasting on a spit.

I stood in a line of passengers waiting to be fed a bit of that pig. I've tasted many dead things in my long life, and few things come close to the magic of barbequed boar. The wait might have been unbearable except for the trio of Filipino musicians singing pirate songs.

A man wearing an eye patch worked his way down the line. He was carrying a tray full of cups. "Rum punch, does ye care to sample, matey?"

"I does," I told him. I drank my punch and finally got to the pig itself, where several generous slabs of meat made their way to my plate. I took my feast to a chair by the simulated harbor and dug in. It was glorious. I ate my pork and drank my rum. Then I fell asleep.

"Sir?" A waiter wearing an eye patch shook me gently. "You dropped your parrot. Are you alright, sir?"

"Yes, yes," I told him. "I was just eating. Hey where's the pig?"

"We cleaned up about half an hour ago," he said, snapping the parrot back on my shoulder. "Sir, have you hurt your eye? Would you like me to call the doctor?"

"No, no. I slipped in the tub," I told him. "I might have to get one of those eye patches. Hey, where did everybody go?"

"They're at Spanish Main. It's already started but you could slip in."

"What's Spanish Main?"

"It's a show," he said. "Just follow the path to the pirate ship. You can't miss it."

I did just that. I passed a couple more shops and came to a pair of large doors. A Filipino wearing an eye patch let me in. Inside, the light was even dimmer, and it took my eyes a minute before I realized I was in a theater. I stumbled into a seat.

On stage was a pirate ship, or a reasonable simulation thereof. And on that pirate ship, three pirates chased three captured lasses around the deck and into the rigging. The captured lasses did some singing. I would say overall, they didn't appear too worried about the events at hand.

Suddenly the room got brighter. Clouds moved on the wall behind the ship, which, as it turns out, was a movie screen. The clouds parted and a Spanish galleon appeared. It was huge, and it was firing its cannons. The pirates jumped into place, manning their own cannons in a highly-choreographed manner. The captured lasses demonstrated an uncanny familiarity with seventeenth-century armaments, helping to load the cannonballs as they sang.

"This is outstanding," I told the fellow sitting next to me, but he shushed me. I sat back and watched for half an hour. I would like to have stayed until the end, but I had work to do. So I waited for a particularly large explosion, and as the pirate captain rushed to aid one of the lasses, I snuck out.

Outside the theater, the Caribbean Quarter was deserted. And the lights were even dimmer than before. I headed back down Privateer's Lane when I saw a colored fellow standing there, blocking the way. He held a sword in his hand, a real one. "I'm disappointed in you," he said, coming toward me.

I looked around, but there wasn't another soul about. I had no interest in being attacked again, so I took out my gun for the second time that day. I did it discreetly, and I held it low as the man moved closer.

"I'm disappointed in you," he repeated.

"Story of my life," I told him. "You should know that the captain is waiting for me right now. He knows exactly where I am."

"Is that a fact, mon? Why do you disrespect me so?"

"What, now?"

"You leave my show before it is even finished. Do you see anyone else leaving my show?"

"Your show?"

"My show, yes, mon." He seemed irritated. "I worked very hard. Why do you walk out?"

"No offense," I told him, "but doesn't it seem like you're tempting fate to have a show about pirates on a ship?"

"Oh, no, mon. We are honoring the pirates of old. They were brave men, free men in a time of slavery, of captivity."

"I've seen pirates," I said. "Two years ago off the coast of Borneo. It wasn't pretty."

"Not those pirates," he said. "I'm talking about buccaneers, men who fought against the Spanish and the English. Some of these pirates were my ancestors."

"Is that right? You're from Jamaica?"

"No, mon, just my accent is from Jamaica. I'm from Haiti. Montrose Royal, at your service."

I reached out to shake his hand, and he drew back when he saw my gun. "Sorry about that," I said, putting it back in the holster. "Hey, I remember you from the crew meeting. You're the guardian angel of the Jamaica Deck."

"The guardian of the Caribbean Quarter, I am."

"And you're a theater director?"

He frowned. "That I seem to be. At home in Haiti, I was apprentice to a houngan, a priest, but things were bad, bad at home, mon. One dark night I paid $1,200 to a man with a boat to take me to Miami. And he took my money and left me behind. So I went back to the houngan. A year later, I got a scholarship to NYU and moved to Manhattan, mon. I studied theater."

"Wow, that's quite a career move; priest to director."

"It is, mon, but it was necessary. Things are bad in Haiti. Have you ever woken up so hungry that your stomach feels like a hard ball?"

"Don't get me started. Hey, do you know who punched me in the eye?"

He frowned. "Now why would I know something like that?"

"Just a shot in the dark. Listen, I'd love to chat more but I have to find my way to Deck 3. Can you help me with that?"

"I can walk you to the elevator," he said, and he did. "If you want to see something truly special, come back here at midnight."

"What's at midnight?"

"A show closer to my heart," he said. "A story of my people, and about the spells we used to defeat the French soldiers, and to bring the dead back to life."

"Zombies," I said.

"That's right. Be here at the stroke of midnight."

"Son, do I look like the kind of man who will be awake at midnight?"

He sighed. "Come tomorrow to the early show. It's at 5:00 pm."

Chapter Fifteen

When the elevator door opened, I checked to confirm I was on Deck 3. I had no intention of getting lost again. I found the security office buzzing with activity.

"Where have you been?" Lester Fung let me in.

"I was at Shave-a-Duck, then the pirate world."

Golan stared at me. "What's that on your shoulder?"

I checked. "It's a parrot. Hey, you guys didn't tell me you had a full-fledged harem on board. Did you know the king was here?"

"I did," Golan said. "I knew he had a girl with him, but I didn't know about the giant. Bashir promised to give me a list of all of his people, but that list has not yet appeared."

I turned to Lester. "Tell me about the cell phone. Did you find out who he was on the phone with?"

"I did," he said. "It's an international number. I called it and reached the private office of Yaffir Salib, Minister of Aviation for Al-Kurbai."

"And who is he?"

"One of Bashir's brothers."

"Why was Bashir talking to him about me?"

"I asked him that very question," Golan interrupted. "He told me he was in the middle of a conversation, and was simply keeping his brother informed as to our affairs. Yaffir is the brother he trusts the most."

"Might be time to keep Yaffir out of the loop."

Golan nodded. "I've already advised Bashir."

"OK, so where are we in regards to the man who attacked me?"

Golan brought up an image of the man on his screen. "His name is Randy Binder. And he's a passenger."

"Is that right? Pick him up."

"He's not currently on board," Golan continued. "He went ashore shortly after the phone call this morning, but we'll grab him when he re-boards."

"Assuming he re-boards."

"Why wouldn't he?"

"Because he did a dumb thing, making the call from the casino. He's not working alone. If he was, he wouldn't have been able to get the key to my room. That means he has help, someone who works on the ship. And they would have told him he was burned. You hold on to passenger passports, right?"

"Yes," Golan said, "we keep them at Guest Services."

"I'll bet he grabbed his on the way out. Find out."

"Tell me about Mr. Binder," I said to Lester as Golan picked up the phone.

"Randy Binder is twenty-eight years old," Lester read. "He's from Las Vegas, Nevada. I asked Cordell to see if the Nevada Gaming Commission had anything on him. Want to guess what he found out?"

I shook my head. "Not much. If he had spent any time at all around casinos, he would have known they had surveillance cameras everywhere."

"You would think," he began, "but when he was seventeen years old, Randy Binder tried to walk out of Caesar's Palace with a coin cart, you know, the little wagons that they use to collect the quarters from the slot machines."

"Is that right? Then why didn't he know about the cameras?"

"That's a good question. Binder was given a probationary sentence, but he was banned from every casino in the state. Eight years ago he tried to join the army but washed out during basic training. Since then he's been only intermittently employed, but he recently decided to try his luck with Soldier World."

"Soldier World?"

Lester typed something into his computer and a photo appeared on the screen.

"That doesn't really look like him," I said.

"He might be wearing a disguise."

It was some kind of advertisement. Randy Binder was wearing military fatigues and holding a machine-pistol in each hand. "Highly decorated American soldier," the ad read. "Armed, capable, and ready for immediate deployment, this Marine will make sure your mission objectives are met."

"Well I'll be goddamned."

Lester shook his head. "Soldier World is an employment service for mercenaries. I read their FAQs. Most of the jobs posted are for security work; guards or bodyguards. And most of the job seekers are ex-military or military wannabes."

"How fun! Let's post a job."

"You're kidding, right?"

"No." I sat back and thought about what I might want a mercenary to do.

Golan put down the phone. "You were right," he said. "Binder picked up his passport. He said he was buying property and needed proof of identity."

I turned back to Lester. "E-mail this to Binder: Retired banker likes your style. I am in immediate need of bodyguard services. Are you available to travel to United Kingdom? All expenses paid, handsome salary to be negotiated. Respond ASAP."

"Why the United Kingdom?" Lester typed in my ad.

"Why not the United Kingdom? It's lovely. Besides, he's already in Europe, so he might jump at it. And we'll be there in a few days. I'm going to need you to help me with some things."

Golan picked up the phone again. "I'm going to contact the tourism liaison at Stockholm police. They can detain him if he shows up at the airport."

"Hold that thought." I wrote out a wish list for Lester. "Can you work with my office and get these things for me?"

"There's a phone right here," he said.

"I don't hear so well on the phone," I told him. "It's the left ear, mostly. Whatever comes out of the phone sounds tinny."

"Then why not use the right ear?"

"I've tried that and it just doesn't feel right. Just do this fast, work with me. I have to talk with Golan for a minute."

Lester fussed but he made the call.

"What time is it now?" I asked.

"It's 6:30," Golan said. "You are wearing a watch."

"6:30? How the hell did it get to be 6:30?"

"We lost track of you for awhile, and then about an hour ago we got a call about a passenger napping after the pig roast. We figured it might be you, but then we lost you again."

"I was watching the pirates. Hey, did I miss dinner?"

"Plenty of places to get food," Golan said.

"Let's hold off on the Stockholm police," I told him. "If Binder was going to the airport, he would be long gone. So either he comes back to the ship or not, right?"

"And you don't think he's coming back."

"No," I said, "so we just have to figure out whether he is still on mission or not. Did he completely jump ship, or is he staying involved?"

I heard Lester on the phone. By the answers he gave, I knew he was talking with Beth Obradors, my capable assistant.

"Yes, he certainly is extraordinary," Lester said into the mouthpiece. "That was exactly the word I would choose. What? Yes, unusual too."

"She loves me," I told Golan. "She desires me, if you know what I mean."

"I'll tell him," Lester said, turning to me. "She said she does not desire you."

"She lies."

"She wants to know if you want her to cancel Binder's credit cards."

"No. I don't want to spook him."

Lester told her as much, and then looked up at me. "Randy Binder just used a Visa card to buy a train ticket to Goteborg."

"That's on the western side of the country," Golan said. "It has a major ferry terminal. He's planning to meet up with us in Copenhagen."

"What time does the train leave?" I asked.

"It's an open ticket, good for a whole year." Lester was still on the phone. "It was purchased online sixteen minutes ago, from a computer leased to OSJ Celebrations. Xana ... what?"

"XanaDoo-Wop," said one of the other security guys, pointing to a flyer tacked on the bulletin board. "It's a party barge."

"In XanaDoo-Wop," I read, "did Kubla & the Five Khans a stately pleasure dome decree, all night long!"

I looked over at Lester, but he shook his head.

"Join us at Djur-Garden pier number four for an unforgettable visit to the 1950s." I looked around the room for some help. "What the hell is this?"

"Party barge," Golan repeated. "They're turning up everywhere. They cater to sailors and off duty military. These northern European ports can be expensive, and crewmembers need a place to blow off some steam at a reasonable price."

"What are we talking about?"

"Music, liquor, dancing girls, and cheap internet."

"Let's go." I jumped out of my chair.

"Hold on a minute." Golan stared at me. "What exactly are we planning on doing once we get there?"

"I'll figure that out on the way," I told him.

"One more thing; they scan everyone going in. No guns."

Nuts. "I'll need to drop by the cabin."

Golan used his radio to have a tender ready to take us ashore. "Meet me at the excursion ramp in ten minutes," he told me. "And you should probably get rid of the parrot."

An inflatable tender whisked us across the harbor. We passed several of the tourist boats, and a couple of ferries tied down for the night. Two cruise ships were in port, but they looked miniscule in comparison to our gargantuan ship. I looked back at Indulgence and couldn't imagine how she stayed afloat.

When we reached the dock, Golan flagged down a cab and told the driver where to go. We passed some lovely buildings and stopped at most of the red lights in Scandinavia on our way to Djur-Garden, one of Stockholm's larger islands. "Look, they have kabobs," I said, as we pulled up to a stop light. "Do you think we have time for …?"

"No," Golan snapped at me. "We have to hurry. We don't even know if Binder is still there. And I don't think we could possibly travel any slower."

The driver tapped at a little sign taped to the dashboard. "This taxi obeys all speed limits," it read.

Nuts. I pulled an ID card from my wallet and held it out for the driver. "We're here on urgent business," I told him. His eyes opened wide and he stared at me in the rear view mirror. He flashed a wide grin and started singing in Russian, but at least we started moving.

"What was that about?" Golan asked.

"Nothing."

"You know we can't just grab him in a public place," Golan said. "He's not going to come with us. We need to bring in the police."

I shook my head. "No police."

"Why not? They can pick him up. We can ask to be present at the interrogation."

"Interrogation? This is Scandinavia. Even snowflakes have civil rights."

"So how do you want to play it?"

"When we spot him, I'm going to line up on him. He'll bolt, so I'll try to flush him your way. Then we take him back to the ship."

"He'll refuse to come. And the party barge has its own security, remember. We can't just cowboy around."

"Then be resourceful," I said. "He's the only lead we have. I don't want to lose him."

The taxi let us off in front of a run-down harbor complex. Golan paid the driver who shook my hand furiously, speaking in Russian.

"Dosvedanya," I said, pulling away.

"Why was he talking about Boris Yeltsin?" Golan asked as we headed toward a brightly-lit barge sitting at the end of the pier.

"Beats me." We passed half a dozen drunk naval cadets, and at least a few dozen Oriental guys wearing identical sunglasses, even though it was night. There was laughter everywhere, and the air was filled with the combined smells of marijuana and grilled bratwurst. It was the kind of party that nobody ever invited me to.

As we made our way down to the gangway, I began to understand why someone would want to come here. The place was amazing. The barge was the size of a football field, and it was lit up from bow to stern with neon. A laser light show played on the wall; two cartoon ladies with giant bosoms were dancing. The bosoms kept getting in the way.

"Welcome to XanaDoo-Wop," said a pretty Oriental girl wearing nothing but leather pants and a bra. "Is this your first visit?"

I could already hear the music coming from inside. "It is," I told her, "but it won't be my last."

"One hundred kroner cover charge," she said, "or fifteen dollars American. I hope you enjoy your visit."

"I'm enjoying it already," I told her as Golan paid.

She opened the door for us. "If you'll just please pass through the arch. Lena can help you through."

Lena was a sterner looking woman, wearing substantially more clothing.

"You're cute," I told her as I stepped through the metal detector, setting it off. "You look like a Chinese Myrna Loy. Have you done any films?"

"Stand here, please," she said, reaching for the hand-held wand.

"Happens every time," I told her. "I've got a nine inch slab of metal holding my pelvis together, along with four screws. You like scars? Let me show you their king." I undid my belt, reached for my fly, and she waved me in.

Golan followed me through the main doors. A pair of doormen in pink tuxedoes pulled back a pair of maroon curtains, and the music hit us like an aural tsunami that had been building since the fifties.

Onstage, a Filipino Buddy Holly screamed out the lyrics to 'Peggy Sue.' He was backed up by a nine-piece band. Dancing girls in off-brand bunny costumes spun around as half of Asia howled in appreciation.

"What can I get you, gentlemen?" I looked down to find a young redhead bunny holding a tray of goods. "I've got cigarettes, Cuban cigars, Toblerones, and SIM cards. Also, gum."

"I'll have a gimlet," I told her, but honestly, I couldn't keep my eyes off the dancing bunnies.

"I'll send a hostess."

I looked around for a place to sit, but there wasn't an empty seat to be had. Laser light zapped from one table to the next, but there didn't appear to be any vacancies. "Next time we need to come earlier," I hollered at Golan.

He grabbed my sleeve and pushed me toward a door marked 'Phones/Internet.' "Can we focus, please?"

I followed him down a long hall where a line had formed for the restrooms. I watched as another redhead bunny worked the line. She was taller; more ample than the last bunny, and her bunny suit was about eleven sizes too small. "Can I get you gentlemen something? I've got cigarettes, Toblerones." She leaned in, "Also condoms, and I might be able to get my hands on a couple of joints, maybe some Ecstasy."

"Oh, my."

"Are you looking for some Ecstasy?"

"All my life," I told her.

"Twenty euros. Then you go over to that man by the phone wearing the orange cap and tell him Trudy says hi."

I frowned. "And what happens then?"

Golan put his hand on my arm. "Can we focus, please?"

"Hold on. I'm dealing with something philosophical here," I told him.

"Twenty euros, OK?" My bunny was getting impatient.

"He's not going to buy anything," Golan told her, and she left.

"That was rude. I think she was starting to like me."

"I need you to concentrate on the reason we came here. Can you do that for me?"

"I can."

"OK. First we'll do a sweep of the internet stations," he told me. It was hard to talk over the music. "If we don't see

Binder, we'll try the cigar bar before heading back into the concert hall."

"A sensible plan."

"One more thing." He opened his jacket discreetly so that I could look inside. "When I told you we couldn't bring guns, I meant most guns."

"Look at that." I knew instantly what it was. "Israeli special forces ceramic pistol, it's the only handgun in the world that can pass through a metal detector. I didn't know they were in production."

"They're not. It's a prototype. But it might come in handy if this goes bad."

"It might," I agreed, "and so might this." I opened my jacket to show him the forty-five holstered on my belt.

"How the ...?"

"You want to see my scars too? Nobody searches an old man."

He shook his head, but he followed me into the internet cafe. The room was cavernous. I counted twelve rows, and each row looked to have about thirty workstations. Half of them featured privacy curtains.

The noise was like nothing I have ever heard. The music from the concert stage mixed with the sounds you hear from slot machines, but it was more than that. It sounded like a thousand video games being played at once.

I pointed Golan to one side of the room, and just as The Big Bopper started singing, I headed to the other side and started poking behind curtains.

I got more than a few frowns, mind you. I hadn't seen so much pornography in weeks. But that wasn't the half of it. Most of the guys seemed to be involved in video chats with nude or partially nude young women. I have never chatted with a nude or partially nude young woman on my computer, and I started getting that feeling you get when you realize you have been missing out on something.

Those who were not video chatting were playing some kind of shooting game, and that is something I don't have any interest in. Why you would come to a concert party only to sit by yourself and shoot cartoon space elves is beyond my comprehension.

It took me about three minutes to poke behind the right privacy curtain and find Randy Binder. He was drinking a beer and looking at CNN.

"CNN?" I screamed at him. "Half of the world's porn is here at your fingertips and you're watching CNN?"

He nearly jumped out of his skin, but he recovered quickly. I stepped inside and pulled the curtain closed behind me. He started to get up but I put my gun on him. "Settle down," I told him, "or I'll shoot you dead."

He leaned back in his chair and stared at the screen. "Old man, you are out of your league. Shouldn't you be back in your nursing home?"

"It's a community of active seniors," I told him. "Now be quiet. He's singing 'Chantilly Lace.'"

"Who is?"

I pointed to the speaker. "The Bopper. Let me ask you a question, Randy. I know you've been in a casino before. How could you not know about the cameras? That is so amateur; it breaks my heart. Now get up slowly. We're heading back to the ship."

"I'm not going anywhere," he said. "Now get the fuck lost or I'll call security."

"This is my favorite part," I said as I sang along with the Bopper. "Oh baby, you know what I like." Then I shot Randy Binder in the foot. It was loud, but I figured I had a minute or so before anyone realized where the shot came from.

He screamed and I slapped him hard across the mouth. "The next one goes in your spine. Now tell me who hired you."

"I won't," he said, wincing in pain.

The Bopper was still singing, but about half of the band

had stopped when the security alarm went off. "Five seconds," I told him. I counted three and then shot him in the other foot. "Who hired you? Tell me now or I'll kill you."

He lunged, knocking me off balance with his chair as he somehow got to his feet. My head bounced off the wall as he tumbled into the aisle, screaming.

"The man needs a doctor," I yelled as five dozen Oriental faces peered over their cubicle walls. "Heart attack or something; he's bleeding all over his shoes."

I waved to the security guys as they spun into the room. "I was just watching CNN," I told them. "Then I heard screaming. I need air."

I met up with Golan at the end of the pier just as the ambulance arrived. "That could have gone better," he said. "You know, your head is bleeding a little."

I nodded. "I would have bet a million bucks he would tell me who hired him."

"But he didn't, right?"

I shook my head.

"So, what now?"

"I don't know. Let's cancel his credit cards."

Chapter Sixteen

I was dizzy by the time we got back to the ship, and Golan insisted on taking me to the infirmary. I must have hit my head harder than I thought. The doctor kept me there for an hour or so, until he was sure that the ice packs were working and the pain pills were working even better.

"I think I'm going to keep you here overnight," he told me.

"No, no," I said. "I'm going back to my cabin. It's not too late for room service, is it?"

"It's never too late for room service," he said, "but this is your second injury in the last twenty-four hours and I'm required to keep you here."

"I'm not a passenger," I reminded him. "And I've been hit harder than this."

"I have to agree with the doctor," Golan told me. "This has become unworkable. I can't have the responsibility of keeping you safe at this point, so I'm going to restrict your activities in relation to this investigation."

"As I told you yesterday," I began, but he cut me off.

"I've already talked with your office. And I told them what happened. They're very concerned. So if you're planning to tell me you're going to pull our security certification, then you go right ahead."

I frowned, which made my head hurt more. "Fine, but I'm still going back to my cabin."

"Lester can help you."

"I don't need help," I said. "Wait, what deck is my cabin on?"

I don't remember who said what at that point. I won't lie. I was feeling very confused and more than a little angry. I had Randy Binder in my sights, and I let him get away. Maybe I was losing my touch. I got my things together and left. Lester tried to come with me but I left him at the elevator. I needed to be by myself.

I made it to Deck 11 without incident. Then I wandered for some time. There wasn't much to look at, just endless corridors flanked by cabin doors, but that was fine by me. I was in need of some reflection, and the mirrored halls seemed to help. There were a great many colors reflected in those mirrors, more than natural light normally allows. At the time, I didn't understand why this was happening, but it wasn't entirely unpleasant. A color bluer than blue filled my vision one moment, followed by something not quite green, almost opaque but liquid too. It had a nice whisper to it. I stared at the colors for hours.

It occurred to me, as I wandered, that it might be time for me to think about my occupational future. Maybe it was finally time to turn in my licenses, even the fake ones.

There comes a time in a man's life, my doctor tells me again and again, when he needs to slow down, to take it easy. And I've always known he was right. I just thought that time was a little ways off. Not a long way off, mind you, I'm nothing if not realistic.

I know that at my age, every day I wake up hale and hearty is a gift of chance. It's not fate, because no course of events is inevitable. It's not karma because I've not gone out of my way to be nice. It's not a blessing because there is no deity watching out for me, of that I am certain. No, it's chance alone, good luck, nothing more. That and good eating. I take care of myself.

Nevertheless, I found myself wondering if the next time I climbed off a ship and headed back home to the condo, maybe that should be the last time. No more jobs; I could hang up my guns, spend more time with Helen. Maybe I could finally take that watercolor class. I already have enough money and enough cable TV. But the idea still made me sad. I don't like to admit than I'm an old man, even to myself.

I made it to my cabin eventually. I was just getting out my keycard when the neighboring door opened and a beautiful young woman stepped out. She was petite, cute as a tiny button, and dressed to party.

"Hello again," she said. "I didn't realize we were neighbors."

"What, now?"

"You don't remember me from earlier?"

"Did we kiss?"

"Did we kiss? No, we sure did not, but you hit on me, remember? Upstairs at the oxygen bar?"

"Not ringing a bell."

She stared at me. "You're kidding me, right? My name is Anne. We had a whole conversation. We agreed you were far too old for me. Also too tall."

"Well that doesn't sound right." I opened my door. "I think we'd be great together, your charm and my good looks. Want to come inside? I have fruit."

"We all have fruit."

"I have rum," I told her. "We could sit out on my balcony and drink rum."

"You have a balcony?"

I turned the light on and had a look around. "No, it seems not. I'll have to bring this matter up with the butler."

"You don't have a butler either. None of us do down here in this neck of the woods."

I looked again. "It would seem not. Let's just sit on the bed. But don't make any moves. I'm shy."

"I'll pass," she said. "Hey, are you OK? You look even more decrepit than earlier. Did you fall?"

"No, I got in a fight with the captain," I said. "He wanted to sail the ship to Puerto Rico, but I said bullshit. I paid to see Denmark and I'll be goddamned if I don't see Denmark."

"Really. And then he punched you?"

"He did, yes," I said. "But then I cold-cocked him. He's probably still unconscious."

We heard chimes from the public address system, and then a voice: "Good evening, ladies and gentlemen. This is your captain speaking from the navigation bridge. I trust everyone has had a wonderful day in Stockholm. The weather was perfect. We're just now getting underway. We're a little late leaving due to some traffic in the harbor but we will still be arriving tomorrow morning in Copenhagen by 8:00 as scheduled. If you are on the starboard side of the ship just now you can see the lovely lights of Gamla Stann coming on. And we have many wonderful shows and events in store for you tonight. I wish you a wonderful evening aboard this most wonderful ship."

"I think he regained consciousness," Anne said.

"I didn't want to be too rough on him. Hey, I remember you now. You're the mean lady who was looking for short love."

"See, you do remember me!"

"Any luck yet with finding that special miniature someone?"

"Funny you should ask!" She locked her door. "I have a date right now, which is why I have to leave you."

"Whoever he is, he won't have half my wit and charm. Or stature."

"Probably not."

"Nor stamina," I added, but she was already walking

away.

    I poured myself a little tumbler of rum and sat on the bed. I spent the next half an hour staring at my TV watching the lights of Stockholm as we pulled away. Then I might have done a little napping. I'm not sure.

    It was midnight when I roused myself and turned off the TV. My head hurt, my face hurt, and for some reason, my back hurt. I was feeling sorry for myself and I was feeling lonely. But self-pity is not something I admire in any man. And a cruise ship is an unforgiving place to be lonely. It was midnight. It was time to start my evening.

    If you thought that onboard activities would be winding down at midnight, you'd be mistaken. A cruise is by definition a vacation, and therefore, normal bedtime protocols must be ignored. Midnight at sea is something like nine o'clock on land. It's not early. You should by that point have some idea of what the night is going to look like, but you still have a way to go.

    Because Golan had more or less relieved me of duty, I was technically on vacation. And I was determined to make the most of it. It was time to see a show.

    'The Loas of Carrefour' had already begun by the time I took my seat at a little cocktail table in the Caribbean Quarter Theater. Per my request, a rum punch was delivered to my table, and I drank from it liberally as I sat back and enjoyed the show. The pirate ship was gone. In its place was a backdrop of palm trees decorated with all manner of unfamiliar symbols.

    A young woman swayed in the breeze to the accompaniment of rhythmic drumming. Behind her, a chorus of colored men wearing top hats danced around an altar. They carried machetes which they used as canes.

    "Michelle asks the loas to avenge her family," boomed the voice of the narrator. "She calls out to Legba, the most powerful of the loas."

The young woman fell to her knees in front of the altar and sang something in Creole as the men in top hats danced around her.

I nudged the fellow next to me and asked him what a loa was, but he shushed me, so I asked the woman sitting on the other side. "It's a voodoo god," she told me.

"But Prosper only laughs," the narrator continued, as a man entered from stage left. He was tall and bald. He wore a white suit and carried a bottle of rum, which he drank from.

I waved to the hostess to bring me another rum punch.

Prosper walked over to Michelle and grabbed her by the hair. "Your gods cannot help you, little girl," he shouted. "You will soon be my wife, even if I have to beat your father and your brothers, yet again!"

The men in top hats shook their heads and raised their machetes as Prosper laughed. Michelle bowed in front of the altar, and suddenly the music stopped.

"Legba hears her prayer," the narrator announced, as one of the top hat men dropped his machete and started shaking. "Legba has taken over the body of one of the apprentice houngans. Michelle will have her vengeance."

The man who had been possessed by Legba did a backwards somersault, and then another, until he came face to face with Prosper.

"Get away, silly man," Prosper told him, "before I beat you too."

Michelle laughed, the chorus sang, the drums grew louder, and the possessed man blew a cloud of powder into Prosper's face. His eyes rolled back and he fell to the ground. The possessed man danced around him, did another somersault and then suddenly stopped, growing completely calm.

"Legba has cast his spell," the narrator told the audience. "But Prosper is not dead, not at all, you see, because he does not deserve death. He deserves something much worse."

The curtain went down as Act I came to a close. I jumped, startled by a hand on my shoulder. "A lady asked me to give this to you," the waiter said, handing me a folded sheet of paper. "Meet me at Crystal Falls," it read. "I'll be waiting for you."

"Who was the lady?"

"I don't know," he said. "I've never seen her before."

"What did she look like?"

He leaned in. "You know how some women are so beautiful, you can't even look right at them because you feel like you're doing something wrong?"

I nodded. "I think I know who you're talking about. Where is Crystal Falls?"

"It's in Rainworld. Deck 6. Two decks up. Take the Forward elevator, and turn left when you see the pandas."

Chapter Seventeen

I found myself alone in the elevator. And when the door opened and I walked out into Rainworld, I felt even more alone. I heard the crickets and the croaking of the tree frogs in the distance as I walked along the deserted path. When I reached the sleeping pandas, I turned around and saw the most beautiful synthetic indoor shipboard waterfall I had ever seen.

In front of it stood Amaranth. Her hair was pulled up in a bun, and she wore a white cocktail dress with a sweater over it. She looked like she had been crying.

"Your Highness," I began, "your beauty is only enhanced by the fluorescent moonlight."

"I wasn't sure you'd come."

"Oh, but I had to. It's not safe down here. There are hunter-gatherers afoot."

"I'm pretty sure they're asleep by now," she said. "Come closer. I don't want anyone to hear us."

"I think we're all alone, unless the pandas get out. Hey, where are you from, anyway?"

"Pigeon River, Tennessee. Have you been to the Great Smoky Mountains?"

"I don't think so."

She took my hand and led me to a ledge. We were close enough to the waterfall to feel the spray. "The cameras can't see us here," she said.

"I understand," I told her. "You're worried that the king will get jealous if he sees you with a more experienced gent."

"Something like that. Look, I need your help."

"With what?"

"I think Abdullah's life is in danger."

"Which one is Abdullah?"

She stared at me. "The king. King Abdullah."

"Right. What makes you think his life is in danger?"

"Within the last year, four of the people he trusts the most have been murdered. The last was Wakim, who was killed not fifty yards from where we are standing."

I looked back into the rain forest, finding it hard to believe that we were actually at sea.

"They're wearing him down. He'll have nobody when they come for him."

"Who is wearing him down? Who is coming for him?"

She threw up her hands. "The sons, the older ones. Each one is worse than the next. Each one wants to be the next king. And they've been isolating him. We have a saying back in Pigeon River: 'If you want to know who your friends are, watch who's crying at your funeral.' And I'm afraid that's what this is all leading to – a funeral."

A tear rolled down a perfect cheek so I got out my handkerchief. "Here's what I don't understand," I said. "If someone wanted to kill him, why not just kill him instead of killing those around him."

"Because Wakim was protecting him," she said. "It would not have been possible to get near him with Wakim around. You should know something about him; he ran a covert intelligence gathering unit that answered only to King Abdullah."

"Like an Al-Kurbai CIA."

"Something like that. Nasr Wakim was a highly-effective hand-to-hand fighter. So whoever killed him was very good. And with him out of the way ..."

"Wait a minute," I said, "I thought the reason he was killed was to make Indulgence fail, to screw over Bashir."

"No," she said. "That's just a smokescreen. There is far more at stake, far more money, and far more politics. And if they win, they will undo all that King Abdullah has accomplished. You should see what he's done with that sump of a country he inherited. Forty years ago, people were cutting each other's heads off in the street. Now, there's universal suffrage, compulsory education. The social services would make a Scandinavian lower his head in shame."

"I had no idea," I said. "You seem to know a lot about the country."

"I have to. I'm doing a Ph.D. in regional development. Or, I was. My studies have derailed somewhat. I had no idea how fascinating this world is. I don't think I could ever leave it behind."

I stared at her. Even crying she was the most beautiful woman I had ever seen. "So you're not really a porcupine?"

She stared at me. "Excuse me?"

"What, now?"

"I think you mean concubine."

"That's what I said."

"No, it's not, but yes. Oh yes, I am a concubine. When he asked me, I leapt at the opportunity."

"And you actually, you know ..."

She stared at me.

"You and he?"

"Did you have a question, Mr. Grave?"

"No, I suppose not."

"I thought not." She wiped the last of her tears.

"Wait, I do have a question. Does the king share your concerns?"

She shook her head. "He won't come out and say that he doesn't trust his own sons, but he shifts them around, changing out their ministries to keep them on their toes. It's a game to him, but it isn't to them."

"So what is it you want me to help with? Why me?"

"Because you're the only one outside of it all."

I shook my head. "You're not giving me much to go on. I think I need to talk with Bashir."

"Bashir is an idiot," she said. "He's got his Harvard Business degree, so he knows something about finance. But he doesn't have the common sense the Good Lord gave a bag of dirt. He wears Italian suits and French leather shoes. He's a dandy, and it doesn't play well back in the Emirate. The brothers all hate him."

"Then give me something to work with."

She was silent for a moment as she stared at the waterfall. "This might not mean anything," she began, "but the ship's doctor, Dr. Faber, have you met him?"

"Once or twice." I rubbed the back of my head which had started to ache again. "What about him?"

"I've seen him before. About two years ago, Abelard and I took the jet to Paris to do some shopping. We spent a day at the Val d'Europe mall. Are you familiar with it?"

I shook my head.

"It's massive, it has all the right stores, and it's near the airport. It's actually right by Paris Disneyland, but we didn't go there. Anyway, I finished with my purchases but Abelard wanted a few more ties, and we had another hour before the car was to pick us up, so I went to the hotel bar to have some champagne."

"A sensible use of your time," I suggested.

"And this man kept staring at me. Finally, he came over. He told me I was ungodly beautiful, and he said he would give me a thousand euros for fifteen minutes of my time."

"Fifteen minutes? He doesn't waste time."

She stared at me. "You understand what he was implying, right?"

"I do."

"So I told him if he remained in my presence, I would have him severely beaten, and he left."

"Fifteen minutes?"

"Are you listening to me?"

I nodded. "And you're certain it was Dr. Faber?"

"I am."

"It doesn't add up to much," I told her. "A lonely man on vacation sees a beautiful woman, has an extra fifteen minutes on his hands, and makes a poor judgment call."

She shook her head. "A short while later, as I was leaving, I saw him step into a meeting room with Hamid."

"Who's Hamid?"

"Hamid Salib, he's one of the sons. He's a little more ruthless than the others. He's the Minister of Defense, and as of yesterday, the new crown prince. In any case, this doctor was at the meeting."

"What was the meeting about?"

"I don't know, but don't you find it too much of a coincidence that this man, an ally of Hamid's perhaps, is now onboard?"

"Yes, I do. Did you tell Golan?"

She shook her head.

"Why?"

She looked up at me. "Abelard was late getting back."

"He was buying ties."

"He was buying ties, yes, but he was late because he saw Mr. Golan standing in front of the train station. He went over to talk to him but lost him in the crowd."

"What was Golan doing there?"

"That is a good question."

"Well I'll be goddamned. You think he might have been at the meeting too."

"I don't know, but it cannot be just a coincidence."

"I have an idea," I told her. Then the lights went out, all

of them.

"What's happening?" she asked.

"Could someone have followed you here?"

"Not possible. I was careful."

"Walk with me," I told her. "And don't say a word."

"Walk where? I can't see a thing."

I grabbed her arm and pulled her along the rail. "I need you to be very quiet, and I need you to trust me."

She started to say something but I squeezed her arm. She might not have understood the true gravity of the current situation, but I did. The whole deck was pitch black as far as I could see, and that is nearly impossible to accomplish on a ship. There are backup lights, and there are emergency lights that go on even when the backup lights fail. So someone put a lot of effort into making Rainworld dark.

I would bet dollars to big donuts that Amaranth had never been through basic training. But I have. It was a long time ago, but I learned that the worse thing you can do if your position is compromised is to stay put. So I led her carefully down the path until we had traveled about thirty feet. There was a tree at my back and I put Amaranth's hand on it. "Stay right here," I whispered.

"No," she whispered back, grabbing my hand. "No, you can't leave me."

"Quiet." I put my hand over her mouth. "There's someone coming." I heard footsteps on the trail. I could hear my heart beating too, and a moment later I saw a flickering light. Someone was coming quickly. Two people; one said something to the other but I couldn't hear anything more.

Amaranth moaned quietly.

"No, no," I said. I held my gun out. I heard the men getting closer, and as they neared our position, I saw them stop at the base of the waterfall. They were short men, and they carried torches. One of them made a clicking noise and they both turned toward us. They came faster now, and I saw who they were. They were the Jipitos.

"You OK?" the older one called out. He saw my gun and backed away. "We come find you when lights gone."

"We were watching *The Fast and the Furious*," the younger fellow said, "and all of a sudden the lights went out."

"You speak English," I said. "What's your name again?"

"Ruspewe," he said. "You can call me Rusty. My dad saw the lady over here before, so when the lights went off, he wanted to make sure she was OK."

"That's very kind of you." I bowed to the father and then felt silly for having done so. "Can you ask him if he saw anyone else?"

It was a strange language they spoke, heavy with the consonants. The father shrugged and then said something back.

"He says he didn't see anyone," Rusty told me, "but someone must have been here because the whole circuit box is crashed. Mom called it in. She wanted to see how the movie ended."

Suddenly the lights went back on.

We followed the Jipitos past the pandas, back down the trail, past their house, to the elevator lobby, where we found Golan staring at the electrical panel. Two technicians examined bundles of wires that had been ripped away.

Golan stared at Amaranth. "Who is this?"

"Don't ask right now. Can you tell me how all the power went off?"

"I'm looking into it," he said. "I thought we agreed you would be taking a rest from this."

"I was just getting a little fresh air," I told him, though in truth I was becoming more than a little angry. "But I have to tell you, I'm growing a little weary of all the surprises. The captain needs to know about this. If you can't figure out what happened, I'll alert port authorities that we need to stay in Copenhagen until you regain control of the electrical systems."

"I'm sure we'll figure it out," he said. "There's no need to alert the captain just yet. We have an act of sabotage here, nothing more."

"Nothing more? You have a killer loose. If you don't want me involved in the investigation, that's your call, but you need to start showing some competence here." At that point I wasn't sure whether Golan was one of the good guys or not, and I was nearly too angry to care. I looked around for Amaranth, but she was gone.

Chapter Eighteen

I planned to get an early start, but as things turned out, it was nearly 10:30 in the morning by the time I woke up. I had a headache that was pounding almost as hard as the person at my door.

"Give me time," I called out. I nearly killed myself stepping on the little minibar bottles from last night.

I opened the door to find Lester Fung standing there. He was holding a laptop. "You need to see this." He followed me in and set the computer on my desk. "This place is a mess. How many bags of potato chips did you eat last night? You had pizza too?"

"Mind your business," I told him. "The butler never showed up. Hey, I'm not sure you're supposed to be talking with me anymore. Golan decided he didn't like me."

"Well, this is just an information item." He typed at the keyboard and brought up Randy Binder's mercenary page. "Binder answered your job posting."

"Well I'll be goddamned." I rummaged around for my glasses and leaned over to read.

> "I am very, extremely, interested in learning more about this position, but am currently unavailable for international work due to bullshit charge of

non-payment of child support (which is bullshit). The hearing is sometime this week. But in the meantime, they confiscated my passport. I do 100% completely expect this issue to be resolved within the week. After that, I'm ready to roll. I hope this works out for both of us!!!"

"Randy Binder can't leave the country," Lester said. "I did some research. Randall James Binder, unemployed, of Las Vegas, does indeed have a complaint filed against him for non-payment of child support. Guess when the complaint was filed?"

"Tell me."

"Two days ago. The man who punched you, the man you shot in the foot isn't Randy Binder."

"I shot him in both feet."

"Still, it's not the same guy. He's stolen Binder's identity."

"Well I'll be goddamned."

"It gets better. Three months ago, Randy Binder opened two new credit card accounts, a bank account, and he applied for a replacement passport."

"So the identity theft was planned in advance."

"And that's the part I don't get," Lester said. "If you're going to steal someone's identity, wouldn't you steal a rich person's identity? Why a rock-bottom loser?"

I shook my head. "Rich people check their credit reports. If you want a whole new identity, something that can get you a passport and a driver's license, you can't go wrong with a rock-bottom loser."

"Good to know."

"So how much does Binder have in the bank?"

"I was hoping you would ask." Lester opened another file. "The unemployed Randy Binder has $672,483 on deposit at Chipley Savings & Loan, of Chipley, Florida."

"He's a man of means." I leaned in to read. "How much do you want to bet the real Mr. Binder doesn't know about the bank account? Hey, where the hell is Chipley? Sounds like a quiet kind of place."

"I think it's in the panhandle."

"Could be. So we have no idea who our mystery passenger really is."

"No, we don't."

I was hungry. I rifled through my minibar and found a tube of nuts. "OK, it's time to reacquire him. It's time the fake Mr. Binder came into some financial difficulty. Did we cancel his credit cards? If we didn't, you can call Beth in my office. She can do it."

Lester grinned. "Done. Unfortunately, there's no way we can touch the bank account."

"Maybe we can't, but I know someone who can. Open this for me." I handed him the nuts. "Hey, I have a huge pounding headache. Can you find a little bottle around here somewhere? It's time I took a pill or two."

Lester found my pills and opened my nuts. I took two pills and went to town on the nuts.

"OK, let's respond to the real Mr. Binder. Send him this message: 'Your timeline works perfectly for my needs. I trust your legal matters will be resolved, and I wish to contract for your services. I have wired an advance payment of $672,483 to a Florida bank, Chipley Savings & Loan. The account is in your name. For security reasons, please transfer the money to your own bank immediately. I will be in touch. Sincerely, Mr. G.'"

Lester sent the message. "Our mystery man is about to have a bad day."

"A very bad day," I agreed. "He might not have any money, or functioning feet, but he does have a train ticket to Goteborg. He might be on his way to Copenhagen. He might try to limp back on board, so I want to be up and running by the time we arrive."

"We docked nearly five hours ago," Lester told me.

"Is that right? OK, I'm going to get some food, and then I need to talk to Bashir. Do you know where he'll be in an hour?"

"I'm not supposed to be helping you," he reminded me, fiddling with his mustache. "I just thought you'd want to know about Binder."

"Bullshit. I have work to do. The king and I are buddies now, so help me or I'll have you beheaded."

"I really don't think he'd behead me."

"Maybe just a maiming. Look, help me out. I need to work on this."

Lester shook his head, but he brought up a calendar on his laptop. "Bashir is currently at a state reception at Amalienborg Palace."

"A state reception?"

"Yes, Al-Kurbai doesn't have an embassy in Denmark, so Bashir is making a formal diplomatic visit. He's meeting with Crown Prince Frederik. Apparently they knew each other at Harvard."

"And what time does the meeting end?"

Lester scrolled down. "11:30. At noon, Bashir will attend a concert at Tivoli Gardens."

"What's Tivoli Gardens?"

"I have no idea. I've never been to Denmark."

"Me neither. OK, off with you." I handed him a list of things I needed him to find out for me. "I need to shower, and I need you to follow up on a few lines of inquiry."

I got myself together and set off to find something to eat. I got in the elevator and hit the button for Deck 4. I still hadn't made it to the dining room, and I was determined to give it a try. For reasons unknown, the elevator deposited me on Deck 5 and it was some time before I became aware that I was not where I should be. In retrospect, I can see that I was having some memory issues as well as some balance issues. I tripped getting into the elevator. And I tripped again getting out. By chance alone, nobody was around to witness either incident, and for that I am thankful. But when older folks start tripping, it is often a sign of things to come, and I was not yet ready to heed that warning.

"Can I interest you in some fine Italian craftsmanship?" a fellow called out from the doorway of what appeared to be a motorcycle shop.

"What, now?"

"Have you thought about getting yourself a scooter?" he beckoned me into his shop. "We have Aprilia, Piaggio, Benelli, Malaguti, all the finest names."

"Do I have to put it together myself? Hey, where can I find something to eat?"

"It comes fully assembled," he said. "Think about it over lunch. If you just keep walking, you'll find several restaurants up ahead. Are you a sushi fan?"

"You bet I am," I said. "No wait, I'm not. What else?"

"There's Napoli for Italian food, and just across from it, the Fox & Swan Pub."

I headed for the Fox & Swan. I ordered a corned beef sandwich with potato salad and chips. I drank dark beer from a generous twenty ounce mug and stared out the window at the port of Copenhagen. It was dark in the pub. I thought I was the only person there until I saw a couple canoodling in the back.

I was still trying to get a handle on exactly what was going on with this ship. Someone wanted it to fail and I didn't yet know who or why. I was getting nowhere, and I didn't know who I could trust. I took out my packet of information on the staff, and looked up the good doctor.

Dr. Manfred Faber, age 60, attended medical school courtesy of the Belgian army, in which he served for nine years.

After a brief stint in private practice, he accepted a position as family physician to a Saudi businessman in Riyadh, where he worked for eight years. Dr. Faber had been at sea, a ship's doctor, for all of three days.

I did the math. It didn't add up. I counted up the years and looked for the holes. Faber had about five years unaccounted for, between the family physician gig and the ship's doctor gig. Maybe he took a sabbatical, caught up on a little reading. Or maybe he got tired of living in Saudi Arabia and just sat at home watching Spicy Mumbai for five years. I myself have been known to while away some quality time just attending to my hobbies and my cable programming. But five years begged an explanation.

I was thinking this through when the woman in the back of the pub pried herself away from her fellow canoodler and stepped up to the bar. I recognized her but I couldn't remember from where. "Come here often?" I asked.

"It's you," she said. "How are you feeling today, neighbor?"

I frowned. "Are you from Pennsylvania too?"

She stared at me. "It's me, Anne. We've met a couple of times. I'm in the stateroom next to yours."

"Is that right? I thought you looked familiar. Hey, you want to join me for a drink? You know what's nice? A gimlet."

"This early in the morning, I'm going to have to say no."

"Is that right? OK, how about this; do you like Kahlua?"

She stared at me. "I do like Kahlua, but again, not in the morning."

"Bear with me. OK, you know that Horsey sauce they have at Arby's?"

"You know what," she said, shaking her head, "I really don't think I want to have this conversation. I'm actually on a date right now."

I turned to look, but it was dark and I couldn't see

the guy. "Well good for you. I trust he's sufficiently petite, diminutive enough for your liking."

"He is, thank you."

"Well, I hope it works out. If it doesn't, don't come sobbing to me, begging me to take you back, because I won't. I have too much pride."

"Are you finished?"

"I am. Hey, if you find out he's not right for you, just give a knock on my door. Day or night, but not too late."

"I'll keep that in mind," she said, waving to her partner.

Chapter Nineteen

I ate my lunch quickly. Let me tell you something, I drink a little bit of liquor now and again to soothe my nerves, settle my thoughts, and keep my demons at bay, so I am not unaccustomed to the effects of drink. But I swear I was drunker than a sailor on shore leave. I wasn't sure why, having had very little to drink all morning.

I used a house phone to call down to the infirmary but was told that the doctor was not currently on duty, so I made my way to Guest Services. A crowd had gathered there in front of the squid tank where a balding fellow was lecturing.

"And that's really what makes infernalis so fascinating to us oceanographers," he said. "Imagine a world with nearly no light, nearly no oxygen, nearly no life. That's what it's like half a mile down. And here's a species that cannot swim fast, has no talons, no venom, only the smallest of teeth. And yet in its chosen environment, it's a top predator. Why? Because it knows how to sit still and wait. And if you sit still and wait long enough, it's just a matter of time before your prey swims right in front of you." He slapped the button for effect, and the crowd yammered in appreciation of the lightshow.

I started thinking about what he said as everyone dispersed. Maybe that's what our onboard killer was up to. Maybe he was just sitting and waiting. Maybe I was going to have to flush him out, put up some fireworks of my own. I asked the young man at Guest Services for Dr. Faber's cabin number.

"I can't give out stateroom numbers," he told me. "But I can get you his phone number." He typed at his keyboard, and read me the number of the infirmary, which I had just called.

I showed him my ID. "I think you'll find that it's OK to tell me his stateroom number."

He eyes opened wide. "You are His Holiness Tenzin Amitaba, the 12th reincarnation of the Rimpopa Lama?"

"What, now?" I took the card back. That's what it said. I really needed a system for keeping track of my IDs.

"I'm a Buddhist myself," he said, beaming. "I had no idea you were on board."

"Yeah, blessings. Listen." I leaned in closer. "I'm traveling under an assumed name." I found my crew ID and showed it to him. "The captain had it all arranged. Now I really need to know where the doctor lives."

He grinned madly, tears welling up in his eyes, but he told me where the cabin was.

On most cruise ships, the doctor's quarters would be up with the officers. But due to Indulgence's size, the good Doctor Faber was billeted in a suite next to the ship's infirmary on Deck 3 so that he could respond in a timely manner to medical emergencies, rather than having to negotiate six or seven decks teeming with seniors.

The Guest Services Buddhist told me I'd find an unmarked door about fifty paces down the hall past the infirmary, and he was right. I was about to knock when the door opened.

Faber jumped back, startled. "You've given me a fright, Mr. Grave."

"Sorry about that, but I'm glad to catch you."

"I was just going to make my way ashore," he said. "I have a couple of hours of unscheduled time and I hoped to pick up a souvenir. Is there something I can help you with?"

"Yes. I wanted to thank you for taking good care of me. I'm especially enjoying these pain pills. I might have to pick up a couple of bottles to bring home with me."

He gave a slight laugh. "I can't help you there. Narcotics are habit-forming. We want you to be pain-free, but we don't want you to rely on the pills for too long."

"Actually, I was kind of hoping you could refill my prescription. I'm out."

"You've finished all the pills?"

"Every one."

He frowned. "I was certain you had enough to ..."

"The pain." I shook my head. "The pain is considerable."

He had a strange look on his face. "I'll have some more sent to your stateroom. And if you stop by the infirmary tomorrow, we'll do a follow-up."

"Actually, could I trouble you for something to drink? I'm feeling a bit parched."

He looked quickly at his watch. "Of course," he said, leading me into the cabin. He had pictures everywhere, photographs in metal frames.

"This is nice." I looked around. "This is a big suite. How many rooms do you have?"

"Excuse me?" He handed me a bottle of water from his refrigerator.

"How many rooms?" I picked up one of the photographs and stared at a younger Faber standing in front of a waterfall with his arm around a heavyset woman.

"Ah, I have three rooms; this living area, a bedroom, and a small office where I do my paperwork."

"Is that right? No bathroom? I worked one cruise a couple of years back and I had to share a bathroom with this Chinese guy who smoked in the shower. I don't know how clean he really got."

"I do have a bathroom."

"What about a butler? I was under the impression that

I would have a butler, but I don't. I have to manage my own spa appointments."

"I do not have a butler, no. But the girls come by to tidy up every day, which is something one misses when not at sea."

"How did you come by a gig like this?" I was looking at his collection of photos. "Hey, that's Santorini. I was there. Lots of good food on Santorini, Greek food mostly. Is that recent?"

"I'm sorry?"

"Santorini. I was there last summer. When were you there?"

He frowned. "It must have been about ten years ago."

"Is that right? So how did you wind up becoming a ship's doctor? I ask because my son Teddy is a doctor, and I think he might like something like this." Faber had a really nice looking leather couch along the wall, so I took a seat.

He stole another peek at his watch.

"Hey, do you have any beer? I could use a belt. Or wine if you have some, but only if it's opened. A beer would be best, something dark."

"I don't keep any alcohol in my suite, I'm afraid. There are many fine taverns on board, but I must advise you to refrain from alcohol while you are taking medication."

"Not a drinking man, are you?"

He took a deep breath. "I take wine with dinner, but I don't drink alcohol alone in my suite."

"Is that right? I like to have a tot when I watch the TV. So how about it, how did you get this job?"

"I had been working for a number of years in an environment that demanded a rigorous pace, and I was simply looking for something more relaxing."

"You're Greek aren't you? I'm good with accents."

"I'm Belgian," he said. "I grew up speaking German."

"Is that right? I learned some German in the war. Check this out. 'Lassen sie die hunde!'" I yelled.

Faber drew back. "Goodness. Yes, you have a good memory."

"Yeah, but do you know what it means?"

"It means 'release the dogs.'"

"That's right. I learned that from the camp guards. You know what? There came a point when there were no more dogs. They ate the last of them that winter. But that's neither here nor there. Let me ask you a question; how did you meet Bashir and the good king?"

Faber grinned. "Forgive me," he said. "I'm just now understanding. You are questioning me as part of your investigation, yes?"

"It's nothing," I told him. "I'm just trying to establish some baselines, see how everyone plugs in to the bigger picture."

"Of course." He took a seat across from me. "I am happy to help."

"Great. How did you get hooked up with Bashir and the royal family?"

He folded his hands. "I spent some time in Saudi Arabia working at a private hospital. It was a lucrative position. My wife wasn't thrilled with it, however. She wanted to go back to Antwerp to be closer to our children. We meant to stay only a few years but each time the contract came up for renewal, the money went up as well, and neither of us could turn it down. In the end we stayed nine years."

"So you met Bashir in Saudi Arabia?"

Faber looked up at the ceiling. "No, I think it was in Abu Dhabi. There was a conference, and I had a meeting with the director of Al-Kurbai's health ministry. He invited me to visit and we became friends. I believe he was Bashir's cousin or uncle. I don't recall."

"So you visited Al-Kurbai and you met the king?"

"That's right." He pointed to a photograph resting next to the television. "In fact, there, that's my wife Pia on the beach at Al-Kurbai. She was an early bird. She liked the sunrises."

I picked up the photo to have a closer look. "Wow. She's hot, Faber. She lost a ton of weight too since that Santorini trip. Did she have the gastric bypass thing, or was it just good eating?"

He stared at me. "She died, Mr. Grave. She lost a great deal of weight in the process of dying. Afterwards, I took some time off."

Nuts. "I'm sorry," I told him. "I lost my wife back in 1944, and I think about her every day."

He looked down at the floor for a moment. "I would very much like to see Copenhagen before we leave. Do you have more questions for me?"

"No, no." I pulled myself out of the deep sofa. "Thank you for your time. And for the pills, they really are first rate. I took two last night with a little Amaretto and I swear I could hear colors. Isn't that the strangest thing?"

"You're not really supposed to take the pills with ..."

"I mean, if I looked at something green, it sounded like a tuba. And purple, purple sounded like the pan-pipes that those poncho-wearing guys play in every public park in the universe."

"I'm sure it's just a harmless side effect, Mr. Grave. But come by the infirmary tomorrow, and we'll conduct a follow-up evaluation, as I suggested."

"Oh, I wasn't complaining," I told him. "I was watching this show on the TV last night about how ships are built, and they had this one shot of the ocean and I swear I could hear jazz in the background. Old style jazz, like Betty Davis jazz."

He stared at me. "You mean Miles Davis."

"Yeah, but it was eerie. I mean it sounded just like it."

"Yes," he said. "Were you watching the program about how Indulgence was built?"

I snapped my fingers. "That's the one."

"It has a Miles Davis soundtrack."

"Is that right?"

"OK, then," he said, opening the door and gesturing toward the hall. "It's been wonderful chatting. I'm glad you're feeling better."

"All thanks to you," I told him.

Chapter Twenty

If you've never been to Copenhagen, then it's about time you visited. The capital and largest city in Denmark, with a population of nearly two million, Copenhagen is an urban fairytale, if my shipboard newsletter was any authority.

"Wonderful, wonderful Copenhagen," I said to the cabdriver just after we negotiated the price to Tivoli. "I heard that in a song somewhere."

He drove, but he wasn't a talkative man.

I had the foresight to snag a few sandwiches from the lunch buffet before leaving the ship, and I ate one as I leafed through my onboard newsletter. 'Founded in the eleventh century ...' I scanned the article until I found the section on Tivoli. 'Tivoli Gardens is one of the oldest amusement parks in the world,' I read. 'A fairytale garden in the heart of Copenhagen, it is at once elegant and picturesque. Children and adults alike will delight.'

That didn't sound right. "Is there more than one Tivoli Garden?" I asked the driver.

He looked up at the rear view mirror.

"It says here that Tivoli is an amusement park."

"Ya. That is correct. It is very famous. Do you enjoy a roller coaster?"

"Do I what? Do I look like the kind of man who enjoys

a roller coaster? I thought it was supposed to be a restaurant."

"There are restaurants in the park," he said. "But you are already eating."

"Mind your business. Why would a prince go to an amusement park?"

"I ... I don't know. What prince?"

"Bashir. He's supposed to be at Tivoli at noon."

"I don't know who Bashir is," he said. "But Tivoli is quite a popular meeting place."

I pondered this as we made our way through the city. I made a mental note to return one day to spend some time in Copenhagen, but that mental note was quickly misplaced.

The driver dropped me at the front gate. Tivoli Gardens was indeed an amusement park. I walked up to one of the entry gates. "Do you speak English?" I shouted at the girl behind the window.

She drew back. "Yes. Please do not yell at me."

"I can't hear you," I yelled.

She opened a little window and stuck her head out. "You don't need to yell."

"Do you speak English?"

"I am speaking it right now," she said.

"That's quick work. Listen, I need to meet someone inside. I'm not going on any of the roller coasters. Can I just go in?"

"Of course. It's ninety-five krone for adults."

"Good Christ," I said. "95 krone. I don't have that kind of money. You'd have to be a millionaire to get in here."

"It's actually only about $16 American."

"Is that right?"

"Or about 12 euros, if you prefer euros."

"Who doesn't? Can I use a credit card?"

"Of course."

I handed my card over but she frowned. "This isn't a credit card," she said. "Touch of Thai. It looks like this is a place to get a massage. It says your tenth massage is free."

"Sorry. Give it back." I handed over my credit card.

"I'm afraid we don't take Diners Club."

"You don't make it easy to pay." I exchanged that card for another.

"I've never heard of this one," she said. "I've seen MasterCard, but not MasterCharge. Actually, this expired in 1978."

I took it back and spent a few moments digging through my wallet. "How about Visa? Did you ever hear of that?"

She smiled. "Would you be interested in a season pass? It costs only 260 krone."

"I would not. Hey, I'm supposed to be meeting a friend here. He's coming for a concert at noon. Where would I find a concert at noon?"

She turned and produced a map. "Tivoli Concert Hall." She drew a circle with a crayon. "Head straight back. If you come to the pirate ship, you've gone too far."

I went in and joined the crowd wandering through the park. It really was quite a lovely place, lots of restaurants, and the map was easy to follow. It didn't take me long to find the Concert Hall. I saw Bashir standing just outside talking on his cell phone. I walked up and tapped his shoulder.

He jumped. "Mr. Grave."

"Call me Henry."

"Who are you talking to, Bashir?"

"Excuse me?"

I took the phone from his hand. "How's it hanging, Yaffir?" I yelled into the mouthpiece. "Are you coming to Tivoli? They have a roller coaster."

The line went dead. "Bastard," I told Bashir.

He stared at me, his mouth slightly open.

"That was your brother, wasn't it?"

"How dare ..."

"Save it," I snapped at him. "You and me are going to

have a little talk, just the two of us, away from the ship, away from your dad, and away from your guards and whoever else you have stuffed away onboard."

"Mr. Grave," he began, "you have no right to follow me. I was at an official state affair. I am currently the guest of the crown prince at an orchestra concert in which his sister is playing. I have known them both for quite some ..."

"And instead of listening to the music, you stand out here talking on your phone."

"I have important state business to attend to, business that is none of yours."

I clapped him on the back. "Indulge me. Get it, indulge?"

He stared at me.

"Like Indulgence, it's the name of the ship."

"I'm aware of that."

"Come on. Walk with me. I'll buy you a schnitzel. I have some questions."

"I have to go back inside. I'm expected."

"Five minutes of your time," I told him, as a dwarf in a costume chased two boys past us.

"Five minutes," he agreed, and we walked.

"That was your brother Yaffir you were speaking to."

"Yes. That's right."

"And he's the one you trust."

He ground his teeth for close to half a minute. "Let's say that of my brothers, he is the one I trust the most. I know he doesn't like me, I can tell you that much. But I've made some good investments on his behalf, so he has recently begun to respect me."

"And yesterday when we were on the bridge, when I got the call, he was the one you were speaking to."

"I don't recall." He shook his head. "I can't possibly be expected ..."

"You most certainly can possibly be expected," I told him. "Lester checked your phone. That was the number you dialed about ten minutes before I got to the bridge. We have footage of you placing the call."

"And what of it? It was very likely Yaffir I was speaking with. I consult with him several times each day about state business. Why is this significant?"

I spotted a guy selling bratwurst from a little cart, and I bought two.

"I'm not hungry," Bashir said.

"I wasn't offering." I led him over to a bench by the artificial lake. "I used to think this was a German thing," I said, holding up my snack. "See how the bun is about half the size of the sausage? That's the way they sell them in Germany. But now I'm starting to think it's more of a pan-European thing."

"Again, can you tell me why this is significant?"

I sighed. "I guess ultimately it means that you can eat more wurst, and instead of purchasing just one, you'd be tempted to spring for two without having to worry about filling up on bread."

Bashir watched me as I ate. "The phone call," he said. "Can we go back to that?"

I nodded. I told him about my conversation with Lester Fung, about how nobody knew I was heading for the bridge, so nobody who was not on the bridge could have known I was there, except Yaffir. So he's the only one who could have told the fake Randy Binder where I was.

"It doesn't make any sense," Bashir said. "Yaffir is a major investor in Indulgence. I went way over budget. The banks would not give me any more money, and neither would my father, but Yaffir came in at the last minute with a hundred million. He's invested. He cannot want me to fail. It doesn't make any sense."

"Then we're going to plug some leaks for now," I said. "Yaffir doesn't need to know anything more about me or the investigation. Can we agree on that?"

Bashir nodded reluctantly.

"So as far as I'm concerned, at this point, Yaffir is my prime suspect. Either that or someone has our bridge wired up?"

"Wired up? What do you mean?"

"Bugged. Listening devices."

"That would not be possible," he said. "Security scans the ship regularly looking for anything like that."

"And security works for exactly who? Because as far as I can tell, you are not exactly running the show here. Golan doesn't answer to you."

"He does. He absolutely does."

"I'm not convinced," I told him. "How about …"

"Look," he said, pointing toward the lake. "Please, it is important that we don't talk in front of them. I don't trust them."

I watched as three clowns came up the path. "I don't think you have to worry about them," I said. "They do a little juggling, maybe ride their tricycles."

"Not them," he said pointing. "Them."

Just behind the clowns came a giant. He was wearing dark glasses and holding a parasol over a nearly translucent woman dressed in white. She was wearing dark glasses too.

"You don't trust Cinderella?"

"It's not Cinderella."

"Whatever. Tinkerbell, Snow White, my point is that you can't just go through life being paranoid."

We weren't the only ones staring at this woman. Just about everyone else in the park was too. She was gorgeous. She stopped right in front of me.

"Does your phone have a camera in it?" I asked Bashir. "I want a picture of me with the Little Mermaid here."

She smiled at me. "I thought you'd be staying onboard, Mr. Grave."

"What, now?"

The giant took off his sunglasses. He looked familiar.

The woman took off her sunglasses too. It was Amaranth. "Do you recognize me now?"

"I do, Your Highness." I tried to get down on one knee but the leg was stiff, so I sat back down.

"You don't call her 'Your Highness,'" Bashir said. "Not her."

"Nobody is speaking to you," Amaranth told him. She turned to me. "Mr. Grave, Abelard and I were just about to have our luncheon at Vinotek. Their wines are lovely. Will you join us?"

"I would be delighted to," I said. "I'll catch up with you. Bashir is teaching me a little about politics, the hand behind the throne, that kind of thing."

She smiled. "Then you'll probably need a tutor. Bashir has a lot to learn about politics."

Bashir smiled back. "I might know more than you think," he said. "But that's understandable. One doesn't expect a whore to understand how power is wielded."

Amaranth smiled thinly. "Listen to me, you cretin," she said. "Call me a whore one more time and I'll show you exactly how power is wielded."

"Whore," Bashir spat. It was too loud for such a nice place, such a nice day.

She turned to Abelard. "Would you please respond to that?" she said gently.

The giant moved quickly. In a single motion he let the parasol fall to the ground and grabbed Bashir's neck, lifting him off his feet.

Bashir screamed as Abelard slapped him hard, then slapped him again with the back of his hand. He loosened his grip and let him fall to the ground.

"I'll have you shot," Bashir spat as he jumped away. He bumped into an ice cream cart and nearly knocked it over. The ice cream vendor stared as Bashir ran away.

"I'm told they have the lovely 2001 Domaine Schoffit

Pinot Gris," Amaranth said. "It's rare, but we called ahead to confirm. We're having it with oysters."

"What, now?"

"At Vinotek. Do you drink wine?"

"Now and again."

"Then let's keep walking. I don't like to attract attention."

"Is that right?" I said. "You know, normally when a translucent beauty queen has her giant slap a prince around, people watch."

She held out her hand, and took me to lunch.

Chapter Twenty-One

It was almost four o'clock by the time I made it back on board. Between the three of us, we managed to polish off three bottles of wine, which works out to about a bottle apiece except for the fact that Abelard wasn't drinking. By the time I passed through the metal detector, I was half in the tank and completely in love.

The metal detector beeped and security pulled me aside. I had forgotten that I'm not supposed to walk through the metal detector.

"It's just my gun," I assured the guard as I opened my jacket to show him. "I have the paperwork for it somewhere in my cabin."

He scanned my keycard. "No need, sir. We have your information in the system. If we could ask, next time you board, please step around the detector."

"The thing is," I told him, "I'm supposed to be undercover. If I step around, people will think I'm special."

"That may be so." He read something on his monitor. "But you will attract more attention by setting off the alarm. Also, there's a package here for you."

I had to wait while he rummaged around, then handed me an envelope.

"Who is it from?"

"I don't know, sir. You'll have to open it."

I did just that. It was from Beth Obradors in my office. "It's from Beth Obradors in my office," I told him. "She desires me sexually."

"I'm happy for you, sir."

I left him, and got into the elevator. My head was starting to bother me again so I popped a couple of the pain pills that the good doctor had thoughtfully delivered. I knew I had work to do, but I couldn't help wondering how I might convince Amaranth to come back with me to my condo at Rolling Pines.

I could tempt her with the bounty to be won at Bingo, or delight her with tales of frolic and mayhem at Square Dance Sundays, which are held twice a month. Or I could excite her with a yarn or two about what really goes on at Knitting for Novices, but I might blush. In the process of developing a plan, I missed my elevator stop and found myself back in Ancient Egypt.

Most of the shops were closed but not Sphinx Drinks, the martini bar. I wandered in but it was nothing but gloom; a room full of seniors huddled over cocktail tables furiously scribbling.

A guy wearing a cowboy hat approached me and I ordered a gimlet.

"I'm not a bartender," he said. "We still have another hour until it opens."

"What, now?"

"The bar is closed. We're just using the space for the hieroglyphs class."

"Is that right?"

"You don't recognize me?"

I looked closer. "Have we met?"

"Max Carder."

"Not ringing a bell," I told him.

"I'm the onboard Egyptologist. You were harassing me yesterday about my employment history."

I remembered. "I never forget a face," I told him. "Hey you want to have a gimlet with me? I have a crime to solve, and I need someone to bounce some ideas off. You kind of have a shady past, so you could help."

"I got it," yelled a woman in the back. "The last line."

Carder went over and read her page. "That's it," he said. "We have a winner."

Several of the others groaned and put down their pens.

"Would you read the entire text for us, Bernice?" Carder clapped his hands. "And let's remember, this is a translation of an actual Egyptian public service announcement written in about 1500 B.C."

"Make not thyself helpless in the beershop," Bernice began,
"Or thy words will slip from thy mouth.
Falling down, thy limbs will be broken.
Thy companions in the swilling of beer will say,
'outside with this drunkard.'"

"Fantastic." Carder led a round of applause. "So what can we know about the Egyptian state 3500 years ago?"

"That they had to deal with a bunch of drunks," a man called out.

"That's about right," Carder said. "It means that the government was concerned enough about alcoholism that it was taking measures to respond."

"So sad," I said, shaking my head. "Why can't we just drink responsibly?"

"That's a good question," Carder agreed.

"No, I mean now. I don't see any bartenders on duty. I'm getting parched."

He stared at me. "I just told you, the martini bar is closed."

"I see."

"So, before we move on to the next text," Carder said to the group, "I have a $25 gift card for Bernice."

More applause.

"This next text," he began, handing out sheets of paper, "dates to 2400 B.C."

"You're good," I whispered in his ear as the group worked furiously to translate their hieroglyphs. "You must have been a hell of a salesman back at Best Buy. I bet you could sell me a VCR, even though they don't make them anymore."

"You're an asshole," he whispered back.

"And you're shady. There's something I don't like about you. It's not your attitude, which I like, nor your clothing, which is rugged but impeccable. I don't know what it is, but I'm going to give you some thought."

"You do that," he said. "I have work to do."

I left him to his hieroglyphs, and I walked back out into Ancient Egypt. Most everything was closed, but the Karnak Art Gallery wasn't. I headed over to see if Isla Rossdale was around. Maybe she had figured out who was behind the crime. Also, my head was starting to feel strange, so I wanted to sit down somewhere.

"She's not in at the moment," a little Oriental girl told me. "Is there something I can help you with?"

"No, no," I told her. "I'm just trying to catch up with Isla. Can you tell her that Murray stopped by?"

"I will. Did you want to tell me your stateroom number?"

"Nice try, but don't get fresh with me. You can't be running off with every virile gent who comes along."

"Excuse me?"

"Nothing. Just tell her Murray stopped by."

Back outside I walked past the pyramids and the statues of Ramses. The whole place was nearly empty. "Where is everyone?" I asked the lone fellow sitting at YouBrew.

He shrugged. "Probably still ashore. Did you get in to

Copenhagen?"

"I did," I told him. "I ate oysters at an amusement park."

"That sounds like fun. I went on the morning tour, but the wife went on the all-day tour, so I'm alone for the next hour. Want to join me for a beer?"

I thought it through. "I'm hard-pressed to see the downside." I introduced myself.

"Art Mellman." He shook my hand. "I'm from Long Island, retired pediatrician."

"Long Island? We're practically neighbors. I live in Pennsylvania."

Mellman shook his head. "I couldn't take the winters. What do you like in a beer, Henry? I'm having some of the house ale. It's nutty."

"Bring me something not nutty," I called out to the bartender. I've never been a fan of nutty beer. "So what brings you to Egypt?"

"Egypt, right," he said. "Hard to believe we're actually on a ship in Denmark."

I watched as the bartender drew me a nice golden lager. "Close your eyes and you'd swear you'd be back in the time of the pharaohs stuffing a teddy bear next to an art gallery."

"Crazy world. We almost didn't make it, you know. We booked the cruise a year ago but then I had the hip replacement surgery."

"Me too," I told him. "I was sore for weeks but that was a few years back. For me it's the ankle that gives me the most trouble." I rolled down my sock to show him.

"That's swelling pretty badly. Plus, you have a nice black eye."

"Yeah." I nodded. "I fell in the tub."

"For me it's the knee." He rolled up his pants.

"You call that swelling?" I took off my jacket and rolled up my sleeve. "Check out that elbow."

"Mercy." He shook his head. "How long has it been like

that?"

I stared at my elbow. "I'm not sure. I think since yesterday. Hey, you want another beer?"

He stared at my empty glass. "That was fast. Sure, I'll have another."

I ordered.

"I fell last April," he told me. "I was coming out of the rec center back at Rolling Maples, and I went down hard."

I drank my beer. I was feeling a little woozy all of a sudden. I was staring at Art Mellman's giant knee, and I swear it was getting bigger by the second. "Did you say Rolling Maples?"

"Do you know it?"

"Know it? I live in Rolling Pines, out in Bethlehem. Same layout."

"I can't believe it." He shook his head. "I almost went up there a couple of months ago when they did the trip, but I had the trots."

"Don't get me started. I've never been out by you, but last year I went on the bus to Rolling Elms, over in Jersey. That's quite a place."

"Yes, I hear they have a general store there. We don't have that."

"Nor do we," I told him. "So anyways, we get there and they have this welcome lunch, and I sit down next to this pretty thing named Mabel Ormond. I never forget a name. Mabel and I both had the Italian beef noodle casserole, and we get to talking about how we both love tango dancing. So she tells me that she has some records back in her unit, and would I like to go listen to them?"

Art Mellman grinned. "I can see where this is going."

I drank more of my beer. "Wait, I think her name was Gaby. Gaby Grossman. She was from Queens originally. So we head back to her unit. She had one of the corner units, the ones with the nook, just like I have."

"Go on."

"Right. So we get to her unit, and she asks if I'd like a little vermouth. Who wouldn't? So she pours me a tumbler and says she is going to change. And she tells me to make myself comfortable."

"Ah, ha. You dog." Art Mellman shook his head. "Hey, you're really going to town on that beer."

I nodded. "It helps me concentrate." I waved at the three garden gnomes that walked into the bar. "Those guys are so cute."

He turned to look and then he frowned.

"So I'm drinking my vermouth thinking about how I might make myself more comfortable, and I decided to take my socks off."

"That sounds about right," Mellman said. "She did say to make yourself comfortable."

"Exactly. So I was checking out her photos, and in the back of my mind, I'm working on taking my socks off. And here's where I got into trouble."

"I'm not following."

"Bear with me," I said. "Normally, when I'm home, I take the pants off first and then the socks. So somewhere in the back of my mind, my brain was doing the normal pants off, then socks."

"You took your pants off?"

"I did, yes. And I think part of the issue was that she had the same unit as mine, with the nook, so part of my brain is thinking that I'm at home."

"But you weren't."

"No, I wasn't. So Glenda comes back into the room, and she looks gorgeous. Baby blue track suit, lipstick perfect, and I'm sipping my vermouth on her couch working off the socks, and she starts yelling."

"Gaby, you mean. She was yelling because you were sitting there in your underwear."

"I know." I shook my head. "Try to understand women, and you're just setting yourself up for failure. She asked me to leave."

"That's quite a story."

"I know it. And that's the last time I visited Rolling Palms."

"Rolling Elms," Mellman said, and at that moment his head became extremely bulbous. The garden gnomes didn't seem to notice, nor did the seven British infantry soldiers who walked in. But I sure noticed.

"Now let me ask you a question about your head."

He stared at me. "About my head?"

"Yes," I told him. "It's really huge, quite a bit larger than any head I've ever seen. And it wasn't that way when I walked in. Does is hurt?"

He didn't say anything for a moment. The gnomes all shrugged in unison. "Are you feeling OK?" Mellman asked.

I thought about that for a moment. I had to admit to myself that I wasn't keeping things together. In the real world, the chance of three garden gnomes shrugging in unison is pretty slim. There were a couple of other things wrong with the picture, but they were eluding me.

"Do you want me to call the doctor?" he asked.

"In time," I said. "Can I ask about the British soldiers standing behind you?"

He turned to look, then shook his head.

"Just as I suspected."

"I think you're hallucinating," he told me. "You might want to ease up on the sauce."

"I think I need to get back to my cabin."

I'm not going to tell you what getting back to my cabin was like. I can barely remember the journey myself, but the parts I do remember are so lovely that I briefly considered taking up scrapbooking.

The elevators moved not just up and down but also sideways, swaying back and forth with the tides. I didn't know where my cabin was, and I got quite lost. At one point I was stuffing little ham sandwiches in my pocket. Ask me where I got them, and I couldn't tell you.

I got scared at one point, I won't lie. I had just turned a corner by the library where a number of ladies were playing cards. I was minding my own business when one of the ladies backed up suddenly and then came toward me on her chair. It was her.

I screamed as I ran but she kept coming. I was running as fast as I could, but every time I looked back, she was closer. This was no ordinary Rascal she was riding; I swear she was moving at six, maybe seven miles an hour. She had giant teeth and there was fire in her eyes. I jumped into an open elevator and made my escape.

I remember stopping to catch my breath by the prettiest waterfall I had ever seen, and then I talked with some panda bears for quite awhile. I even offered them some of my sandwiches, but they declined. They were so polite. Then a bushman helped me to the elevator, which was full of beautiful women and old men. And when the door opened next, we were all of us standing in front of the biggest restaurant I had ever seen.

I didn't care where I was or what shape I was in, it was time to eat. I'd work on the hallucination issue later, but turning one's back on food has just always just seemed wrong to me.

Chapter Twenty-Two

"Your table, sir?" A waiter approached me as soon as I got to the door.

"What, now?"

"If you tell me your table number, I'll escort you." His nametag read 'Sonny' and he was from Poland.

"No, no," I told him. "I can find it myself, Sonny. Which table am I at?"

He frowned. "Have you forgotten your table number?"

"No. I just haven't been here yet. I've slept through most of the meals; this is my first time. I ate at the sushi place but it gave me gas."

"Certainly, sir." He walked me over to the maitre d' and we learned that I was at table 238. But when we got there, it was empty.

"Don't put me here," I begged. "I want to sit with other people."

"It's a little early still," he assured me. "They'll be coming. My good friend is the head waiter at this table, so I know that it always fills up. You're going to have a wonderful dinner."

"Well that's grand. Hey, can you bring me a gimlet?"

"Yes, sir. I'll send the sommelier right over."

He did, but it wasn't until gimlet number two was halfway down the hatch that my tablemates arrived. I'll be honest with you, the hallucinations were still with me, but by this time I was able to exert some measure of control. Stare at a nonexistent garden gnome long enough and he'll fade away. The same thing goes for imaginary infantry soldiers. There were quite a few walruses in the dining room, and they weren't responding as easily. You really had to stare them down, and I was doing just that, clearing the room one walrus at a time.

I remembered the envelope that the security guard handed me when I re-boarded. I hadn't yet had a chance to look at it so I opened it. It was the information I had requested from Beth at the home office.

"I don't see anything here that troubles me," she had scribbled in the margin, "but trust your instincts."

I read the report. It was a financial profile.

> Richard "Tuck" Savoy, age 69, lives at 2309 Glendale Terrace, Bethesda, MD, with his wife, Margaret "Meg" Savoy, age 60. Mr. Savoy is a retired land developer who enjoyed great financial success in the 1980s. He has broad assets in the stock market and a joint portfolio that contains in excess of eleven million dollars in liquid assets.
>
> Credit score of 820. No arrests, no warrants, no addictions, no known affairs. Donates regularly to a number of philanthropic causes. Plays tennis and bridge recreationally. Collects high-value impressionist art.
>
> None of our current risk algorithms suggest any issues or concerns with Mr. Savoy.

Nuts. I generally like to assume the husband is involved somehow, but there are a great many husbands walking the earth, and they can't all be guilty. Or can they? I was thinking about this when a little boy sat down next to me.

"Remember me?" he asked. "Hey, did you eat all the breadsticks?"

"No, no," I said. "The basket was empty when I got here."

"You have crumbs all over you."

"Casper," a woman called to him, "please do not harass Mr. Grave. I'm sure we can get more breadsticks."

"I remember you," I told Meg Savoy. "We talked at the sushi restaurant. What are the odds that we'd be at the same table?"

"I think they set it up so that we'd be at the same table," she said as her husband took the seat next to her. I blanked on his name.

"Nice to see you again, Henry," he said.

"Likewise, Grover. So did you folks get out to Copenhagen today?"

"We saw the Little Mermaid," Casper told me. "And we went to Tivoli Gardens. It's an amusement park."

"I went there too," I said. "I saw Snow White."

He frowned. "I don't think they have a Snow White."

"They did today. Let me ask you something." I turned to Meg Savoy. "If it turns out that this question is strange, it's because I'm having some hallucinations, but there is a man who just sat at the table behind you. Don't look now, but he appears to be interested in you. And I saw that same man at the sushi restaurant. Is this something I should be concerned about?"

"I'm sorry to hear about the hallucinations," she said, "but the man sitting behind me is Lieutenant Bill Gandy. He's a member of my staff. He's my bodyguard."

Her husband chuckled. "He better not be interested in you."

"You know what he means, Tuck."

Tuck; that was his name. "Is that right?" I said. "It's good for me to know about things like this, you know, because if I get to shooting, I'm going be shooting anyone I can shoot, and it would be nice to know who not to shoot."

Casper stared at me. "You have a gun?"

"I do," I said. "I'm like a police officer."

"Do you have a badge?"

"Somewhere. I'll show you some time. We'll fire up the grill, down some brews, make a day of it."

Our waiter arrived just in time. "I am Wagus," he told me. "I will be your head waiter. I have not yet met you, but I am sure you will be pleased with your meal."

"I'm sure I'll be delighted," I told him. I looked through the menu. It was glorious. I love food the way few men do. If a screaming comet made quick work of most of our earth, and the only things left were me, the items on the menu, and the staff to prepare them, I think I could get by, make sense of things, and start fresh.

He started with Meg Savoy, and then moved on to her husband.

"What are you having?" I asked Casper.

"T-Bone steak," he said. "I love T-Bone steak. I've had it every night so far. I get it with fries and onion rings."

"Tempting," I told him.

"And the young gentleman will be having the usual?" Wagus asked, "but with extra carrots."

Casper frowned, then nodded as his grandmother wagged her finger.

"And for you, sir?"

"French onion soup, captain's salad, and a shrimp cocktail please, and can you bring me a couple of those melon balls wrapped in that ham? I love that; it tastes so wrong but also so right."

"Very good, sir."

"And for an entrée, I'm going to have to go with the

seal. I was mightily tempted by the beef tenderloin with warm cabbage salad, but in the end, I had to go with seal." I slapped the menu shut.

"I don't think they have seal," Casper said.

Wagus didn't miss a beat. "Veal scaloppini for the gentleman," he said. "It is my personal favorite."

"I can't wait," I told him, "and bring me another gimlet."

"I'll send the sommelier right over."

"You drink a lot," Casper told me.

"Mind your business. OK, listen folks, I'm trying to do a job here, so it's important that I understand the players involved. So do you have just one bodyguard on board or is there more than one?"

"More than one," Meg Savoy said.

"Who, and how many?"

"I won't tell you," she said. "There are several members of my staff on board, undercover. As I think I mentioned to you, I am interested in cooperating with you. But at some point, my own safety is my own concern, and I've taken what I think are appropriate precautions."

"I don't like it at all," I told her.

Tuck Savoy pointed to the window. "See anything strange?"

I saw a number of cars parked in front of warehouses, and an assortment of vendors selling ice cream and souvenirs.

"We should have left by now," he said. "We were scheduled to depart at 6:00."

"Maybe someone didn't make it back to the ship on time," Casper suggested.

I shook my head. "No, unless it's one of the tour busses returning late, they won't wait. It's probably traffic in a shipping channel."

"I hope it won't be too long," Tuck said, "We have big plans for Oslo."

"It's the land of the Vikings," Casper said as the sommelier returned with my gimlet.

I turned to Meg Savoy. "Let me ask you something, how did you come to pick out this particular cruise?"

"She didn't," Tuck said. "It was my idea. It was meant to be a birthday present for Casper. Also, we have an anniversary coming up."

"Congratulations," I said. "But isn't this kind of an odd choice for a gift?"

"Odd?"

"Yes, odd. With all the publicity surrounding this ship, were you worried about bringing a high-ranking military officer into a potential security risk?"

"No," he said. "As we've just discussed, we've taken precautions."

"So you picked this ship?"

"I did," he said. "I thought it would be fun, and so far it hasn't been a disappointment."

"Why this ship in particular?"

"I think he just answered you," Meg Savoy said.

He put his hand on her arm. "This ship had everything I was looking for. I play bridge. It has bridge. It has a lot of activities for children. Casper is crazy about two things; rainforests and dinosaurs, and I couldn't find any dinosaur-themed cruise ships."

"They're hard to find," I admitted.

"Also, there's a painting I've been interested in for some time, and it turned up here for sale."

"Is that right?"

"Yes." His eyes lit up with pleasure. "It's a little known Mary Cassatt called Lydia and The Cradle. Lydia was Mary Cassatt's sister. Mary painted her often, but this is one of the first Lydia portraits. She's standing beside a cradle. It's not evident in the image, but there is presumably a baby in the cradle. And Lydia would have been about fifteen years old, which might alter our understanding of the Cassatt family."

"And you want to buy it?"

"I do. I currently have the highest bid."

"Well, if it's that important a painting, then maybe I want to buy it myself."

"You could do that," he said, "if you had a spare million and a half dollars."

"I might have to move around some funds, make a few calls, but in the end, no. So I'll wish you luck."

He nodded.

"We're going to Holography World after dinner," Casper told me, breaking my concentration. Something was gnawing at me but it wasn't Holography World.

"Have you been there?"

"I don't think so," I said. "What is it?"

"It's a room that has all its walls and ceiling and floors made of TV screens. You go in and you tell them what kind of world you want, and then you stand in the middle of a 3D movie."

"That sounds scary."

"No, it's not scary. Yesterday I did World of the Amazon, and it was just like being in a real rainforest, even bigger than the one they have on board. And then I did it again, but this time, I did the cartoon world. They have 3D glasses, so all of the characters were right in the room. You should try it."

Wagus tapped me on the shoulder. "Mr. Grave?"

"That's me."

"A message for you, sir." He handed me a folded sheet of paper. I learned that a security guard was waiting just outside the dining room to accompany me to the security office.

"I have to go," I told the Savoys. And I was very sad. Leaving dinner before dinner has arrived is a terrible thing, something nobody should have to do.

"But you didn't even eat your food," Casper said.

"I'm not happy about it either," I told him. "Don't touch my seal. See if you can get them to box it up for later."

Chapter Twenty-Three

I found Golan and Lester Fung and a couple of other guys in the security office staring at a large TV. It was showing passengers returning to the ship.

"We have a problem," Golan told me.

"I can see that. Network television has really gone downhill with these reality programs. Nobody should be forced to watch a show about people boarding a ship. There's no drama."

"Oh, there's drama." He ignored my joke. "We have a stowaway."

"What, now?"

"One of our crewmembers was pick-pocketed today while he was onshore. His name is Manuel Bacod. He had been drinking with friends at one of the party barges: ShangriLaBamba. And someone lifted his wallet. He had his crew ID in his wallet."

"I see."

Golan picked up a card from his desk. "And here it is."

"Well I'll be goddamned. So how did he get back on board?"

"He returned to the ship and reported th~ He met with the deck officer and they iss~ card."

I nodded. "And this is the replacement or the original card?"

"This is the original," Golan said. "This is the card that was stolen. Someone used it to get on board."

I stared at the picture of a smiling Filipino man. "Wouldn't the person who used it have to look like Mr. Bacod?"

Golan shrugged. "If it was busy enough, he might have gotten lucky."

Lester called over. "There's nothing here. He pointed to the screen showing passengers boarding the ship. "No single men. We've looked at the same timeline three times now."

"He's got to be there," Golan said.

"But he's not," Lester insisted. "We have the ID scanned at 5:30 exactly, and these are the people coming on board at 5:30. I don't see anyone out of the ordinary."

"What about him?" I pointed to the screen. "Guy in the hat with all the shopping bags. He's standing right next to the woman in the track suit."

"Which one?" Golan asked. "All of them are wearing track suits."

"Over there." I got right up to the screen. "Can you freeze it here?"

Lester paused the image.

"Look, this guy in the hat with the shopping bags is right in behind the woman in the pink track suit. If you weren't paying attention, you'd think he and pink track suit lady were together. But I don't think they are. If you play it again, I'll bet you don't see his face. He's being careful."

We watched the guy in the hat board, and then we watched it again.

"No shots of his face," Golan said. "He knows where the cameras are."

"Tell me about Manuel Bacod," I said. "Let me see his profile."

"He's fine," Golan said as he brought up Bacod's employee records. "This is his first tour on Indulgence, obviously, but he's done two tours with Carnival and four with Crystal. He's a model employee."

I read the file. Manuel Bacod, age forty-five, of Manila, Philippines, held the rank of Motorman, which meant he worked in the engine room under the direction of the engineering staff. He had a monthly salary of $1,400. "I want to talk with him," I said.

"Lester already did," Golan told me.

I shook my head. "There's no way he got pick-pocketed and then an hour later someone is using his ID to board the ship."

"IDs get lost all the time," Golan said. He took a call on his cell phone. "We're leaving port now."

"Not yet." I dug through my wallet to try to find the right card. "Here's what we're going to do. Call the bridge and tell them to wait half an hour. I need a little time with Mr. Bacod. You come with me. We're going to visit him right now. Where's Lester?"

"Right behind you."

"Lester, I need your ID holder." I snapped it off his shirt and replaced his ID with mine.

"It's in French," he said. "That's a picture of you. Is that a fake ID?"

"No, very real, I'm afraid."

Golan leaned in close. "You are Chief Inspector Gaston Lamarque of the Paris Metropolitan Police Department?"

"Oui."

"Is that a real mustache?"

"No, they glued it on for the picture. It's nice though, isn't it?"

"So you're impersonating law enforcement?"

"Oui," I repeated. "Lester, I need you to do something for me. Get on the internet and find a picture of a dead hooker at a crime scene. I need you to print it out and bring it down to me ASAP."

Lester stared at me. "You want what?"

"You heard me. Work with me here. I have to break him before the ship sails. Now hurry."

Golan was back on the phone talking to the bridge. He put his hand over the mouthpiece. "They're going to fine us a thousand euros every fifteen minutes if we don't get underway. There's another ship waiting to dock."

"It will be a thousand euros well spent," I told him. "Let's go." I asked Lester to find one more thing for me, and then I followed Golan out the door.

"You want to tell me what your plan is?" Golan led me to the elevator. He keyed in the code that would take us down to the crew deck. "Or maybe you just want to start shooting."

I ignored the last part. "The plan is that I'm a policeman and I came onboard to talk with Mr. Bacod. The ship is being detained so that I can arrest him."

"For what?"

"I'm thinking it through as we speak."

The elevator opened onto a different world. I'm always shocked whenever I descend to the crew areas of a ship, shocked by the different crummier world that exists just under foot. I've seen some bad crew decks and some awful crew decks, but this one was actually not bad. The ceilings were noticeably lower than the ceilings upstairs, and I instantly felt cramped. The carpet was of lower quality, and there were sheets of paper taped up all over the walls, announcing parties and items for sale or barter.

I followed Golan through a door, and through a plastic vapor and smoke barrier, and entered the world of the crew. I nearly choked on the smoke. Run your air filters day and night, as every cruise ship must, but you're never going to get rid of the pooled exhalation of two thousand smokers emptying their lungs at once. Someday soon, someone will figure out how to channel that energy, harness those exhalations and use them to propel a sail or turbine that will open up a new world of green energy cruising. But not today. I followed Golan up to a large desk, much like the Guest Services desk upstairs, only the folks down here weren't dressed so nicely, and the fixtures were much cheaper. Indulgence was only three days old and already the counter was marred by cigarette burns.

Golan spoke with a man behind the desk who was reading a newspaper. "It's important, Yuri," he said. "I hope it's nothing, but it's important that we speak with him right away."

Yuri looked irritated. Golan was clearly violating some norm of onboard jurisdiction. Still, the man typed away and pulled up a record on his monitor. "Bacod is not on duty until midnight," he said in a thick Russian accent. "I will find where he is."

We waited only a minute or so while he made some calls, but during that time, two naked men walked by, followed by a naked girl carrying a poodle and a gallon bottle of vodka. The girl was very polite. She smiled and inquired about our evening.

"My evening just got better," I told her, but she just kept walking. I turned to Golan.

"Don't even ask," he said. "What happens down here can only be understood by the people who live down here."

"But that actually happened, right, the naked people? It wasn't something I imagined."

"It happened."

"I have found him," Yuri told us triumphantly. "He is in TV lounge number four. He has just purchased four twelve-packs of beer, perhaps to share, perhaps not. Very popular movie is beginning soon. Movie is of zombies."

"Which way?"

"Downstairs, halfway to bow on starboard side."

"And you keep this conversation to yourself, Yuri."

"I will do that," he said, picking up his newspaper. "I

have no friends."

I followed Golan down a narrow flight of stairs to the crew cabin deck. Here the hallways were narrower. Bare light bulbs lit the way, as did light pouring out from the occasional open door. I heard a lot of music but most of it was pretty low. I knew from experience that at any given time, most of the crew and staff were either on duty or sleeping. The pace of this life is extremely fast, and the shifts are long. Once off duty, most people want nothing more than to unwind a little bit, drink something, get something to eat, and then sleep as long as possible.

Golan entered a cramped lounge on the starboard side, and I followed him in. Four couches had been squeezed into a space that could comfortably hold two at best, and each of the couches was occupied by three or four Oriental men smoking Marlboro Light cigarettes and drinking beer or jug wine, or both, as they stared at a flat-screen TV. On the screen, a pack of zombies chased a woman down into a valley. She wasn't going to make it.

"Gentlemen," Golan said, "I need your attention for a moment. Can someone pause the movie?"

Someone did.

"Manuel, this man needs to speak with you. Can we have everybody else clear the room, please? This won't take long."

Nobody grumbled. They left, leaving Manuel Bacod alone on the sofa with his beer, his cigarette, and his wine jug. "What did I do?"

"Manuel," Golan began, "this is Chief Inspector Lamarque, and he's here to ask you some questions."

"Is this about the ID?"

"It is," Golan said. "And you're the reason the ship is still in port. We can't sail until we finish this."

"It is not about the ID," I said, angrily, in my best French accent. "It is about what you did this afternoon."

Bacod looked nervous. He frowned at Golan and then at me. "I was at the party barge with the other engine room guys. What are you talking about?"

"I think you know what I'm talking about," I told him. "I'm talking about your little hobby. How many prostitutes have you killed by now, Bacod? Ten? Twenty?"

"What?" he shouted. "Prostitutes? What are you talking about? I have a wife."

"I have been following your career for a long time," I said. "Wherever you go, you leave a trail of dead prostitutes, like poor young Emilie Santine who you killed this afternoon."

"What?" he shouted again.

"She was just seventeen years old," I shouted back, trying to sound as French as I could. "She liked the beach and playing ball with her nephews, and you took that all away from her. It was you."

"Hold on," he said nervously. "Just hold on. I didn't kill anybody. I was at the party barge all afternoon with the guys, as I said. I've never killed anybody. You have the wrong man."

"Non," I said. "Monsieur Golan, please handcuff this man so that I might bring him ashore with me."

Golan stared at me. Lester Fung walked into the room and handed me a folder.

"Your handiwork," I sneered as I let the photograph spill out onto the coffee table.

Bacod frowned. "This is the prostitute?"

"Oui." I leaned in closer to get a better look. It was a photograph of a middle-aged woman in a bathrobe smoking a cigarette. It wasn't what I had in mind. I turned to Lester. He shrugged and pointed to his watch. I looked at the photo again. The words 'Harlan, Texas, case #443-383,' were scribbled in the margin.

"This is seventeen year old, Emilie something?" Bacod asked. "This is the prostitute you're saying I killed?"

"Oui."

"But she isn't even dead."

"Believe me," I said, staring into his eyes, "she is quite dead. You thought you were clever posing her body with that cigarette, didn't you?"

"She doesn't really look seventeen," he said, "and we're not in Texas."

"The years have not been kind to her," I admitted. "Harlan is her nickname, and Texas is a code we use for prostitution."

"This is ridiculous," Bacod spat. "I haven't done anything. This is some kind of joke."

"I'm afraid it is not," I said quietly. "You will go to jail for a long time, Mr. Bacod. You were careless this time. Your crew ID card was found in Emilie's hand. You are a murderer."

"What?" He started looking a little more afraid.

"Your crew ID card."

"Look," he said, "my ID was stolen. I already reported it."

"Then you can explain that to the jury," I told him. "Do not worry, sir. Danish juries are some of the fairest in the world. It is unlikely they will impose a death sentence. I think you can safely hope for life behind bars." I turned to Golan who took out his handcuffs.

"OK, look," Bacod said. "Look, some guy offered me five hundred euros for the ID. He said he collected maritime paraphernalia. OK, I lied when I said I got robbed. I'm sorry, but it was a lot of money."

I reached into Lester's folder and took out a second photo. "Is this the man you sold the ID to?"

"Yeah," he said. "That's him! That's the guy. Mother fucker."

The fake Randy Binder was back on board.

Chapter Twenty-Four

We got a late start to Norway that night, but far more worrisome was the fact that I missed dinner entirely. I mean, I could have jumped in for dessert, but that gets in the way of my dinnertime groove. It nearly broke my heart. I was telling Lester Fung all about it as we stared at the monitors looking for any signs of our stow-away.

"This isn't going to work, is it?" Lester said as Golan switched from one camera angle to the next.

I shook my head. "Presumably he used his time ashore to change his appearance. And on the topic of appearances, Lester, can we discuss the photograph? I asked you for a picture of a dead hooker."

"You didn't give me enough time."

"Maybe, but that wasn't even close. You did a really bad job."

"Well, I'm sorry. Next time I'll be sure to have some hooker photos on hand."

"A sensible thing. Look, we're not going to find him this way. We don't know what he looks like, and with more than seven thousand people on board, it's unlikely we're going to spot him in a crowd."

"What do you suggest?" Golan asked.

"I don't know. I can't think without food." My head was

killing me too. After questioning Bacod, I stopped back at my room to clean up and take some pain pills. The bottle said to take one or two with meals. But I didn't have any meal. I took three pills. I don't like being told what to do.

"You could order room service," Lester suggested.

"By god, you're right," I said, and I did just that.

Golan was in a foul mood. I mentioned that to him and it didn't appear to cheer him up any.

"Our situation is deteriorating," he noted. "There's no reason for him to come back on board unless he plans to make good on his threat to start killing passengers."

"That's what I'm afraid of too," I said. I had seriously underestimated this man, and in doing so, I put more than seven thousand lives at risk.

"He might come after you," Golan suggested.

"Let's hope so. At least we'll know where he is. But I'll tell you something, next time I see the bastard, I'm going to take him down."

"Not before I talk with him," Golan said. "I'm going to have a good long talk with him, the kind of talk we used to have back when I was in the armed forces and we had a troublesome captive."

"He wants the passengers off the ship," I said, thinking aloud. "That's what he told me on the phone. He told me he was going to start killing people if I didn't make that happen. So what is he after? What does he want?"

"He wants Indulgence to fail," Golan said. "He wants Bashir to be ruined, humiliated."

"I'm going to hunt him," I said.

"Yeah, that sounds like a great idea," Golan said. "You can barely keep your eyes focused. I have half a mind to take you into protective custody."

"Then work with the other half of your mind. I have work to do. I'm going to need a few things from you. Do you have a pen?"

He found one on the desk.

"No, you write," I said. "My hand is shaking from hunger. I also don't feel so good."

"Do you want me to get you something?"

"No, I'll be fine when the food gets here. OK, here's what I need you to do," I said. And I told him.

At some point I must have eaten. I know that because when I woke up the next morning, I had pudding and some rice on my jacket. But I have no coherent memories of that night, or of anything, really, until I shot my cabin.

Lester Fung worked with me later to piece it all together, but here is what I remember about my evening. First, I flew through the air. Then, I went for a long walk on a beach in Puerto Rico. It was a little breezy but I had my coat on. Next, I climbed through a medieval castle somewhere in Bavaria. There were gargoyles everywhere. After the castle, I swam with dolphins and an octopus, and danced the tango. Then I flew in a Russian fighter jet over some mountains.

At some point, I wandered through the streets of seventeenth-century Jamaica where I drank a seventeenth-century piña colada with a voodoo priest. Then I had some drinks in the hot tub, and later smoked something from a water pipe with a sheik. A crazed old woman mounted on some kind of demon chased me for an hour. And later, I brewed a batch of beer, stuffed stuffing into a whale doll, and then hunted frogs with a blowgun just like the hunter-gatherers taught me to.

Apparently, I returned to my cabin just as the sun was coming up, and as soon as I opened the door, I saw him there, King Tut. I had no intention of letting him get the drop on me again, so I shot him. I shot him three times. But he did not fall down; he kind of expanded, getting bigger and bigger until he popped. And then there was nothing left of him.

Then the security guys came for me. They were angry because I had shot my cabin. They brought me to the infirmary, and Dr. Faber examined me.

"You've been through quite a lot," he told me.

"I don't really understand what's happening," I said. "I feel like my brain isn't working."

"You seem to be experiencing some episodic dementia," he told me. "You're hallucinating quite a bit, and I don't like it."

"I don't like it either," I said. "I have a terrible headache too."

"Yes, I'm going to give you something a little stronger for the pain."

"That sounds like a wonderful idea."

He gave me a shot. "Have you been taking your pills?"

I assured him that I had. I even held up the little bottle.

"That's good," he said. "We don't want to make too many changes to your brain chemistry at this time. So please continue to take the pills as I prescribed. Once we make port in Dover, you're going to be admitted to a real hospital for some tests."

"No, no," I said. "I'll be just fine. I don't think a hospital is necessary."

"Mr. Golan is making the arrangements as we speak," he said. "Now, I'm due to go make my rounds, if you will excuse me."

I shook my head. This was not going well at all. Not only was I not doing my job, but I was also going crazy.

I slept. I don't know for how long. When I woke up, Lester was sitting next to my bed. "I have the information you requested." He opened the file. "You did some wandering around last night. You won third place in a dance contest."

"That's fantastic!"

"Yes, you danced the tango with one of our bartenders, Lyudmila. Then you grabbed the microphone and asked her to marry you in front of everyone?"

"And?"

He shook his head.

Nuts.

"At 8:45, you showed up on a surveillance camera walking into the Oxygen Bar on the Riviera Deck. Shortly after that, you were photographed as you rode the zipline from the bow to the stern."

I stared at the photograph he handed me. Sure enough, there I was flying through the air. I had kind of a demented grin on my face. "Looks like I had fun."

"Then, a little after 9:00 p.m., you made it to Holography World and ordered the Three New Worlds program."

"That explains this." I pointed to the sticker on my jacket that said 'I visited three new worlds.'

"Right," he said. "The computer randomly kicked out a Caribbean beach holiday, a Romanian castle exploration, and an undersea experience."

"So I did swim with dolphins."

"In a manner of speaking, yes. And it does feel very real when you're standing in a room where every wall is a movie screen."

"Three new worlds," I repeated.

"Well, technically four," Lester told me. "There was nobody else waiting at that moment, so they gave you a fourth world. You spent three minutes flying in a Soviet MiG fighter."

"So I'm not crazy, see. It only sounds crazy when you take it out of context. What else? I think there was a fifth world, the Jamaica one."

Lester shook his head. "No, we lost you for a little bit, but around 10:30, you were in the Caribbean Quarter drinking at the pirate bar with Montrose Royal. We checked with him, and he confirms that you were with him. He said the two of you spoke for some time about the case you were working on."

"Is that right?"

"It's what he says. I asked him myself if it seemed like

you were acting funny, and he kind of grinned. He said that you were eccentric."

"Go on."

Lester returned to his notes. "By midnight, you're back upstairs in the hot tub, unless the surveillance cameras lie, and they don't. Then we lost you again, but Bashir confirms that you came to his suite and met with his father for about an hour."

"Not ringing any bells," I said.

"Shortly before two in the morning, when the last of the shops and restaurants were closing down in Ancient Egypt, you purchased a fractional ownership contract for a 1/13 annual, which means you bought a cabin onboard Indulgence for four weeks each year."

"Good Christ." I sat up too quickly. The blood rushed out of my head all at once. "I really am going crazy. How much did I spend on that?"

He shook his head. "$264,000."

"Well I'll be goddamned. I don't have that kind of money. That's a lot of money for a timeshare."

"It is."

"Can you get me out of it? Tell them I'm demented. Hell, tell them I'm senile."

"There's a remorse clause. You can still go back and cancel the purchase."

"Thank god," I said. "I am really losing it. I can see that now. OK, so that's quite a night. That leads us up to the point where I shot my cabin."

"Not quite yet." He turned back to his file. "Just after 3:30 in the morning, you were picked up by security in Rainworld where you were using a blowgun to shoot tree frogs."

"Why would I do a thing like that? That makes no sense. Are you sure it's not just another of the holograph worlds?"

"No, we're sure. The elder Jipito confirms that you paid

him $200 in cash to teach you how to hunt with a blowgun."

I shook my head.

"And then at 5:00 this morning, after you fired three shots into your stateroom wall, waking up half the passengers on board, you were brought here to the infirmary."

"I just cannot wrap my mind around this," I said. "Why would I buy a timeshare?"

"I don't know."

"OK, I need to get myself organized, Lester." I stared down at the little pill bottle I was still holding in my hand. I sure felt like taking one, but at that moment, I felt like I needed all the lucidity I could get my hands on. I've taken enough pills over the long decades of my life to fill several aircraft carriers. And I know they can sometimes interfere with the clarity of thought.

"Are you alright?" Lester asked.

"Yeah, one more thing, there's an older lady on board who has been chasing me around the ship every chance she gets. Did you catch any of that on any of your surveillance cameras?"

Lester shook his head.

"I think she's possessed." I slipped the pills into my pocket. "OK. How much time do we have before we get to Oslo?"

He stared at me.

"Come on, I don't want to waste all morning in here."

"We left Oslo hours ago," he said. "It's after eleven at night. You slept all day."

I stared at him, trying to make sense of it all. "That's a whole day of my life that I'm never going to get back. That's three whole meals plus assorted snacks."

"I'm sure you can make up for it."

"I'm sure too. What about our friendly neighborhood stowaway? Any sign of him?"

"Not a peep. Golan thinks he's cooling his heels somewhere below decks. We've done sweeps, but so far we haven't found him."

"He'll be disguised," I reminded him. "Also, probably limping."

Lester's phone rang. "It's Golan."

I couldn't hear the conversation, but I could see that something was wrong. Lester turned a few shades paler. "I'm on my way," he said into the phone.

"What happened?"

"Bashir's father, King Abdullah. He's dead."

Chapter Twenty-Five

Lester took off running. I could not keep up, so I was a few minutes late getting to Bashir's suite. Two security guards manned the open door. They waved me in.

Bashir sat alone on the couch staring at the wall. I took a seat across from him. "Tell me what happened."

"I don't know what happened. The doctor is examining him now. I had lunch with my father this afternoon. He was in good spirits. He complained about shortness of breath, but he said it was of no great concern."

"Any history of heart trouble?"

"No."

"Let me ask you something. Do you think this could have been foul play? Was someone else with him?"

Bashir shook his head. "No. He spent much of the day by himself. He was tired after your late night visit. He's not usually up that late."

"Me neither. So no other visitors after I left?"

"Only the people he normally interacts with, his cook and his valet, as well as Abelard and the girl. I'm certain none of them wish him any ill."

"Well, I'm sorry for your loss, Bashir. He was a good man, and I know you loved him."

He ground his teeth, getting ready to say what he had

to say. "I've just spoken with my brother Hamid," he said. "He'll be airborne within the hour, en route to Dover. He's very angry."

I put my hand on his shoulder. I could feel him trembling. "You're afraid," I said. "Don't be. This isn't your fault."

"Tell that to Hamid. He's king now. He can do with me whatever he wishes."

"Then we're going to have to sort this out before we get to Dover," I told him. "And I think we can do that. I've had a good long nap, and some memories are starting to come back."

I left him and walked through the hidden doorway behind the mirror. The beads had been pulled back, and my path was clear. Just inside the great room I found Abelard. He was weeping. I saw the king just beyond him, lying on his carpets on the floor in front of the giant TV. He looked peaceful, and very dead.

Golan and the doctor were speaking quietly, so I moved in closer. "He's really dead?" I asked.

Dr. Faber turned. "I think you're supposed to be back in your hospital bed. I'd be most upset to have two deaths in the same day. You're not well, Mr. Grave."

"I'm fit as a fiddle. Are you sure he's dead, not just in a coma or something?"

"Quite sure. He has no pulse and no heartbeat. I've given him a thorough examination, as I was just telling Mr. Golan."

"Can you determine cause of death?"

"Not without performing a post-mortem exam," he said, "which we're not equipped to do on board. I'm certain his heart gave out, but we'll learn for sure once we reach Dover. I would be interested in the opinions of a medical examiner, but there is, however, the issue of Islamic rules regarding burials. The new ruler, King Hamid, will be meeting us in Dover, and I suspect it will be his decision."

"Is there anything here that would lead you to suspect foul play?"

Faber shook his head. "He was an old man." He turned to look me straight in the eyes. "Old men die."

I left them to their conversation and went looking for Amaranth. I found her outside on the verandah. She was sitting on an ottoman, wrapped in a blanket and staring out at the ocean. She looked up when I put my hand on her shoulder.

"He was perfectly healthy yesterday," she said, "perfectly healthy. I need you to tell me what you talked about with him last night?"

"Last night?"

She turned. "Yes, last night when you asked me to leave the room so that you could discuss something privately with him. That was rude of you, and rude of him to agree to your request. We have no secrets between us. Or had, I should say."

"I didn't mean to be rude. I was working on some strategies to catch a killer."

"But you didn't catch him, did you? And now they've killed someone very important to me."

"You think he was killed?"

"Oh, yes, Mr. Grave. I do. I don't understand how, not yet. But I will. Now will you please tell me what you two discussed last night?"

"I'm working on remembering it," I told her. "I'm having difficulty remembering things. Sometimes it feels like I've been drugged, but as soon as I can piece it together, I promise I will tell you everything."

She looked down at her hands. She opened a small box and took out what looked like a button. "I have so little to remember him by," she said. "We promised we would love and protect one another, even into another life. And I'm going to honor that."

"I'm not sure what that means," I told her.

She stood and put her arms around me. "It means that

I'm in the process of getting really angry, and often when I get angry, I feel like hurting people. Have you ever felt that way?"

"I have."

"He was poisoned, you know."

"Why do you think that?"

"Because people don't just die. No. Someone poisoned him. Someone got to him last night. I'm going to find out who did it, and I'm going to kill him. Even if I have to tear this ship apart."

I left her and went back inside.

Abelard was still weeping but he grabbed my hand as I tried to leave the suite. "You promised all would be well," he said.

I pulled away and left. I didn't know what to do. I didn't know what was going on. I didn't even know if I was still sane. I went back to my cabin, ate nachos from room service, and slept through the night.

Chapter Twenty-Six

There's nothing quite as exciting as a full day at sea, unless it's a kidnapping. I woke up the following morning to a pounding in my head and a pounding on my door. I'm not sure which was worse. I took a pain pill and opened the door to find Golan standing there. Casper Savoy had gone missing.

"So does this mean I'm officially back on the job?"

"At this point, I can think of no compelling reason why not," Golan said. "Things are getting out of control."

"Have you issued a public alert?" I stepped out into the hall and shut the door behind me.

"No." He held up a hand to stop me. "Two things: first, it is extremely important that we keep this low profile; and second, you need to put on some pants."

I nodded. I didn't have my keycard with me, so Golan used his master key to open my cabin door.

"The boy might just be wandering around," I told him as I dressed.

"We've checked everywhere. Also, it's not his nature to take off in the middle of the night. General Savoy wants to call in the FBI."

"The FBI doesn't have any jurisdiction here," I reminded him.

"But the British might intervene. We'll soon be coming into British territorial waters and they might feel compelled to investigate an active kidnapping, especially if help is requested by a senior American military official."

"Assuming this is a kidnapping," I said as we made our way to Meg Savoy's cabin.

"Oh, it's a kidnapping," he said. "In any case, she's asking for you. I've already told her we're conducting a full search of the ship, and we have two of her bodyguards with us."

Meg Savoy was on the telephone so I went over to Tuck. He looked exhausted.

"When did you notice he was gone?" I asked.

"About an hour ago. We looked up in the loft but he wasn't there. I put him to bed myself last night."

"And you didn't leave the room after you put him to bed?"

"No. We watched TV for a while. That's all."

"He could have just wandered off."

Tears welled up in the man's eyes. "Mr. Golan told us that the door had been unlocked from the inside, just after 5:00 in the morning. Apparently, the computers record every time the doors open."

"So Casper opened the door himself?"

"He wakes up in the middle of the night. If someone knocked on the door, he might have answered." He wiped his eyes with a napkin.

Meg Savoy put the phone down. "David is a mess." She was considerably more composed than her husband was. "David is our son, Casper's father. I felt it appropriate to tell him."

"I'm going to find your grandson," I told her. "This is a closed environment. It's only a matter of time. We'll be in Dover tomorrow morning. If by some chance we have not found him by then, I suggest you contact the British authorities to do a full sweep of the ship."

"Mr. Grave, you told me several days ago that you thought the best way to get to me would be to kidnap my grandson. Do you think that is what is going on here?"

"Yes, I do," I told her.

"But it's still possible he might just be on his own."

"It is, but that would be an extraordinary coincidence." I told her about our stowaway and about the dead king, and about me shooting my cabin.

"Why would you shoot your cabin?" she asked.

"I was hallucinating. I need to know what he liked to do, where he liked to spend money. Did Casper use his own keycard to pay for things, or did you pay?"

"Both."

"OK, I'm going to get printouts of your transactions and see if I can recreate his movements. It's highly unlikely that a kidnapper came to the room and grabbed him in the hall against his will. So probably, Casper made a friend."

"Oh god."

"No, no. He's going to be OK. I told you before, I think whoever did this is going to try to use him to get to you. So they're definitely not going to hurt him."

"What if he went overboard?"

"Nobody goes overboard," I lied. "There are cameras everywhere, and motion sensors at the waterline. No, he's still onboard."

She nodded.

"I want you to stay here," I told her. "Eat room service. Don't leave the cabin. If anyone contacts you, they will likely impress upon you the importance of you acting alone. Threats will be made. You are to ignore those threats and contact me immediately. If you do not, this is not going to go well. Do you understand me?"

She nodded again.

"You said you had several bodyguards on board with you. How many?"

"Three," she said. "Two of them are helping with the search. Bill Gandy is just across the hall. He's been on the phone, but he'll be coming back shortly."

"You're sure you can trust him?"

"With my life," she said.

"And forgive the next question, but it has to be asked." I gestured toward her husband. "Are you sure you can trust him?"

"Absolutely."

I left feeling her fear. I knew that if it were my grandson who had been taken, I would feel some combination of fear and rage, and I would be quite willing to tear off chunks of the world in my effort to find him. But my grandson is forty years old, not as vulnerable as an eleven-year-old boy.

Back at the security office, Lester Fung printed out a report of everything the Savoys had purchased since the cruise had started.

"Lots of money on alcohol," Lester said. "It looks like he's a drinker."

"It's a crying shame," I said. "Wait, this can't be right. It says they've spent a total of $503,190. That's a lot of money. Did they buy a timeshare too?"

Lester leafed through the pages. "No. This is strange," he said. "Tuck Savoy put down a half a million dollars on a painting."

"Right. Yeah, he mentioned that. He's trying to buy some famous painting."

"For half a million dollars?"

"Crazy, I know. But it's his money."

"No." Lester shook his head. "I've been on lots of cruises. I've seen some good art and some crappy art, but not at that price. Nobody comes on a cruise ready to drop half a million dollars. That's too expensive."

I thought about what he was saying as I made my way to the Karnak Art Gallery. Normally the gallery would be closed at this hour of the day, but we were at sea, and on sea days, all the rules change. I found Isla Rossdale talking with a passenger who looked eager to become a customer.

"And of course Salvador Dali is one of the greats," she said. "This is an original lithograph, sure to increase in value."

The man nodded, still needing a little convincing.

"Let me tell you a secret." Isla leaned in. "This print didn't come with the main shipments from our gallery. It came, like some of the other pieces, from a private collection. But this one is undervalued. If you pick up this piece for $4,300, and like I said, I can make one phone call and probably get it down to $3,900; I'll bet you could flip this in New York for $6,500 minimum."

"Then why is it so cheap?"

"It's cheap because the seller doesn't have a good handle on its value. This piece was in a private collection in Houston. The seller probably got it appraised in Houston, and the appraiser did a poor job. Hell, I'd buy it myself and flip it in a week, but that would be a conflict of interest."

Two more exchanges, and he handed over his keycard. I stared at some of the artwork waiting for Isla to finish.

"Murray," she called out to me. "We're going to make a collector out of you yet. Do you like landscapes or portraits?"

"I was thinking more along the lines of Impressionism."

"So you do know something about art." She led me across the gallery to a tiny painting of a bridge in Venice. "This is a lesser-known piece but it's lovely. It's by an Italian artist named Giacomo Belotta."

"It's the size of a postcard."

"And priced to match," she said. "$1,695 is a good price, a really good price, but for you, I'll forgo my commission. You can walk out of here with this beauty for $1,350. What do you say? Shall I box it up?"

"Let me think on it," I told her. "Actually, I had a particular painting in mind. I've always been a huge fan of Mary

Cassatt."

She didn't say anything right away. "I'm sure. That brings us to a whole different price point when you start talking about paintings like that."

"But you have one on board, don't you?"

"From time to time, something comes along, when the gallery thinks they might be able to find a placement."

"I want to see it."

She laughed nervously. "I don't know exactly what we have on board at the moment. This is my first time on this ship, right, like everyone else. So I'm still trying to figure out exactly what's in stock."

"I want to see the Mary Cassatt painting," I told her directly.

"Is there a problem, Henry? I'm not sure how a painting fits into whatever it is you are investigating."

"There is a problem, Isla. I need you to answer my questions, or we can have a more formal meeting with the captain and the security staff."

"Fine," she said stiffly. "There are a number of high-end paintings currently on board. To celebrate our maiden voyage, we planned a special art auction. We alerted some of our high-value customers. I believe we do have a Mary Cassatt on board, along with several other originals. They would be stored in the ship's main vault behind Guest Services on Deck 5. Does that answer your question? I have work to do."

"I have work to do too," I told her. "I've been on a lot of cruises, but I've never seen a painting sell for half a million dollars."

Isla took a deep breath. "It doesn't cost half a million dollars, Henry. It's priced at a million, five. And for your information, we already have a nearly full-price bid, with a half a million dollar deposit on hand. So yes, paintings do apparently sell at this price point."

She was getting a little too defensive for my comfort.

"I'm not sure they do," I told her. "I think there's only one person on board who has expressed any interest at all in this painting. Am I right?"

"I wouldn't know."

"Well I do. He came on this cruise to chase this painting. So that begs the question, Isla. Where did the painting come from? Because you know what I think? I think someone stuck this painting out as bait."

"I have no idea what you mean." She waved as a younger couple entered the gallery. "I'll be right with you, Melanie," she called out. "I think you and Ed made a fine choice."

"I need you to focus right now," I told her. "It might be a good idea to close the gallery for a little while."

"Why are you being such a hard ass?" She elbowed me in the side. "Come on, Murray, you and I go way back."

"We do, Isla, and that's why we're going to be honest with each other. Let me start," I told her. "You're going to tell me where the painting came from. And don't feed me some line about the gallery sending you an expensive painting, because they didn't. My new best friend Lester just made a few phone calls. Nobody at your gallery has any record of a Mary Cassatt being on board. So tell me who, how, and how much, or I'm going to have you arrested in Dover as an accessory to kidnapping and murder."

She stared at the tiny painting of Venice and shook her head.

"That was me being honest with you, Isla. Now it's your turn."

"OK," she said. "Look, I didn't do anything wrong, but I might have stepped into something. From time to time I act as an independent consultant, offering appraisals and referrals to collectors, and to individuals interested in liquidating some of their works."

"Go on."

"About three months ago, I got an inquiry from a man

claiming he had a Cassatt for sale. I told him that that was way above my pay grade, but he was adamant and very specific. He wanted the painting on Indulgence's maiden voyage, and he'd pay me $50,000 to represent the piece. If it didn't sell, I still would get to keep the commission."

"What was the seller's name?"

She shook her head. "I don't know, and I didn't ask."

"British prisons are musty," I told her. "Dank in the winter."

"I don't know his name," she said. "Everything was done by e-mail, but the owner was somewhere in Saudi Arabia. I can show you the e-mails, but there's never a name, I swear."

"And you didn't think there was anything funny about this deal?"

She shrugged. "You know, it was odd, but it wasn't anything illegal. Maybe there would be a buyer on board, and as it turns out, there is."

"So you got the money?"

"Yes," she said. "Is that going to be a problem, Henry? I didn't mean to do anything wrong. And it was an easy $50,000."

"How did they pay you?"

"By wire transfer, to some little bank in south Florida. I transferred it to my regular account a day later."

"Do you remember the name of the bank?" I asked.

"Let's see, something like Chippingham or something like that."

I got out my little notebook and leafed through. "Was it Chipley Savings & Loan?"

"Yes," she said. "That was it."

Chapter Twenty-Seven

"It means that this is about Meg Savoy," I told Golan. We were sitting in the security office drinking coffee. My heart was beating fast, not from the coffee, but because I finally felt like I was getting somewhere.

"But we're still no closer to catching our murderer or finding the boy," he said.

"No, but we're figuring a few things out. I want Bashir out of this loop."

"You think he's involved?"

"No," I said, "but we're finally one step ahead of the bad guys and I don't want to tip them off. We know that whoever is paying the fake Randy Binder is also paying Isla Rossdale. They're using the same Florida bank to move their money. They used the painting to lure the Savoys on board so they could kidnap the boy. So that's what this whole thing is about. It's not some family squabble, and it's not a plan to bankrupt the ship or mess with Bashir. It's about Meg Savoy."

"That boy has been gone five hours," Golan said. "Every additional minute is bad news."

"So search the whole fucking ship, bow to stern."

"We already have."

"Then do it again. How hard can this be? You have a twenty-nine member security team, and you can't find either the boy or fake Binder."

"It's harder than you think. This is a big ship, with lots of places to hide."

"Fine," I said. "So think it through with me. Fake Binder is hiding in plain sight. He's changed his identity and he's cooling his heels in some cabin or closet. But the boy is being held against his will, so he's either gagged or they have him in a far-away place. If it was me, I'd have some help from some of the engine room guys."

"We've already done a sweep of everything below decks, engine room, crew quarters, every last locker. My teams are finishing that up just now, but if I was kidnapping the boy, I wouldn't put him there because that's the first place we'd look."

"Then where would you stash him?"

"In a lifeboat," he said, "in one of the big ones hanging from a davit, I'd stuff him under the floor in a utility locker."

"Then search the lifeboats, but have guys that don't usually work with the lifeboats do it. This is almost certainly an inside job of some sort."

"I'm already on it."

"Then I'm going to get back to work," I told him. "I'm going to trace Casper's movements. Remember, if his keycard gets used for anything, jump on it. Take down whoever is using the card. And one more thing, can you please ask Lester to cancel my timeshare?"

I left him, and I wandered the ship, trying to learn something about Casper. He was an energetic young man, I'll tell you that much. Up on the Riviera Deck, I had a look around the arcade. I almost played a game of pinball because it has been awhile since I last did that, but I had work to do. Casper wasn't there.

I showed his picture around to several game players. Some recognized him but nobody had seen him recently. The teen disco was closed but I was concerned about some locked doors behind a curtain. I got a staff member to open them for me, but no Casper.

Apparently, Indulgence has a planetarium that Casper spent time in, but he wasn't there now. Nor was he at the whirlpools or the waterslide or the zipline. I checked the printout of his onboard purchases and learned that he spent a lot of time at Holography World, so I headed there.

A sign on the door invited me to visit three new worlds. It sounded tempting. The door was closed but I could see a young woman inside. I knocked.

"We're just closing up," she said, opening the door a crack. "We have a staff meeting, but they've promised us it will be a short one. We'll open again in an hour. You must have really enjoyed your trip if you're back for more."

"What, now?"

"You were here just last night. You seemed to enjoy it very much."

"Yes," I said. I showed her my investigator's license and a picture of Casper. "Have you seen this boy?"

She took a close look. "He's been here quite a lot."

"Have you seen him today?"

She shook her head.

"When was the last time he was here?"

"I can check." She led me inside the small entry chamber and closed the door behind us. She brought up her log on the monitor. "He was here last night at about 9:30."

"Is that right? Does it say what program he was watching?"

She stared at me. "They're not programs; they're experiences. And yes, we do keep records so that people can refresh their experience. Each individual world has five frames, so the more often you come, the deeper you can immerse yourself into a particular world."

"And what is the boy fond of experiencing?"

"Let's see," she said, scrolling through a computer file.

"He generally likes the same files; Star Fighter, Caped Avenger, and Amazon Adventure."

"Is that right? Let me ask you another question. I have a distinct memory of the floor actually moving. That's not real, is it? I mean that's just a sensation you get from having the images all around you, right?"

"No," she said, "the floor actually moves. Hydraulics tilt and pan the floor panels during the action sequences. It feels like a lot of movement, but it's not."

"Do you mind if I go in and look around?"

She shrugged. "I have to go to my meeting, but I can leave you here if you promise to lock the door on your way out."

"That sounds good," I told her. She turned the lights on and I stepped into the chamber. It looked different all lit up, like a big white box with video panels everywhere. I walked around the perimeter looking for something that Casper might have left behind. It was a long shot, but it seemed like the only shot I had.

Casper's choice of programming was also interesting. A star fighter program suggested escapism, part of a young boy's fantasy, as did a caped superhero. But an Amazon adventure was something different, something tangible and real. And we had an actual rainforest on board. I was making a mental note to have a chat with my friendly neighborhood hunter-gatherers when the lights suddenly went off.

"Hello," I called out. "Hello, I'm still in here." It was really dark. I moved around looking for the door, but I didn't have a good sense of where that might be anymore. I heard the crackle of a sound system, and a moment later a recorded voice welcomed me to Holography World. "Be prepared for the adventure of a lifetime," it said.

And then another voice took over. "You should have let it go, old man." It sounded like the fake Randy Binder's voice, but I couldn't be sure, not with all the reverb and echo.

"Let's talk about this," I called out. "Let me take you in. I promise I'll be reasonable."

"Oh, I'll be reasonable too," he said. "It's just about time you exited the picture."

I called out again but the screens lit up. "Be prepared for five long minutes of sheer terror," came the recorded voice. "You've chosen Transylvanian Castle."

Even as I started getting scared, I was still impressed. The entire room transformed into a dark castle. The walls were lit with torches. I tried using the light to find the doorknob, but I don't think there was an actual doorknob. I didn't know how to get out.

The vampires came from my right; three lady vampires with red lips and long fangs. I instinctively moved to the left and nearly bumped into some kind of werewolf or devil dog. I don't know what exactly it was supposed to be, but it was a little off-putting. It howled, and the floor pulsed with the vibration. I turned around and started walking away but the vampire ladies were scurrying away down a hallway, evidently afraid of something.

I have to admit, I felt a little uneasy as the floor began to shake more violently, and a pair of rotting zombies ran at me, only to turn away at the last minute.

"Fuckers," I called out. "I'm safe as long as I stay in the middle of the room." But I knew that wasn't true. My real worry was standing outside the door in the control room.

I survived my five minute monster ordeal, and the room went dark again. "Get ready," called out the recorded voice, "for five harrowing minutes on Bug Planet."

"Oh, brother." The ground shook as some kind of demonic tarantula filled up one wall, mirrored by a leering caterpillar behind me. The tarantula was kind of scary, but the caterpillar just looked disgusting.

I was thinking that I wasn't getting my money's worth when the floor fell out from under me, and the ground was overrun by horned beetles.

The room went black for a moment, and my heart skipped a beat when the lights came back on. I knew exactly where and when I was – the Imperial Party Congress Ground in Nuremburg during a Nazi rally in about 1940.

German soldiers marched by the thousands, holding their swastika flags high. And each time they stepped in unison, the floor shuddered. It was quite unnerving. Hitler was arriving just to my left, standing in a Mercedes convertible and saluting the crowd.

Let me tell you something, I have not for a moment in my life been afraid of vampires or zombies or giant bugs, but I've been around long enough to sense the presence of evil. And even now, sixty-five years after the fact, Nazis still creep me out.

The scene shifted to a battlefield where a Panzer division trained its tanks on a French town and pounded away. I sat down on the floor and tried to calm myself, breathing deeply. I understood at that moment what I understood back in the prison camps in the winter of 1945, that this evil was unsustainable, that somehow the world would devour the lot of it, end it forever. And it did, we did, back in the day. And this time, I only had to make it through five minutes.

It quickly became clear to me that sitting on the floor was not a great idea. Every time the Luftwaffe planes dropped a bomb, the floor shook, and I could feel it in my spine. So I stood up and I heard something behind me. I spun around and came face to face with a sniper. He was hiding in a bell tower taking shots at Allied soldiers, and they were having a bear of a time dislodging him.

I don't know how they put this program together. Some of it had to be newsreels, but it had been stitched up with some manner of technical finery, because even though I wasn't actually walking, I was getting closer to the sniper. He was getting bigger and bigger, closer and closer until I could see his eyes. And he could see mine.

And I remembered a similar moment, way back when, when I turned a corner in a little Belgian town and came face to face with a Nazi scout who pointed a gun at me. He took me prisoner, then led me to five months of hell in a rancid prison camp. I promised myself a long time ago that I would never let anything like that happen again.

So when this sniper pointed his rifle at me, I did what I should have done many decades ago. I shot him. I fired two shots. Then the room went black.

Chapter Twenty-Eight

The gunshot woke me up; the acrid chuck of a Karabiner 98k, the most common infantry rifle used by the Germans in World War II. It was morning, almost dawn, and the sky was lighting up. My friend Buster Pullman was sharing a bunk and a blanket with me, and we were cuddled together, I'm not ashamed to say, to stay warm and alive as 1944 came to a close.

"Do you think that's Kaufman out there shooting?" Buster whispered.

I shook my head. "Kaufman isn't on duty until the afternoon. My money's on Remer. He says his day isn't complete until he kills a Russian prisoner."

"Bastard," Buster said. "Who told you that?"

"Walter Bremmerman."

"Bremmerman is a bastard too. Don't get too friendly with the guards, Henry. They'll turn on you in a heartbeat."

"I trust him," I said. "I have a good feeling about him. I trust him just as much as I trust you."

"There he is now." It was a whisper. The German accent made my blood run cold.

"Where am I?"

Dr. Faber tossed the smelling salt into the garbage pail.

"Please don't be alarmed, Mr. Grave, but you are once again in the ship's infirmary."

I was lying in a hospital bed hooked up to a monitor. "In the morgue?"

"Yes, in the morgue. Unfortunately we've had a number of slips and falls today, so we're short of space. And this will give us a little privacy."

"What happened to me?"

"You don't remember?"

I tried shaking my head but the pounding inside made that inadvisable.

"Please don't move around. I've given you a sedative, and it is likely that your equilibrium is a bit off."

"What happened?"

He chuckled. "You've shot up our ship yet again, Mr. Grave. But it won't happen again, I've been assured. Mr. Golan has confiscated your weapon."

"I'm having difficulty thinking clearly," I told him.

"So it would seem. I believe you are experiencing some degree of senility. It's quite common among the extremely aged."

"Hey, now!" I tried to sit up but could not. I wiggled around and found my arms were strapped to the bed, as were my legs.

"The restraints are for your own protection," Faber said. "You were thrashing around and I didn't want you to fall. In your condition, a fall could be disastrous."

"What, now?" I was getting a little worried. The doctor's head was expanding and contracting, and I saw a walrus behind him.

"Just calm down now," he told me.

"I think I am hallucinating,"

"Yes, the dementia is progressive. It's been worsening since you came on board. I'm sure you've noticed it yourself."

"Dementia?"

"Dementia," he repeated. "A profound loss of cognitive ability; it's very often the result of Alzheimer's disease."

"Alzheimer's," I shouted. "I don't have Alzheimer's disease."

"No," he said. "I really don't think you do." He rubbed my shoulder. "In your case, the dementia is more than likely an effect of the Ketamine. The drug can be quite unpredictable, especially at the doses you've been taking."

"Ketamine?"

"Yes. It's most commonly used in veterinary medicine as an anesthetic, but it's more than that, really. It's a dissociative drug that can, over time, unhinge your consciousness. Reality just trundles on without you," he said, walking his finger up my arm. "And reality is about to trundle on without you, Mr. Grave."

"What in the hell are you talking about?" I demanded. "Take these straps off me right now."

He smiled at me. "As I mentioned, they're for your own protection."

"I'll take my chances," I said. "I want them off now. And bring me that phone."

He picked up the phone. "What number, please?"

"I want Golan in here right now. Tell him it's urgent."

He pressed the button for the operator. "How odd, there seems to be something wrong with the phone." He held it up. It wasn't plugged in.

I felt my heart race, which isn't good at my age. "Can you tell me what's going on, please? Why am I on Ovaltine?"

"Ketamine."

"That's what I said. I don't take any drugs. Just the blood pressure medicine, and the pills that you ..." It was at that point that I understood everything. My consciousness re-hinged, and with that, a great deal of fear came online.

"It wasn't difficult to increase your daily dosage," Faber said. "You've been quite clumsy, and you have required frequent need of my services."

"Why?" I asked. "Why are you doing this?"

"You should have done your job," he told me. "We killed a man in Helsinki. Your job was to alert the authorities. But you did not, so we beat you in your cabin, stole your gun, and you still did nothing. This cruise should already be over."

My head was spinning, and I was having a hard time making sense of what he was telling me. "You did all this just to cancel the cruise?" I was trying to stay calm but it wasn't working.

"No, no." He shook his head. "We did this to get the passengers off, so we'd have some alone time with General Savoy, so that she could share, in studious detail, the Predator command and control algorithms. How long do you think she could hold out, knowing what we could do to that little boy?"

"So that's what this is about?"

He held up his hands. "That's what this is about."

I could feel my color fading.

Faber turned to look at the monitor he had me hooked up to. "Goodness, Mr. Grave. A man of your age has to keep the excitement to a minimum. Your heart is racing a mile a minute. I wonder how long you can keep that up before something ruptures."

"Why did you need the passengers off?" To be honest, at that point I didn't care. I was just trying to buy time. "What good would that have done? I wouldn't have signed your security clearance, but so what?"

Faber sighed. "Look, if you failed to certify the ship's security parameters, then we couldn't sail to the United States. Bashir's grand experiment would have failed, and his loans would be called in. The ship would be repossessed, would become the property of the monarchy. Are you following me?"

I nodded weakly.

"We would disembark the crew in Copenhagen. There's no reason you would know this, Mr. Grave, but Al-Kurbai does not have an embassy in Copenhagen. Yet, if we had our lovely ship parked there, a ship that could not sail, well the logical next move would be to declare it an embassy. This is where Bashir unwittingly becomes part of our little plot. He has great friends in the Danish monarchy. Can you understand why we would want to do this - turn the ship into an embassy?"

I closed my eyes. "Because an embassy is sovereign territory. Nobody could come on board, nobody could search the ship. Nobody could check to see if General Savoy was still on board."

"Very good."

"But I didn't alert the authorities," I said, still trying to buy time, "and the passengers stayed onboard, so your plan failed."

"No," he said. "It was always going to work one of two ways. If the first plan didn't work out, then we'd go with the backup plan. We'd wait until we left Dover and then grab the boy. Then we'd have six glorious days at sea to meet with the general and her grandson.

"In fact," he continued, "with our good king out of the way, we can afford to speed things up. We're behind schedule as it is. We'll take the boy this afternoon, probably just after lunch. Then we'll have all afternoon, all evening, and a long night at sea for young Casper to convince his grandmother that his life is worth saving."

"You're working for one of the brothers, aren't you? What's his name, Hamper or Bovid, something like that?"

"Very good, Mr. Grave. Now, as I mentioned, we're behind schedule, so I'm afraid it's time for you to leave us."

"I can't let you do this," I told him. "Let's you and I go have a drink and talk about this. You'll find I'm a reasonable man."

"You'll find I'm not."

"Golan won't let you get away with it. And Fester Lung is probably looking for me right now. He's supposed to keep an eye on me. I'm surprised he's not already here."

"Oh, but he is here." Faber moved across the room. "We'll put an end to Mr. Golan's life early this evening, but you're right about Mr. Fung. He is already here." He opened one of the large doors on the mortuary refrigerator and rolled out the tray. Lester Fung was lying on it. He was dead.

"And the beeping starts now," Faber said.

He was right; a moment later my heart monitor started beeping. I felt myself start to shake.

"You probably should have retired a long time ago," he said, pressing a button on the monitor to stop the beeping. "But you've had a long life, a good life, I hope. And all things come to an end."

I struggled against my restraints but I could barely move. Just moving my head caused massive pain. "Wait a minute; you said you were behind schedule. Behind schedule for what?" I was trying to stay calm but it wasn't working.

He picked up a syringe from a tray on the counter. "I can't see the harm in telling you. Look, we have two functioning Predator drones fueled and ready. The Syrian government will pay handsomely when those drones destroy an Arrow 2 anti-ballistic-missile defense battery just across their border. Then the missiles will really start to fly."

"You want to start a war?"

"No, Mr. Grave, I only want to make a great deal of money. What Hamid Salib wants out of this is his own business." He came at me with the syringe.

I tried to free my hands but they were strapped tightly.

"Heart rate is 146 and climbing," he told me, pointing at the heart monitor with the syringe. "148. I was going to shoot a little adrenaline into your heart, but you might render that unnecessary. 152."

I knew I wouldn't last much longer. I managed to kick out of one of my leg cuffs, but that didn't help me much. Then I saw the door open. Amaranth stepped into the room. She was wearing a blue tracksuit and a baseball cap, and she was pointing a gun, a big one with a silencer.

"Shoot him," I told her. "Shoot him."

Faber turned.

"Step away," she said. "Drop the syringe."

He stared at her. "Who are you?"

"Once again, step away, and drop the syringe."

"No." He shook his head. "I am administering to my patient. You have no right to be here." He took a step toward me, and Amaranth shot him in the back. The bullet spun him around so that he was facing her.

"Drop the syringe," she said. "That shot went through. It looks clean. You can make it."

Faber looked at the bloodstain on his shirt. I stared at the one on his back. I knew a little about guns, enough to know that she was lying to him. He wasn't going to make it. "It's still not as bad as what they'll do to me if I fail," he said.

"Who are they?" Amaranth asked, but he didn't answer. Instead, he turned back to me and took a step, and she shot him three more times, dropping him to the floor.

"160," she said, reading my heart monitor. "Calm down, Henry. Can you do that?"

I stared at her.

"Can you do that?"

I nodded. "Get me out of these straps?"

She did, but she also pulled something off the back of my lapel. She tried to hide it in her pocket but I caught her hand. "What's this?"

"Microphone."

"That's how you knew I was here."

She nodded. "I would have come sooner but I needed to hear what he had to say."

"So you were willing to put my life at risk."

"That's right. Look, we're going to say that you shot him, OK?" She wiped the gun and handed it to me. "He came at you with the syringe, and you pulled the gun and shot him. I was never here."

I grabbed her hand as she turned to go. The effects of the dissociative drugs were still vivid, and she looked like she had a halo. "Are you an angel?" I asked.

"No, I'm not." She pulled her hand free. "You need to get organized. I can't be here."

"You might not be an angel," I said, "but you're not really a porcupine either, are you?"

"No," she said as she left. "No, I'm not."

Chapter Twenty-Nine

"They were going to kill you too," I told Golan. "And I have to tell you, I was happy to hear that."

He looked ashen. He was staring at Lester's body. "You were happy to hear that they were going to kill me?"

"Yes. I had my doubts about you. I had some reason to believe you might be working with them."

He turned. "Do tell."

"About two years ago, Dr. Faber traveled to Paris to meet with Hamid Salib, the man we now know to be behind all this." I told him what Amaranth had shared with me. "You were at that meeting, Golan."

He shook his head. "I don't know what you're talking about. I've run into Hamid Salib many times over the years, but I've never had an actual meeting with him. And I never met Dr. Faber until two weeks ago."

I looked him in the eye. "Bullshit."

"Not bullshit. What are you talking about?"

"I have an eye witness than can place you at the train station in Val d'Europe France. That's where the meeting took place. Still not ringing any bells?"

"Val d'Europe?"

"All coming back to you, is it?"

He took out his wallet and handed me a photograph. "Yes, I was at Val d'Europe two years ago. Last year too. My children love it. Want to know why?"

I found my glasses and looked down at the image of Golan and two children holding hands with Minnie Mouse in front of a castle. "Because that's where Disneyland Paris is," I said.

He nodded. "That's right. Any more questions?"

"No," I said, "not at this time."

Art Mellman, my new friend from Long Island, stood over me, measuring my blood pressure with a cuff. He was a retired pediatrician, I remembered him telling me, and he'd been pressed into service as interim ship's doctor.

"It feels like my heart is racing," I told him.

"It is."

"Can't you give me a sedative or something?"

"No."

"Why not?"

"Because I don't know what is already in your system. Now stop yammering and relax."

"I need to get up. Stuff to do."

"Absolutely not."

I turned to Golan. "Stuff to do," I repeated.

Art Mellman shook his head. "I'm pretty sure that the ship's doctor has ultimate authority in these matters. As ship's doctor, I say you're staying right here in this bed."

Golan shrugged. He looked weary.

"Hey, that reminds me," I told him. "They don't have the boy."

"What?"

"Remember what I was telling you about Hamid and about the Predator drones, the stuff Faber was telling me?"

"Yes."

"Well, he said they were going to grab the boy today

after lunch."

"Today?"

"Yeah, that means they didn't kidnap him."

"You're sure you heard that right?"

"I'm positive."

"Because you've been saying some pretty strange things over the last half hour. Are you still seeing walruses?"

I looked around. "Not as many as before."

"Then where the hell is that boy?"

Art Mellman kept me in the hospital for most of the afternoon. At some point he gave me a shot of diazepam and I slept for hours, then I was under strict orders to remain in my cabin. It felt good to be home.

I was feeling quite a bit better after my nap, but out of the loop. I tried calling Golan but he was out and about somewhere. Half a dozen times I thought about calling Meg Savoy to tell her that Casper hadn't been kidnapped, but I wasn't sure that would cheer her up any. And until I knew exactly who was involved, it wasn't an especially good idea.

I turned on my TV and saw a video message from the captain informing the passengers that we would be arriving in Dover a few hours early, at 4:00 a.m. rather than at 7:00, and that we would be staying in port an extra day. They would make up the lost time at sea, en route to Miami.

That's because they've alerted the British authorities that something is amiss, I realized. Just then a photo of Casper Savoy filled the screen, Antonio Grassi asked anyone who knew of the boy's whereabouts to contact Guest Services.

I needed to get some food, so I got myself dressed, cleaned up, and got ready to go. Then I suddenly became very sad. I was thinking about my new friend Lester Fung. He didn't deserve what happened to him. And I had a suspicion that this whole mess wasn't over yet. I still had some unanswered questions. I poured myself a little rum and Coke and quickly reviewed my notes. I was still having difficulty putting it all together, but I was remembering more and more. I remembered most of my conversation with Montrose Royal, and I remembered hunting the tree frogs. And more importantly, I was starting to remember why.

I picked up the phone to call Bashir Salib when I heard noises coming from the cabin next door. It sounded like sobbing. I got up and put my ear against the wall but I didn't have my hearing aid in, so it didn't do much good. I sat back on the bed but the sobbing got louder, so I gave a few knocks on the connecting door. The sobbing stopped.

"Who is it?" called out a female voice.

"It's the butler."

"Say again."

"Security," I called back. "Open the door."

"What?"

"Security. Please open the door. Passengers are reporting a disturbance."

Then silence.

"I just opened the door," she said, a moment later. "There's nobody there."

"The other door," I said.

"That's not a door, that's a mirror. Wait a minute, you're that creepy old guy next door."

"Just open the mirror," I said, as I opened mine. "I'm a police investigator. Trust me or call security yourself."

She opened the door. I stared down at her. She was gorgeous.

"Wait a minute," I said. "You look familiar."

"I look familiar," she repeated in kind of a crabby tone. "I should look familiar. We've met half a dozen times. You hit on me each time."

"Did I? Hey, you want to come in and have a drink with me?"

She stared at me. "Are you serious?"

"I have a minibar."

She moved to close the door.

"Hold on a second," I called out. "Who is doing the crying?"

"None of your business, OK?"

"No."

"So you are a police investigator? Is that what you're telling me? Or were you a police investigator, like back in the thirties?"

"I am right now an investigator. I was a young man in the thirties, very handsome, and there's no reason to be rude."

"Do you have a badge?"

"No."

"A gun?"

"Yes." I checked my holster but it wasn't there. "I had two, but I don't know where either of them is right now."

"Bye, now," she said, closing the door.

"You need to open it and let me have a look around, or I'm calling security. There's a missing boy onboard, and I think he's in your room."

She cracked the door open. "Why would you think that?"

"Because I heard sobbing, and it sounded like a boy."

She sighed. "Did you ever stop to think that what you heard was not sobbing, but something more related to lovemaking?"

"No, it never crossed my mind. Look, I just need to have a look at the lucky gentleman, if you please. Then I'll be out of your hair."

She turned around. "Rusty, would you please oblige this man?"

I heard a voice inside, a male voice. "Huh?"

"It means can you do as he asks?" Anne continued. "Please just put a robe on and come over here."

He did. He wasn't Casper. He was a short little fellow.

He wasn't a child but he was about the size of a young boy, and he looked kind of silly wearing one of the adult-sized Undulgence robes. The mirrored sunglasses were also a bit anomalous.

"What's your name, son?" I asked.

"Rusty," he said.

"Is everything alright, Rusty?"

"Yes," he said, sniffling. "I miss my mother, that's all."

"Your mother?"

He nodded.

He looked kind of familiar. "Rusty, can you take off your sunglasses for me, please?"

He did. His hair had obviously been dyed blonde, but the bowl haircut wasn't working. "I know you, don't I?"

He nodded. "Yes, Mr. Henry."

"Where do I know you from? Are you from Pennsylvania?"

"No," he said. "I'm from Rainworld."

"Well I'll be goddamned." I turned to Anne.

"What?" she said. "He's an adult. We're in love."

Rusty nodded. "It's true. I'm in love with her. She's perfect."

"He's coming home with me," Anne said. "We're getting off the ship in Dover, and we're going to spend a few weeks in London before flying back to New York."

"What about your mother?" I asked, and he began to cry.

"He still has some mommy issues," Anne admitted. "We're working on them."

It was about at that moment that I realized what was going on. "But you can't get him off the ship, can you?"

She took a deep breath, but I was too angry to let her say anything. "He doesn't have a passport, does he? He needs one to get past immigration control. You had to find him a passport."

"It was supposed to be a win-win situation," she said.

I stepped through the door into her cabin. "Rusty, can you give me your passport, please?"

He stepped around the bed and opened a night table drawer.

"I told him to wait until tomorrow morning before switching places," Anne said. "It was only supposed to be for a couple of hours. But they got creative."

I couldn't even look at her.

"I'm sorry," Rusty said, as he handed me Casper Savoy's passport.

I held out my hand. "Come on, let's go get the boy."

I didn't call Golan until after, because I wanted to be sure. The three of us, Anne, Rusty, and I made our way down to Rainworld. It was just about a quarter to six when we got there, nearing dinner time, so we found it mostly empty. The tree frogs were chirping as we came up on the Jipito compound. Only a few passengers remained, sitting on benches as the father, Jispewe, demonstrated how to make an arrowhead from bottle glass.

We found Casper inside the hut weaving a basket with the Jipito mother while watching CNN.

"You have everyone worried," I told him. "Shame on you. CNN isn't even that interesting."

He burst into tears just as Rusty burst into the hut and ran to his mother, devouring her in a big hug as he cried. She cried too.

Casper's hair had been dyed and cut, so if you weren't looking directly at him, you might mistake him for a Jipito. He wore a loincloth and a necklace of beads and teeth. "I don't want to go back," he said. "I want to be a real hunter-gatherer, and this is where real hunter-gatherers live."

I glanced over at the room service tray next to the flat-screen TV. Casper and the Jipitos had dined well. Scraps of pizza, egg rolls, and waffles vied for space with a few remnant fries and three empty ice cream dishes. "It's a hard life," I said, "but I can see the appeal."

He wiped his tears as Rusty endured a swift rebuke from his mother. She hugged Casper too, but I led him away. I didn't know quite what to do with Anne. She stood in the doorway watching as Rusty sank deep into his mother's embrace, so I left her there.

I called Golan. Then I took Casper back to his grandmother.

Chapter Thirty

Indulgence docked in Dover, England just after four in the morning. An hour later, Crown Prince Hamid Salib came on board. Marched on board is actually more like it. And if you want to get technical, at this point, he was King Hamid Salib though he hadn't been crowned yet. Or maybe he had, I don't know, but he wasn't wearing a crown. He wore a black suit and dark glasses, as did his entourage. He had four guys with him, bodyguards by the looks of them. I was standing with Bashir next to the squid tank when he arrived.

Bashir gave him a little nod.

Hamid took off his sunglasses and slapped him across the mouth. "I trusted you with the life of our father," he spat. "Your failure is complete."

Bashir wouldn't meet his eyes after that.

I held out my hand. "Pleased to meet you, your princeliness," I said. "I'm Henry. Hey, do you wear a crown when you're at home?"

He stared at me for a moment and then he grinned. I didn't think he was going to bother shaking my hand, but he did. "I've heard about you," he said. "I was expecting you to be younger."

"And I was expecting you to be thinner. You're a bit chunky. You might want to take it easy on the falafel."

I don't think he was accustomed to people talking to him like that; his mouth hung open. "I can have you detained for quite some time," he said finally, "quite some time."

"No," I told him. "No, you can't. You have no authority here. We're in Great Britain. If you look out the window you can see Dover Castle. Real kings used to live there. But guys like you; you're just a regular nobody here."

He glared at me then turned to Bashir. "Take me to my father."

Bashir looked him in the eye. "You had Wakim killed, didn't you? He was like a brother to us, and you had him killed."

I didn't think Hamid could get any more angry-looking, but his face turned kind of a beige-red, and that was fine with me. Angry people make mistakes. He held up his hand and started to say something but then thought better of it. "Brother," he said, "you are in no position to question me. And after today, when this is sorted out, you will not again enjoy my presence."

"You killed Wakim, didn't you?" Bashir kept at him, just as I had coached him. I wasn't really expecting a confession, but I wanted Hamid off balance. And only Bashir was in a position to accomplish that.

Hamid took a step closer and I did too. Then Hamid's four goons came in, and we all stood there, like a football team in a huddle.

"Here's how this works," I told Hamid. "You're going to tell your little playmates to go upstairs and eat a taco by the pool and have a nice non-alcoholic Muslim-friendly beverage. You might think you're tough, but I'm tougher. Take a look around, and you might see one or more of the sixteen security officers we have watching you right now."

Hamid looked around but he said nothing.

"How about it, Hams?" I said. "Not getting any younger here. We have some things to talk about."

He nodded at his men and they fell back. They were good, well-trained. I could tell because they didn't take my advice and go get a taco. They stayed on point, alert, but they weren't obvious.

"Take me to my father, now," Hamid said calmly. "I wish to see his body."

Bashir was shaking, all the years of bullying and threats had added up, but he held it together. "Tell me why you had Wakim killed," he said, "or I'll have you removed from my ship."

Hamid glared at him. "Your ship? This is a monstrosity. It will be sold before the end of the month. Once you reach Miami, you will terminate all crew and staff employment contracts. This nonsense is over."

"I will not terminate any contracts," Bashir said. "This is my ship."

Hamid sneered. "I have already signed the paperwork that removes you from your position as Minister of Finance. When you return to Al-Kurbai, you'll find your bank accounts seized. Then you'll be tried for fraud and embezzlement."

"Yaffir won't let you get away with it," Bashir said, "or Nezim. My brothers will side with me in this matter."

Hamid slapped him hard across the mouth, and this time his own men pulled him back. "Your brothers despise you as much as I do," he yelled. "Your failure will be a blessing to us all. Yaffir is calling in his loan as we speak. You have until the end of the day to pay back his hundred million dollars. If you cannot, and you cannot, we will take possession of the ship. I'm certain we'll find a buyer in Miami. Enquiries have already been made."

"You might want to watch the blood pressure," I told Hamid. He was still bright red. "I might have to confine you to the ship's hospital. I can do that. I really can. See that man sitting over there on the couch?" I pointed to Art Mellman, who waved at me.

"That's our ship's doctor. Did you know the ship's doctor is the most powerful man on board? He can even relieve the captain of his duties if he sees fit. In any case, one nod from him and you're in for a day in sick-bay, and maybe even a high-colonic."

Hamid Salib stared at Art Mellman. "That man is not the ship's doctor. I know that for a fact."

"He is," I told him. "We had another one, Dr. Faber, but I killed him."

"You killed him?"

"I did, yes. I shot him. I'd shoot you too but Golan took my gun away after I shot the ship the second time." I showed him my empty holster. "In any case, I killed Dr. Faber in self-defense, but not before he told me about your plans to get the drone codes from General Savoy, so I think we have enough evidence to lock you up."

He took a deep breath. "Enough evidence to lock me up," he repeated. "In what world do you think you live? I am a sovereign monarch on board a state-owned vessel. Exactly who do you think is going to lock me up?"

He had a point. "Hey, check this out," I said, slamming the big button on the squid tank. Whatever electrical current or burst of bubbles that triggered, I don't know, but it worked. That squid lit up like a strobe light, and then went through all the colors of the rainbow. Hamid jumped back in shock, but it was really quite pretty.

"That was Henrietta," I told him. "She's a werewolf squid."

Bashir shook his head. "No, that was Woodrow. He's smaller and not as red. And they're vampire squid."

Hamid looked like he wanted to kill me, which he probably did. "I will see my father's body now," he told Bashir. "I will bring him back to Al-Kurbai for burial."

I nodded. And we walked, all of us, two princes, four Arab bodyguards, sixteen security guards, Art Mellman, and me, to the elevators. "Race you to the top," I called out to Hamid as our elevator door closed, but in fact he got there first.

Bashir swiped his keycard and we filed in through the door into his suite. Abelard stood in front of the mirror, blocking entry to the royal quarters. "You should be ashamed of yourself," he whispered to Hamid.

"Get out of my way, woman." Hamid shoved him aside.

Abelard glared but he moved aside and opened the door.

We walked single file past the mirrors and into the throne room where King Abdullah bin Salib sat on his carpet eating lunch with Amaranth and Montrose Royal. They were having duck with what looked like a white sauce. I was getting hungry. They had stuffing and mashed potatoes too, and I had to look away because my mouth was watering.

Hamid was stunned. Bashir fell to his knees and began to sob. Then he ran over to his father and knelt in front of him.

"How ... how is this possible?" Hamid demanded.

The king looked up at Hamid. "You are not happy to see me, my son?"

"But ... but I was told you were dead," he stammered. "The doctor confirmed it."

"Yes," the king said. "I have made a remarkable recovery. I'd like you to meet my friend, Mr. Royal."

"Peace, mon." Montrose Royal waved.

"Mr. Royal was once an apprentice houngan," the king continued. "I can see that you are not familiar with that term. I wasn't either until yesterday when Mr. Grave presented his plan to me."

I elbowed one of Hamid's bodyguards. "He's talking about me," I said.

"A houngan is a voodoo priest," the king continued, "one who is adept at preparing toxins that make an individual appear to be dead, even to a medical doctor."

"Zombies," I whispered to the bodyguard, but he didn't even look at me.

"Mr. Grave procured the toxins from our rainforest frogs, and Mr. Royal was good enough to administer them in the proper dosage."

Hamid shook his head. "What would be the point of this?"

I cleared my throat. "The point, as far as I can recall, was to force your accomplices on board to make mistakes, and they did, just as you have."

"I don't know what you're talking about," Hamid said.

"Tell me, my son" the king began. "Did you have Wakim killed?"

Hamid stared at him. "Of course not."

Amaranth flipped open a laptop, pressed a few keys, and we listened to a recording of Dr. Faber telling me more or less how he and Hamid planned to kidnap Casper Savoy to get the drone codes.

The king picked up a duck leg and began eating it. "If you lie to me a second time," he said, wiping his mouth, "I'll hang you from the ceiling fan."

Hamid looked around the room, tried to make eye contact with his bodyguards, but they weren't giving him any love. They had already assessed the situation and figured out who was going to come out ahead.

"Yes," he said quietly.

"Yes what?"

"Yes, I had him killed. It was necessary, father, because you have refused to do what is best for our country. With those drones, we could finally take our rightful place on the world stage and deliver a crushing blow to ..."

"Enough," the king shouted, louder than anyone in the room expected. "I'm having my luncheon, and I have guests. Your reasons are of no concern, but I accept your resignation from the Ministry of Defense."

Hamid closed his eyes.

"You will find that I am a forgiving man. After your sentence, you will assume your new position as Minister of Entomology. You will oversee all matters relating to our national insects."

"My sentence? Entomology?"

"But first, you will meet with Mr. Golan to discuss your accomplices, at least one of whom is still onboard."

Hamid stared at the floor.

"And I have assured Mr. Golan that if you require persuasion, he may use any techniques at his disposal. Leave me now, while I confer with the new crown prince of Al-Kurbai." He held out a hand to Bashir.

Chapter Thirty-One

"Don't most pop stars party through the night and sleep till afternoon?" I asked. I had just stopped by the oxygen bar for my morning fix, and now I was having breakfast with a young woman I met there. My breakfast consisted of English-style sausages, hash browns, a bagel and a big fluffy waffle. The young woman's name was Emily Ashberg, and she was apparently some kind of pop star.

"Maybe they do," she said. "But not me. I have a concert tonight and one the next night as well. Want to come?"

She was adorable. "A concert," I said. "It must be nice to have that kind of free time, going to concerts and all. Hey, how can you afford to take a cruise like this if you're only eighteen years old?"

"I am working," she told me. "It's my concert. I'm a performer. We just discussed this, remember?"

"It's all coming back. And you're staying in the executive suite."

"That's right. It's really something, three stories. I've never seen anything like it."

"Let me ask you something, do you have a butler?"

"You're not going to believe this, but we actually have two."

"Well I'll be goddamned. Did they unpack your bags?

Arrange your cocktail parties and manage your spa appointments?"

"They sure did."

I shook my head. "And you can afford this?"

"Well, it's all free, right, because I'm the featured performer. But yes, I can afford this. Last year I made almost nine million dollars, and I graduated high school."

"I'm in the wrong line of work," I said. "Do you need any backup singers?"

"No, but can you dance?"

"Can I? I'm an international tango champion. I have awards."

She frowned. "We don't do a lot of tango."

Let me tell you something, I was so happy at that moment. I had done my job, and solved my crime. I had largely recovered from my drug-induced dementia, saved a kingdom, and eaten most of a big fluffy waffle while engaged in meaningful conversation with a beautiful girl. I stared up at Dover Castle which loomed over the port. I wondered how many medieval English kings had ever been as happy as I was.

I tried to picture Emily Ashberg back with me at Rolling Pines, but even the vision seemed inappropriate. I'll tell you something though, if I were sixty-five years younger, I would have given this girl my every last lustful intention. I told her as much, but she frowned. Then she waved to someone behind me. I turned to look and then froze with fear. It was her.

"Have you met Wilhelmine?" Emily asked me. "She's a countess."

I was too frightened to answer, too frightened to do anything except watch in horror and she came towards me, her Rascal speeding at what seemed like a hundred miles per hour, but which in fact couldn't have been more than five.

"She's my neighbor," Emily said as the woman pulled up in front of me. She was a big woman, an old woman, older than myself by a long margin, but she was a fiery one, I could tell by the gleam in her eyes.

"Call me Winnie," she said in an accent I couldn't place. She held out a surprisingly dainty hand. "Have we met, young man? You look familiar."

I introduced myself as best I could, quaking with fear as I was. "I've seen you around," was all I could manage.

"No," she said, "I'd remember you. You remind me of Charles de Gaulle. We were lovers, he and I. I remember the day the Nazis stormed into Paris. I was to meet Charles at the train station. We were leaving France, you see, but I had recently learned that my husband was still alive, leading the resistance. So I had a letter delivered to Charles at the train station, a letter I was certain would break his heart."

I frowned. "That sounds a lot like the movie Casa...."

"Break his heart," she repeated. "It was the last I saw of him, though I'm told he kept my photograph at his bedside until the day he died."

I summoned up my courage. "Have you been chasing me around the ship?"

"Excuse me?"

"It just seems like you've been coming after me."

"Young man, do I look like the kind of woman who has to chase men?"

There was only one way to answer. "No, I suppose not." Maybe the whole thing was in my head, another of my hallucinations.

"It was lovely meeting you," she said. She held out her hand again, and as I took it, she gunned her motors and came at me hard for half a second. I nearly jumped out of my seat. Then she winked and she was gone.

Emily finished eating her waffles. "She's a cool lady, you know. Since we've been on board, she hasn't missed a single one of my parties."

"Is that right?"

Just then, the cruise director came over to chat. "I trust

you're enjoying yourself, Miss Emily?"

"Yes, Mr. Grassi. Everything has been lovely. I've just been chatting with my friend Henry. Did you know he was a tango dancer?"

"I didn't, but I'm not surprised. He's a man of many talents." He put a hand on my shoulder. "Mr. Grave, you have a phone call."

It was Abelard. "Miss Amaranth has a matter she would like to discuss with you," he said. "Would you meet us in the throne room, please?"

"I'm just now having a little breakfast, but I'll head over as soon as I'm done. Or you all could come up here. It's nice out. We could sit in the pool."

"It is a matter of some urgency," he said.

"OK, I'm on my way." I told Emily to guard my breakfast.

"Guard it from whom?"

"I don't know. Sometimes people like to take the trays away, even if they're not empty." Max Carder, the Egyptologist, was heading our way. It was still morning, so he had the Atlanta Braves cap on. "And watch out for guys like him."

Carder stopped in his tracks when he saw me. He tried to pass without incident, but that wasn't going to be possible.

"Hey, it looks like I was wrong about you," I told him. "I hope there are no hard feelings."

He shook his head. "Whatever."

"I'd stay and chat," I told him, "but I have a lady to meet. Hey, I'd like you to meet Emily. She's a pop star. Emily, I'd like you to meet my good friend Best Buy."

"Why do they call you that?" she asked, but he walked away in disgust.

"Some people just don't know how to behave," I said. Then I headed back to Bashir's suite.

I found the door open, which gave me pause. I walked in slowly but didn't see any sign of Bashir, or Abelard either.

Instinctively, I reached for my gun, but I still hadn't gotten it back, so I moved slowly, as quietly as I could. The mirrored door was unlocked; I opened it slowly and made my way inside. I had forgotten about the beads, which tinkled as I passed through them. So much for being quiet.

The first thing I saw was Abelard lying on the floor, clutching his abdomen. He'd been stabbed. I saw the king over in the center of the room, sitting on his carpet, but I couldn't worry about him just yet. I rushed over to Abelard.

"Keep her safe," he gasped. "No matter what cost, you must keep her safe."

I took a look at the knife wound. I'd been stabbed twice so I knew what to pay attention to. This one wasn't good. "I'm going to get you a doctor," I told him as the door slammed shut.

"No, you're not." The voice came from behind me. "You have been a pain in the ass from day one." He limped toward me, holding Amaranth by the hair. And he had a gun at her chin. My gun.

His hair was shorter, and he had a beard. "Well, if it isn't the fake Randy Binder," I said. "Why don't you hobble on over so I can get a look at the new you."

He was angry. "Old man, you stole $672,000 from my account. That was smart. But shooting me in the feet was not smart. It's time for payback, and I'm going to start with your knees."

"Shoot him," Amaranth told me. "Shoot him now."

"Let the girl go," I said. "What's your name, son? Or should I just call you Fake Binder?"

"You can call me whatever you want during the last few moments of your life," he said. "And by the way, the real Randy Binder will be arriving shortly. I used your name to get him to come. He was quite pleased with your little advance payment."

"So why do you want him here?"

"I'm going to make him wire my money back before I kill him."

"I look forward to meeting him," I said. "I'll bet he's not as big a dick as you."

"You won't get the chance," he said. "I'm going to need your other gun too. Take it out slowly."

"Shoot him now," Amaranth repeated.

"I can't help either of you," I told them. "They took my gun after I shot the ship during the Nazi movie. That was you, wasn't it, you fucker? Hey, you know what? The bug planet wasn't even scary."

He didn't say anything. He walked Amaranth over to the carpet in the center of the room where King Abdullah sat. "First he's dead, and then he's back alive. Craziest thing I've ever seen. The idea was to kill you tomorrow night, fairy Prince Bashir too, make it look like a murder-suicide. Then six beautiful days in the Atlantic before anybody knows you're dead. But you know what they say about plans."

The king glared at him.

"You have some vicious fucking children." Fake Binder turned to me. "Now, what I need you to do, old man, is help the good king with the computer. He says he's never used one, and since you managed to empty my bank account, you're going to help him fill it back up."

I shook my head. I've known guys like this my whole life; hard guys who fail to grasp the concept that power is given, not taken. This guy was a bully, and I wasn't about to give him any power.

"Let me tell you something about shooting a gun on a ship," I began. "Remember that day back in Stockholm, back at Shama-Lama Ding-my-Dong, when I shot your feet?"

"I don't think it was called ..."

"Remember how loud that was? I do. That means you've got one shot before the entire security team shows up here. So stop spouting off about how you're going to shoot me in the knee. You're not scaring me, son. There are only two ways you get off this ship; I walk you down the gangway and make it look like we're old poker buddies, or I stuff you in a body bag."

"Tough talk," he said. "You're right about the noise, but I can still stick a knife in this whore's back. I'll put my hand over her mouth and drop her slowly to the ground, quiet as a church mouse." He tugged hard on Amaranth's hair, causing her to gasp.

He waved me over to the carpet, and I sat next to the king. In front of us was a laptop. It was logged on to a bank account. That much was clear, even though the writing was in Arabic.

Let me tell you something, I might have been talking the talk, but I was having a hard time seeing how we were going to get out alive. Once the money was transferred, none of us would be of any utility.

I turned to look at the king but he didn't acknowledge me. He looked very calm. "We will do as you ask," he said, clearing his throat, "but only under one condition."

"You do not set conditions," Fake Binder spat. "You'll do as I say."

"In fact, that's not the case," the king told him. "I will not comply until you take that gun out of her face. Point it at the floor or at me, but as long as she is in discomfort, I will not comply."

Amaranth gasped as Fake Binder tugged hard at her hair, drawing her head back. He had the gun jammed up in her throat, but it wasn't having the effect he was looking for.

"That's going to cost you another million," he said, but he lowered the gun.

"Now take your hands off her hair," the king said. "You can still threaten her if you must, but if you take your hands off her hair, I'll make it an even twenty million dollars. That is the maximum I can draw without a series of phone calls."

"Yes, she does have nice hair." He let go of Amaranth's hair and held her by the arm. "You have a deal."

King Abdullah bin Salib recited a series of numbers, and I entered them into the appropriate field. "I will do the passwords myself," he said. He pulled the laptop close and angled it so that I couldn't see. Then he typed in his code, and hit the return button.

"Is that it? All done?"

"Yes, you may see for yourself," he gestured to the screen. Fake Binder came around, pulling Amaranth with him.

"Long ago," the king said, "men would come down from the mountains to steal our jewels and our women. There was a way we dealt with such men."

"Save it." Fake Binder leaned in and stared at the screen. The computer issued a series of beeps. "Hey, asshole, this says two hundred dollars. This is no time for fucking games."

"No. Let me see that." The king leaned in, and as he did so, he pulled a curved dagger from his robe and drove it into Fake Binder's abdomen. He grabbed the gun with his free hand. "This is how we dealt with the men who came down from the mountains," he said, slicing upwards.

Chapter Thirty-Two

In the six days I'd spent onboard Indulgence, four people had been killed. On the bright side, I solved a kidnapping that wasn't really a kidnapping, and I found a killer, or a series of killers. Well, technically they found me each time, but it was my quick thinking, sleight of hand, and silver tongue that kept everyone safe.

Actually, Amaranth killed the doctor, and the king killed the fake Randy Binder, but I'd like to think that I played at least some small part in sorting it all out.

It was me, after all, who hunted the tree frogs to provide the toxins that Montrose Royal used to make the king a zombie, and that's the part I'll remember most. I don't actually remember too much else, but what can you expect? I spent most of the cruise high on animal tranquilizers.

I was thinking about Amaranth as I sat in the hot tub, drinking a gimlet and staring at Dover Castle. I still don't know if she was CIA or Mossad or just your garden variety concubine. And I didn't imagine I'd get the opportunity to inquire. She was no longer onboard, having accompanied Abelard to Dover's hospital where he was recovering from a knife wound to the abdomen.

And I was thinking about Hamid Salib, who confessed everything under Golan's withering gaze. It took him less than three minutes to give up his accomplice. The fake Randy Binder was a highly-accomplished ex-U.S. marine turned contract killer named Alonzo Ortiz who had spent the last decade working as a mercenary in Yemen. It was Mr. Ortiz who killed Wakim with a spear, and Lester Fung with a bullet.

Hamid didn't have a lot more to say on that matter. He had trusted the good Dr. Faber to take care of the details, but Faber had ultimately been a disappointment. Hamid himself had a long future in insect conservation to look forward to, but not until he completed a fifteen-year sentence for murder and treason. And the icing on the cake was that he was going to have to serve those fifteen years in Indulgence's brig. I had to laugh every time I thought about that, but then people nearby started looking at me funny, so I stopped laughing.

I was also thinking about my neighbor Anne, who had made the life-altering decision to join a rainforest tribe. I was thinking a lot about her because she was sitting next to me in the hot tub. Coincidences happen in life, but this wasn't one of them. I spotted her in the tub about an hour ago. She looked so gorgeous in her bathing suit that I ran down to the cabin and came back wearing mine.

"Will you help me do the back?" I handed her my tube of sun block.

"You don't stop, do you?" she said. "There are so many clouds in the sky you'd doubt there was even a sun up there, and you still want to play the sunscreen game."

"What can I tell you? Hey, so mission accomplished; you found short love."

"I guess I did."

"I think you snagged yourself the shortest fellow on board."

"Maybe I did, but you know what? He's perfect for me. He fits me."

"He's a keeper, no doubt about that. But you're sure about this; you're really ready to become a hunter-gatherer?"

"Well, they're not really hunter-gatherers, you know. They have room service. But why not? I have nothing going on back in Miami, just a dumb job and a lonely condo. This will be good for me, and for Rusty too."

"I'm sure. I hear the legal papers are already in the works. Once you're married, you will be a vested member of the Jipito tribe. You can stay on board as long as you like. Though I'm told you have to be topless when the passengers are around."

She smiled. It was the first time I'd seen her smile. "I do not. And I know what you're dying to say, so I'll beat you to it; yes, I am thirty-two years older than Rusty, but I don't look it. And I don't care."

"Cheers to that," I said, waving to the waiter to bring me another gimlet. "I wake up most mornings, and you know how I feel? I feel young."

Just then, the most amazing thing happened. A woman came walking toward the hot tub, and I swear she was the spitting image of my beloved girlfriend, Helen Ettinger.

"Hello, Henry," she called out.

And she sounded just like her too.

She stared at Anne. "Are you happy to see me, or am I cramping your style?"

I think my mouth was hanging open.

"No, that's just Anne. She's a headhunter. Helen, what on earth?"

"Your son called me. He was worried about you. He told me you had taken a few lumps, and he said he'd spring for the ticket if I wanted to join you for the Atlantic crossing."

I can't tell you how happy I was to see her. I jumped up to give her a big kiss.

"Your eye looks awful," she said. "Does it hurt much?"

"Terrible pain," I said as she kissed it.

Helen turned to Anne. "He's off the market. You're going to have to find someone else."

"I'll manage somehow," she said.

I reached for my towel. "Helen," I said, "tonight, I'm going to take you to dinner at the largest restaurant in Dover."

"I can't wait," she said. "But I was hoping we could swing by the cabin first. I'm in the mood for a pre-dinner nap."

"That sounds like a fine idea. I could use a little shut-eye myself."

She stared at me. "That's not the kind of nap I had in mind."

"Well I'll be goddamned." I gave Anne a final wink and led Helen to the elevators. We were making out like teenagers when the door opened and Golan stepped out.

"Just the man I was looking for," he said. "You have company."

"Don't I know it." I gave Helen a little squeeze. "We're just now heading to the cabin for a pre-dinner nap, and by nap, I mean energetic love-making. After that, we're going to have dinner. Then TV."

He stared at me. Then he gestured to the man standing next to him. He looked to be in his mid-twenties and he was dressed in army surplus fatigues. He looked vaguely familiar but I couldn't place him.

"Are you Mr. Grave?" he asked. "Or should I say, Mr. G?"

"What, now?"

He held out his hand. "I'm sure pleased to meet you, sir. Randy Binder reporting for duty."

Golan wouldn't meet my eyes.

I didn't know what to say. I think I just stared at him for most of an hour. "Well, here's the thing, Randy," I began. "Our circumstances have changed somewhat over the last few days, and I'm afraid I no longer require …"

"You'll find I am quite flexible, Mr. G. I can blend into the woodwork if that's what you need. You've already paid me up front for about eleven years of my time, so whatever you require, I can provide."

I had an idea. I pulled Golan aside. "Can he bunk somewhere below decks until we get to Miami?"

Golan shrugged. "Well, the ship is completely full, but since we've had a few killings, I'm sure we can find him a spot."

"Fantastic." I turned back to my new friend. "Mr. Binder," I said, reaching out to shake his hand. "You just became my new butler."

If you enjoyed reading **Grave Indulgence**, be sure to check out the other Henry Grave novels. Available at www.amazon.com; or order from a bookstore near you!

The Glencannon Press
Palo Alto, CA
ISBN: 978-1-889901-49-7
277 pages

When retired FBI profiler Robert Samson is murdered onboard the cruise liner Contessa Voyager, Henry Grave is sent to investigate. Samson was giving a series of lectures on cold case crimes he felt he could crack. But he got cracked first. Henry has just five days before Voyager reaches Miami. There, the FBI will question the passengers, but the case will have grown cold and the killer will walk free unless Henry can find him first. With the help of a television actress, a cosmonaut, and a Venezuelan general fighting extradition, Henry draws on skills honed in a Nazi prison camp to track down a couple of passengers who might have their own reasons for taking this particular cruise, reasons unrelated to the sumptuous meals, delightful shipboard activities, and exciting ports of call.

MEDITERRANEAN GRAVE
A Henry Grave Mystery
WILLIAM DOONAN

BookYear Mysteries
ISBN: 978-0-9831354-0-1
274 pages

Mediterranean Grave explores crime on the high seas, and establishes a valiant and original protagonist. Henry Grave is an investigator for the Association of Cruising Vessel Operators. A World War II P.O.W., Henry is as cunning as he is charming, and at 84 years of age, he fits right in with his fellow passengers. The cruising yacht Vesper is anchored off the Greek island of Thera, in the caldera of an ancient volcano when Henry comes aboard. An Egyptian federal agent was onboard to guard a valuable Minoan cup, but the agent was murdered and the cup, stolen. With the help of a Nicaraguan soap opera star, a New Age spiritualist, and a blind pickpocket, Henry draws on skills honed in a Nazi prison camp to track down a killer who might have his own reasons for taking this particular cruise, reasons unrelated to the sumptuous meals, delightful shipboard activities, and exciting ports of call.

```
12 million people take a cruise each year.
Most have fun.
Some die.
Henry Grave investigates.
```

About the Author

William Doonan is a professor of anthropology in Sacramento, California, where he lives with his wife Carmen, and his sons Will and Huey. To contact William, or to learn more about Henry Grave mysteries and other novels, please visit www.williamdoonan.com.

CPSIA information can be obtained
at www.ICGtesting.com
Printed in the USA
FSOW03n0547260816
24091FS